LAST BID FOR
A DYING EARTH
BOOK ONE OF
THE ANISIAN CONVERGENCE

Mike Wyant, Jr.

Theogony Books
Coinjock, NC

Chris Kennedy/Theogony Books
1097 Waterlily Rd.
Coinjock, NC 27923
https://chriskennedypublishing.com/

Publisher's Note: This is a work of fiction. Names, characters, places, and incidents are a product of the author's imagination. Locales and public names are sometimes used for atmospheric purposes. Any resemblance to actual people, living or dead, or to businesses, companies, events, institutions, or locales is completely coincidental.

Cover Design by Shezaad Sudar.

Ordering Information:
Quantity sales. Special discounts are available on quantity purchases by corporations, associations, and others. For details, contact the "Special Sales Department" at the address above.

Last Bid for a Dying Earth/Mike Wyant, Jr.-- 1st ed.
ISBN: 978-1648554124

To Amy Wyant, for always supporting me and always pushing me to finish the next book. To David Farland, for inspiring me well after I lost my own inspiration. And to my writing group, the One Ring, for cutting me off when I trashed my work and for rapid turnarounds on beta reads (thanks Alicia Cay, Ari Officer, Leah Ning, Michael Kortes, and Rebecca E. Treasure!).

Without all of these wonderful people, the Anisian Convergence wouldn't have happened. Thank you all.

Here's to many more!

Chapter One

Sarah shouldn't remember the blood, neither the hovering crimson globules nor the harsh stink of bleach and cleaners.

When you became Staff, you were supposed to black out. It should be as easy as closing your eyes, then opening them twelve hours later.

But Sarah remembered. Usually just the strain of scrubbing floors or a flash of a face, but that wasn't supposed to happen. And if she wanted off the doomed Earth—if she wanted a chance somewhere safe, somewhere with a future—no one could know. The NDA had made it very clear any deviance was cause for termination.

They won't find out. Sarah squeezed her eyes shut. *They're nothing. Just glimpses. It doesn't matter.*

But there'd never been so much blood before.

Her gut twisted. Bile splashed the back of her throat. The ache of a dozen hours cleaning the Ladder, the space elevator leading to her salvation in orbit, settled into her limbs. Her bones.

Outside, a howling gale swept by, sending the high-rise vibrating through the soles of her work boots. The chill of her tiny, stark-white apartment settled into her skin, somehow amplifying the smell of sweat and the citrus cleaners speckling her baby blue Staff jumpsuit. Before her sat the toilet, right next to the pod-like UV shower and porcelain pedestal sink. The wall behind was a tile backsplash, its grout darkening and cracking with age and lack of maintenance.

And secured to that wall was the mirror she avoided.

She made to rub her eyes, to try and push away the memories, but froze as her skin came into focus. Burnt sienna flecks raced along the backs of her hands, up her forearms. A hum built in her brain, drowning out the summer nor'easter building beyond the walls.

Cursory inspection sent one splotch flaking off toward the floor. Her vision blurred; her stomach flipped.

Sarah fell to her knees and vomited.

ALIZA, the AI that controlled her during the day, had been nice enough to plop her right next to the toilet, at least. Like she knew this would be too much.

Sarah's stomach swam as she devolved into dry heaving, then she leaned against the porcelain throne for dear life. The acrid bite of stomach acid and puke mingled alongside the strangely comforting aroma of toilet water. She sat like that for a long while, hacking and cursing until the toilet grew warm beneath her elbows and the hard, white tiles of the floor scored her knees. Limbs rubbery and throat burning, she forced herself to her feet and leaned against the sink, careful to avoid the mirror. She didn't need to see her splotchy face right now.

From behind her, the telltale sound of the Processor let her know dinner was served. Her stomach turned again, but the sink kept her up this time, her bronze skin standing out in stark contrast to the white porcelain. Her fingernails were nub-bitten, skin chapped and dry.

It'll be fine, she lied to herself, staring hard at mint-green toothpaste splotches in the sink. *It wasn't blood. It was something else. ALIZA wouldn't make me clean a murder scene. No one died on the Ladder.*

Sarah blinked away blurred vision, clenched her hands in and out of fists as a rocket launched from her stomach and roared its way up her throat.

A ragged wail worked its way up from her stomach. It caught in the back of her throat as the world vibrated. From the blood on her hands to the base of her spine, it filled her. The wrongness.

The violation.

The water kicked on. Soap, too much soap, poured into her hands. Sarah scrubbed. Dug under her nails. A numb fear drove her forward.

Old memories buried for years threatened to burst from her mind. A broken window. A busted door. Two bodies piled in the middle of a room.

Sarah shook her head. She wasn't a child anymore.

She could handle this.

Maybe it'd been an animal? Some sort of accident?

But why would they use her? She was in janitorial, but as far as she knew, she'd never had to clean a blood spill. Maybe an errant thumbprint—she'd had a flash of memory once where she'd cleaned up broken glass and a few specks of blood—but nothing like what popped into her head this time.

Then again, maybe she just hadn't remembered. It didn't happen every shift.

But a burning certainty told her this was different. There'd never been a floor and part of a wall covered in blood spatter before. And the few times she remembered cleaning bio-spills, she'd used gloves.

That was protocol, at least as she remembered it. And then there were the floating, coagulated bits. Had she gone to the top of the Ladder? Had she ever been there before?

She didn't know, but ALIZA wouldn't put her in danger like that, not on purpose.

Right?

Sarah lifted soap-bubble-covered fingers and stared. The water shut off automatically. She could still feel the crusted blood in there, staining her skin, even if it wasn't visible.

Her hands went back under the faucet. Steaming water shot out like a hose, burning her skin as she scoured unseen splotches away. She rubbed until her hands hurt and the mirror blurred with mist.

Still, she scrubbed and worried.

If she left the UILB—the Unified InterPlanetary Launch Base, the company that owned, operated, and controlled the Ladder and the ARK—she'd lose her spot to New Eden. She'd lose her only chance at a future, at finding a real home. And if she contracted any sort of disease, they'd dismiss her. Even if she got it on the job.

She raised her dark, red-limned eyes to the mirror and saw her mother staring back.

Sarah turned away.

Maybe it was just an accident? Maybe if she went in and talked to Human Resources, she could ask them to be more careful? No. If she reported this—talked about it—no space. No ARK.

No New Eden. *You can't trust an automaton if they remember.*

"I won't die on Earth," she hissed at the voice twisting in her mind.

A small noise rang through the ALIZA cranial implant. Cursing, she tapped behind her left ear. Black block letters appeared in her line of sight. They didn't reflect in the mirror.

Reminders for Friday, July 24, 2076:

Mandatory Reproductive Exam in thirty minutes (19:00)

Camila's B-Day in two hours (21:30)

"Oh, fuck me," Sarah said, laying hands rubbed raw on the sink. Her fingers dripped water into the sink.

The reproductive exam. There was one every goddamned month. Can't be taking some sterile loser to the first colony. And Camila… could Sarah even pull that off after today? She and Camila had been friends since grade school. It was Camila who'd helped Sarah through some of the worst parts of foster care, who'd helped her enroll in the astrobiology prep course that got her into the Ladder Staff Program.

Sarah owed her, even if she didn't think she could follow the "dress sexy and be ready to get nasty" guidelines Camila had sent her. Hopefully sweatpants counted as sexy because, outside of her work jumpsuit, Sarah didn't think she had anything left to wear. Maybe a single black dress from her ill-advised high school prom. If it still fit.

But, Jesus, how the hell was she supposed to go out tonight after this? Could she just pretend this hadn't happened?

She took a calming breath. "Been doing it my entire life. Just another day."

Sarah dried off with a hand towel then risked another look in the mirror. She fixed her shoulder-length black hair and turned away from the ghost in the glass.

With a shake of her head, she took another shuddering breath and smoothed tears from her face.

She'd do what she needed to do, what she'd always done. What had gotten her through her parents' murder-suicide. A decade in abusive foster homes.

Sarah stared in the mirror. Took in a breath then let it out.

And smiled a smile that came nowhere near her eyes.

* * * * *

Chapter Two

The AI-controlled guy had dead eyes. Most did.

And even though Dave would never admit it, it freaked him out. Sometimes Dave wished there was still a physical currency so he could throw coins at the poor bastard—try to pull him out of their voluntary thrall.

"Thank you for shopping at OmniMart."

"Yep, lots of variety to choose from nowadays," Dave murmured and snatched the perfectly packed biodegradable bag from him.

The man—or rather, the AI-controlling said person—plucked a smile from someplace. His pale skin flexed into a disconcerting grin and turned blue eyes to the short lady with the baggy jacket and mussed hair behind Dave.

Staff creeped Dave out. Why anyone would let a computer control their body for a work shift was beyond him. Mostly. He'd helped make ALIZA for the UILB project fifteen years back for just this purpose. Okay, maybe he hadn't helped "make" her, but Dave had overseen all the deep dive quality control. Didn't want ALIZA burning out someone's optic nerve on accident, after all.

The idea had made sense back then. Robots were expensive, and human labor was cheap, but unskilled. Replace the higher-functioning human with an AI for a few hours, and you got the best of both worlds.

Boom. Profit.

Which was exactly what ALIZA turned into: a profit-making machine. All the instances spun off to companies that licensed the StaffTech™ software.

Like OmniMart.

And that goddamned space elevator, the Ladder. A pall fell over him, a familiar ache squeezing his throat.

What was the point? The ARK? Abandoning Earth? To do what? Destroy another world?

No, no one was ever leaving this godforsaken planet.

Since the last StaffTech update, he couldn't even mess with the AI anymore. He used to love breaking the algorithm to get a chance to chat with the human behind the mask. Like the young lady who'd worked here until a few years ago. She'd really liked his dad jokes. Or at least she'd pretended.

Apparently, he wasn't allowed to have fun anymore.

With a sigh, Dave grabbed his groceries. Bourbon and pickles sloshed around inside the bag as he made his way to the exit. He tried to ignore the dull ache building behind his left eye, the hazy halos around everything. Unnatural whiteness flooded every inch of the place. That must be what messed with him.

Besides the constantly puddling melt at the entrance, the store was immaculate. The thrumming of asynchronous automation rang through the building. Tiny little robots buzzed about, scouring corners and whisking away slush and dirt, before scurrying away between booted feet. Any items tossed about in a panic were swiftly adjusted by the adept hands of dozens of Staff.

The only thing wrecking that architected perfection were the people. Not the Staff people, of course. They were frustratingly immaculate.

But everyone else? Dirty and filthy in all their unwashed humanity.

That made Dave smile ever so slightly. He didn't get out much anymore, not since Rose passed. She'd been the people person, but it was still nice to see some semblance of actual life in what was left of the world.

Sometimes it got a little lonely.

Grimacing, Dave straightened his knee with a painful pop. It was best to limber up before going outside when there was a storm. A proper Jacket—a mid-level exoskeleton built to help folks adapt to ever more intense weather—protected from a lot, but nothing helped you if a gust overwhelmed the hydraulics, and you blew out a joint.

One needed agility. Finesse.

Both of those were in short supply in Dave's old, beaten body.

"You look like you're warming up for the Olympics."

Unfortunately for Dave, he hadn't warmed up quite enough for that. He jumped, cursed, and almost blew out the knee he'd been so worried about.

"Oh, Jesus, I'm sorry!" The young woman in a mundane sky-blue coat grabbed him as he slipped on a patch of gray slush that'd formed beneath his snow-speckled boot.

Dave gripped her shoulder for dear life, cheeks reddening, and tried to pretend she wasn't the only reason he wasn't sprawled on the ground. Getting injured wouldn't be a good idea. Not at his age.

Not since he'd retired from UILB. No health insurance, but at least they'd given him a nice plaque for his seventeen years of service.

He'd burned it after Rose died.

God forbid Dave catch a cold and get pneumonia. Choking to death on your own fluids didn't sound like a good time. His credit check wouldn't go through if there was an emergency, anyway. He hadn't paid off Rose's hospital stay yet, and likely wouldn't. Sometimes he was happy they'd decided against having kids, or they'd inherit his debt when he died. At least paid off property still transferred without adding liens.

"Y'all right, Dave?" the woman asked, her floral perfume tickling his nose.

Dave grunted and got his feet firmly under him. A little box scurried beneath to mop up the puddle. He only just tamped down the urge to kick the damn thing across the room, which was probably a good thing. It was OmniMart property, and they'd probably sue him to death.

Groaning, Dave turned to his savior—and froze. Rose looked right at him, a ghostly angel bathed in pure glistening light.

But her eyes were wrong. They were almond shaped, and hazel.

And…

Dave rubbed at his own eyes, hoping she hadn't noticed him staring. "Yeah, Janet, I'm good. Just pretending I'm Iron Man." Dave smiled, tapping his Jacket. "How're the kids?"

The slight purse of her lips told him she'd noticed but was kind enough not to say anything.

A good kid, Janet. It'd been, what, twenty years since the family had realized she looked almost identical to her aunt? She and Rose used to dress up and try to trick people. Rose had barely aged by her forties, so it had worked a lot better than you'd expect. Hell, even into her sixties, Rose hadn't looked a day over middle-age. Dave was always getting harassed for being a cradle robber, even though she'd been older than him. It wasn't his fault he'd gone gray at twenty and started balding in his early thirties. Genetics, right? What a kick in the balls.

Rose's chemo had changed all that.

Janet turned to look out the glass doors at the wall of swirling snow. Her face lost a little of its luster. "You know. Enjoying their summer vacation. The nor'easter kind of killed the beach plans, but what're you going to do?"

Dave nodded and cinched up his Jacket.

"I guess you just try to raise 'em right and wait for the ARK," Dave mumbled, intoning Rose's old standby.

Wait for the ARK. Lot of good it'd done her.

Janet nodded, stray hairs—some gray now—pulling out of her hood. There wasn't anything left to say. You just hoped you survived long enough for the next breakthrough, the next thing keeping humanity around longer.

The ARK had "almost" been complete for fifteen years. Seven of those, Dave had spent hopeful. The last eight, well, at some point you just hoped you didn't die a lingering death from a broken hip in the bathroom. He almost never took his Jacket off anymore.

An errant whiff of his own body odor hit him in the nose. It needed washing.

He needed washing.

"Oh!" Janet hopped suddenly, clapping her pink and green knit mittens together like the excited child she still was in the back of Dave's mind. "Did you hear?"

Dave allowed a smile to creep onto his face. "Probably not?"

Janet grabbed his arm and walked toward the door, pulling him along with. He sighed and shifted his groceries so the exoskeleton took most of the weight. The actuator at his elbow squealed a bit as the machine adjusted. He made a mental note to check it during to-night's maintenance.

"We finally cracked the light speed mass problem!" she said, swelling with pride. "We sent a piece of matter the size of—" Janet stretched her arms out into a one-meter by one-meter square, "—I dunno, a safe? Anyway, it landed on Luna Base in a little over a sec-ond."

Just as smart as her auntie. "Congrats!" Dave nodded and looked out the doors. Whorls of snow buffeted the few vehicles visible in the old parking lot. Deep inside, a little flutter of hope sparked backed to life. "Does it scale up?"

"To the ARK?" Janet asked as she stared outside. "It will. We just need to get the fission reactors ramped up so we can power the jumps. Though we need to do testing now. Large scale tests, destina-tion missions so we can verify the other Eden planets. New Eden only has a thin habitable line since it's tidally locked, so we need some more space for everyone. Three years more, tops."

The excitement died as soon as it sprang to life. Dave nodded, no longer listening to her positive recount of mission objectives. The ache in his chest built as she rattled off likelihoods of habitation, gravitational effects on lifeforms (which needed further testing, of course), and on and on.

He smiled and nodded, remembering his Rose saying similar things fifteen years ago after they'd first managed to send a piece of matter from two points at light speed. Then it'd been neutrinos.

For Rose, though, it had been all about the cryogenics. With the working lightspeed calculations, it'd still take several hundred years to get to any far-off destination since the energy usage for a lightspeed jump required a decade of charging from several fission reactors. How do we store humanity for one hundred, two hundred years? Clothe them? Limit the impact of travel on Earth biology? And how the hell do we avoid vaporizing a planet's atmosphere when we take off?

She hadn't lived long enough to see her work complete, but the team had dedicated the cryogenics wing in the ARK to her memory.

Real nice of them.

"Doesn't that sound exciting? I think we're almost there!" Janet beamed. Her eyes were bright, cheeks flush with excitement. Tiny crows' feet bent around the edges of her eyes as she smiled.

When had that happened?

And how long had she been working on this now? Five years? Six? It seemed like yesterday he'd given her a hug at her doctoral graduation. Now she had kids and clung to the hope that they'd live through all this.

"It sounds spectacular, dear," Dave repeated an aged maxim he hadn't used since Rose passed. "I can't wait."

With that, Dave disengaged himself from Janet and waved at her now-frowning figure. He stepped out through the shimmering shield of the OmniMart secure zone and into the "summer" blast of wind and whipping snow. The sudden roar thankfully drowned out any calls of farewell.

The Jacket whistled to life as the temperature plunged. Goosebumps tickled across his body, and the hairs in his nostrils froze with the first frigid breath. His face was buffeted for only a moment by the ice and wind before a tiny energy field sprang to life in front of him. A HUD flickered on, and the world became a wire-framed parody of itself, all lit up in wavering orange lines on a background of grayish white.

The snow swirled so thick and viscous he could only make out the closest of the vehicles in the parking lot without the Jacket's assistance. As it was, Dave saw them all, or at least a light representation of them as a series of orange streaks.

"Get me home," Dave whispered to the Jacket.

Dave's Jacket began the long trek back to the solitude of his house, his body following the motions as if on puppet strings.

A little over an hour later, the white roaring mess around him had sunk into a deep gray. Night fell beneath an arching canopy of overgrown trees. And still the arrows led Dave home. Out of the darkness, amber-outlined trees and bushes sprang up around a squat, one-story ranch. Even through the artificial wire-frame—or maybe because of it—you could tell it was in desperate need of preventative repairs. The roof no longer had the stiff lines of a sturdy structure. Half the gutters hung vertical to the ground, swaying as the wind pounded them.

Once upon a time, Rose had run around putting up those gutters while he struggled to control the now-wild bushes surrounding the house.

"'Gotta keep the rain off the foundation,'" Dave mumbled and walked the last few steps to the front door.

His hand wrapped around the door handle. With a high-pitched whine, the HUD disappeared, and the roar of the storm filled his ears. Dave cursed as icicles solidified in his facial hair. His cheeks went first cold, then hot as the frigid temperature bit into him.

Dave tried to open the door.

His wrist didn't move.

A trickle of fear blossomed in Dave's chest as he realized the entire Jacket had powered off. The exoskeleton seized as well—which shouldn't have happened—locking him in place, spare inches away from home.

Cold numbed his cheeks. Icicles snapped to attention on the gray goatee coating his upper lip and chin. Snow swirled between him and the door, spinning up and down the gap between his face and the edge of the Jacket. A harsh cold settled across his chest.

Don't panic, he told himself, even though it absolutely didn't work. *You can do this.*

A low, whining giggle escaped his lips at the thought. *I can't do shit anymore. Just a lonely prick waiting to die.*

"Stop that," Dave growled to himself, "and get your old ass inside."

He took a frigid breath and focused. Dave forced his wrist to turn against the dead weight of the Jacket. It was an arduous process, as the door handle creaked millimeter by millimeter, but eventually the catch snapped open.

A crack of heat hit him in the face. Tiny beads of sweat frozen to his skin melted as warm air rushed forward, trickling off his mustache and into a previously unknown crack that'd formed on his upper lip.

It burned.

"Janice!" Dave yelled through the gap in the doorway, watering eyes catching the corner of his easy chair.

"Yes, Dave?" a smooth, cheery automated voice responded from the speakers around the living room.

"Initiate Jacket cleaning mode!"

"Yes, Dave."

The small shield materialized in front of his face as the wireless charging system kicked into gear. With a lurch, the Jacket walked him through the front door to the charging panel. Dave gritted his teeth as it stepped over to the wall in the corner—his hip clicking painfully—and spun around quickly enough the world swam.

It popped open. Thick folds of wet, black cloth disconnected, slid down off his shoulders, and hit the floor heavily. His shopping bag fell to the floor.

Dave managed to stumble away just before the Jacket fell backward into the wired nook and struck the charging plate with a dull *thunk*. A heavy bass note rang out as the connection was established. Blue charging indicators lit up on the left forearm of the Jacket, then dropped back to a single, flickering LED.

The battery was almost dead.

Well, shit. That wasn't right. Another expense he didn't have the money for.

A set of mechanical claws flicked out from underneath the charger, grabbed the fabric part of the Jacket, and pulled it in.

Along with his bourbon and pickles.

Dave fell to his knees, hip sending a shriek of lightning up his spine, and grabbed the bag. Straining, he pulled it away as the fabric slipped through the opening with a soggy swishing sound.

"Goddamn thing is trying to kill me," Dave said, then stumbled to his feet, leaving the groceries behind. Grumbling, he made his way to the front door and shoved it closed.

There was almost an inch of snow on the floor by then. Dave glared at it with unconcealed scorn. It was fine. The floors were already cupping, anyway. A little more water wasn't going to break the place.

The house went dreadfully silent with the shutting of the door. Quiet left too much room for thought, so he changed that. "Janice? Can you queue up some instrumental music, please?"

"Do you desire a specific category of instrumental today, Dave?" Her voice filtered through the hidden speakers in the house, a calming, psychoanalyzed, robotic simulacrum of humanity.

Janice was technically an ALIZA 1.0 he'd snagged back in the early days. Better than all the other home assistants of the 2060s, but not smart enough to be scary, she'd seemed awesome at the time.

Nowadays it was nice to have someone to talk to, even if she didn't remember everything. He'd named her after his niece originally, Janet, but then she'd come over one day, and he'd realized how weird that was. It was crazy how adding a few letters made it less strange.

Sometimes he wondered if he was just a lonely old man too afraid to connect with real people. Luckily, there were ways to stop that train of thought from going much farther.

The steps back to the groceries were more than a little painful. The forced marching, and his valiant attempts to save his booze, had done a number on his hip. Dave found himself babying the hell out of it to avoid learning if it would pop out completely. It'd happened once in his thirties, and he had zero interest in experiencing *that* shit again.

Whispering a silent prayer to no one in particular, he knelt and grabbed the bag.

"Dave? Do you have a music preference?"

"Yeah, uh..." Dave opened the bag and stared at the contents, which included a box of bourbon and a jar of real deal pickles. The latter were made with actual cucumbers and were one of the few real foods still available and affordable at OmniMart. Besides those two prized items, he had a couple vacuum-sealed packages of smoked meats, and a dehydrated powder called 'Vitamin Paste' that provided the rest of his nutrients on any given day. "Since I have intact bourbon, let's go with a smooth-jazzy New Age playlist."

"Of course, Dave."

A low, mellow tone filtered through the house. The light, tinkling keys of a piano and a steady walking bass danced alongside a quietly riffing guitar. He ambled carefully to the kitchen, only sparing a glance for the small coffee table in the hallway where he kept the .38 revolver Rose had purchased for "protection."

As far as he was concerned, all guns did were kill good people. But still, there was a fine line between principle and reality. The only people who'd come out here nowadays weren't selling Girl Scout Cookies, after all. Fuck, everything had fallen apart so quickly. He'd thought they'd have more time…

Dave put it out of his mind and set his bag on the kitchen countertop.

A true smile appeared as he poured a glass of bourbon into a small, dusty tumbler on the cluttered kitchen table. Equipped with the bottle and a full glass, he went into the living room, following the worn, scraped path running through the wooden floors.

"Janice, please kick on the fire."

"Yes, Dave."

The fireplace roared to life, and he collapsed into a well-worn easy chair, purposefully ignoring the cluttered mess that filled his once-tidy domicile. The flickering fire burned the cold from his bones, easing the tension at his hip and knee. The walls had the golden glow of polyurethan-coated pine, even after all these years.

Two of four were covered with similarly finished bookshelves Rose had built with her own hands. He hadn't touched the titles there in years and wouldn't ever again.

Those were Rose's books.

No picture frames or awards littered the empty walls. Discolored spaces were the only indication anything had ever hung there. No more lavender-scented candles or heady cinnamon brooms. Just the moldy stink of decaying books and the underlying stink of an old man who didn't give a shit anymore.

Grimacing, Dave turned his attention away from the past and grabbed Rose's old tablet. He took a burning sip of liquor, savoring the lingering touch of vanilla and oak on his tongue.

Rose's face flashed to life as the tablet detected his presence, and a passcode prompt popped up. Dave didn't do anything right away. Instead, he took a few minutes to stare at her face, ignoring his own much younger self over her shoulder. It was a close-up of them at a company event six years before everything went to hell. Rose had worn that green knit sweater she'd loved, despite the unseasonal heat. Her hair was pulled back into a loose ponytail, tufts sticking out like a halo.

In the photo she leaned into him, pressing her cheek into his shoulder, infectious smile wide, arms wrapped around his middle.

God, the twinkle in her eye… so much life.

"Agh, fuck." Dave scrubbed his eyes clear.

This wasn't healthy. He wasn't stupid. Dave knew he should've moved on years ago. Should've been more social. More adventurous.

Should've done a lot of things.

Like every night, he sat there far longer than he'd planned. Two full pours of bourbon longer. Usually took three to float him past the tears, to numb the emptiness in his gut. To banish the lingering memory of the perfume of her hair and the bright tinkle of her laugh.

Through blurred vision, his finger traced Rose's cheek.

Then the tablet vibrated.

"Sonuva—" Dave set the glass down and wiped his chin, where his fifth bourbon now dripped through his facial hair.

There hadn't been a message sent to this device since before Rose's passing. He'd managed to purchase it as "surplus" before his "retirement." Rose's old team had been helpful in making that happen.

But now there was a priority message on the screen containing a single word.

ARK.

Any other time, Dave would've called Terry, his old employee in Ladder IT, and let them know someone'd made a mistake with device enrollment, and he was getting classified notices. Any other day, Terry would've thanked him, then sent along a bottle of wine as a thank you.

But the truth was, Dave was a little drunk, and seeing Janet at the store had made him more than a little nostalgic. Just the idea that there was a message Rose would be reading in that moment had she still been alive… well, it wasn't something he could turn away from. And it wasn't like he hadn't had similar security access when they'd worked there.

Dave tapped the message open and started reading.

And immediately wished he'd just called Terry.

* * * * *

Chapter Three

The goddamn light was too bright.

"Dave? You okay?" Terry asked.

"Yeah," Dave said. "I'm fine, just really bright in here."

Security had made him check his Jacket. He felt naked. Vulnerable. Squinting against the light, Dave rubbed his arms, surprised at the terrycloth fabric of his shirt. He couldn't remember the last time he'd been someplace outside his home without the support of the exoskeleton and the enclosed comfort of the interior wrap.

At least he'd showered this morning. No more old man stink.

Terry laughed in his rich baritone. "You need to get your eyes checked, old man. I've only got this one lamp on."

"What?" Dave asked.

There was a pause, then Terry's voice. Softer. Concerned. "Are you sure you're okay, Dave?"

Everything came into focus slowly, like his eyes had decided to take a break without telling him. The room dimmed, splashing his old office in dark earth tones, until a single lamp lit the space around Terry's mahogany-stained desk.

Across from him sat Terry. He was a rail-thin man with a massive nose Dave still couldn't quite stop staring at and skin as dark as the table between them. Back when Dave had occupied this desk, Terry had been a twenty-something fresh out of Syracuse University, with a master's degree in Philosophy, an array of work inappropriate t-shirts, and a need for a job that actually paid the bills. Dave had only

25

been in his thirties when they'd first met, back before the oceans had risen and Central New York had turned into prime real estate.

A lifetime ago.

Now Terry sat at *his* desk wearing a gray polo with the UILB logo on it—a single pea-pod shaped ship surrounded by a field of stars. His once stark black hair was now a woven mesh of salt and pepper.

Dave rubbed his left eye, massaging away the tension just beneath the surface, an itch he couldn't quite scratch. "Yeah, I'm okay, but I got a message for Rose last night."

Terry leaned back, exposing a potbelly that hadn't been there thirty years ago. He raised an eyebrow. "What kind of message?"

Dave rolled his eyes. "Not some sort of spirit shit, Terry."

"Just checking," Terry replied, a sardonic smile pulling at his lips.

"But really." Dave reached into the canvas bag he'd brought in with him, the tremor that'd shown up this morning in his right hand—which he'd decided was from stress—just visible in the lamp light. He pulled out Rose's old tablet, unlocked it, and slid it across the table between them. "This thing got the message and, I'll tell you, it's a lot."

Terry leaned forward, spun the tablet on the desk, then picked it up. The smile that'd been teasing his face disappeared. Then he tapped the screen a few times. When he finally glanced at Dave, there was a worried look in his eyes.

After a long pause, Terry locked the tablet and slid it back to Dave. When he finally spoke, it was in a whisper. "This says the ARK is already transporting passengers to New Eden. But I thought these trips were supposed to take decades?"

"Centuries is what Rose used to say."

Terry nodded. "She did. But I checked the ARK update site this morning. They're waiting on large-scale testing. I mean, your niece works in that department, doesn't she?"

Dave nodded.

"Don't you think she'd tell you?"

"Not if she doesn't know, either," Dave replied, snagging the tablet and dropping it into the canvas bag like it was on fire. "That's why I came to you. I wanted you to check the mail server and see if it's legit." Dave rubbed at his eye again until the sparks shone. "I mean, there are diagrams and plans for the thing in that email."

Terry stared at him for a long moment before drumming his fingers on the wooden table and falling heavily into his chair. It creaked beneath him with the effort.

"You want me to check the mail server to see if the CEO of UILB sent an email to a private distribution list that, for some reason, includes Rose?"

"Yes."

"Your dead wife?"

Dave grimaced. The pulsing in his head was getting worse. "Goddammit, Terry. Yes."

Terry nodded. He sucked his teeth. "You already checked the headers?"

Dave nodded.

"And all the IPs are right?"

Dave shrugged, then knocked his knuckles on the table. "I've only been gone three years, Terry."

"Okay," Terry said. "Forward me a copy, and I'll look into it."

Dave sat there, stunned for a long moment.

Apparently, too long a moment.

Terry shook his head. "Dave. Are you sure you're okay, man?"

"Yes," Dave snapped. "I'm fine, I just want to find out what the fuck this is all about. I need to know if this is true."

I need to know if it's real. If she died for nothing. And then the thing that really made his gut clench. *I need to know if Rose knew.*

"Okay," Terry said. "I'll run it up the grapevine and see if someone can shed some light on it."

That's not what I want. I want you to verify the sender right now, Dave wanted to say, but didn't. "Thanks Terry. I appreciate it."

A twitch flickered Dave's left eye. He rubbed at it, the pressure in his head growing. Was it normal to start getting migraines in your sixties? Who knew anymore?

Dave got to his feet, joints groaning with the effort.

Terry followed suit, dark hand bridging the space between them. He flashed a toothy smile. "Take care of yourself, Dave."

"I will," Dave replied, gripping the offered hand. "Just let me know what you find, okay?"

Terry squeezed, then let go. "Don't worry. I will. I want to know if this is legit, too."

Dave grunted. "I know. Take care." Dave knocked knuckles on the old mahogany desk. The thud of the old wood brought a smile to his face. "And make sure you keep this thing polished. It's one of a kind nowadays."

"Get out of here, old man—" Terry grinned, waving him out, "—and stop touching *my* desk."

Dave waved back with a sarcastic flick of his wrist, and left the office, exiting into the long, blisteringly white hallways of the Ladder. Everything about it screamed artificial, from the seamless plastic walls to the omnipresent glow. Even the low *thrum* that ran through everything as the Ladder rose and fell endlessly around its central spire.

That was one of the reasons Dave had originally purchased that heavy wooden beast of a desk. It had helped stave off the artificial tone of the rest of the Ladder. Dave would like to say he'd gotten used to all of it during his decades in the lower-level office—there from the day the Ladder's construction had reached this level to the day they'd booted him from it—but he'd never been able to get over the feeling of wrongness permeating the space.

Everything felt so... sterile. Which was important for a building that reached into the stars, he guessed. But still. It didn't make for a hospitable work environment. Dave missed the desk, but certainly not this place.

However, despite all his discomfort, for some reason, the transition into this hallway didn't trigger the headache again. Small victories.

The passage itself was on one of the lowest levels of the Ladder, a mere thirty stories in the air. For the most part, the stark white walls were empty, though the periodic Staff member walked them in their gray and blue jumpsuits, a mop or bundle of papers in hand alongside their flat-eyed stares. Just like in the OmniMart, they freaked him out, so he avoided them.

In the years following Rose's death, when UILB had decided to use Staff in the Ladder, Dave had argued against it for security reasons. When it had become mandatory for everyone with access to the Ladder to have an optical implant installed, Dave had refused. He wasn't getting something grafted into his damn brain, especially not in his sixties. That was insane.

But then again, maybe that was the point.

While his forced retirement technically hadn't had a "reason," he was pretty sure his stance had a lot to do with it. He'd just never bought into the idea that all these people walking through classified areas wouldn't remember details, or that the implants were safe, despite his testing. Too much trust that technology would fix everything was what had gotten humanity into trouble in the first place.

Shuddering, Dave made his way to the exit, following a long, curving sweep of the windowless hallway. When he'd been here every day, he'd often wished something would happen. Something excit-ing. Something not having to do with IT work.

Today he'd gotten his wish.

Something slammed into him as he came around the final swing of the corner. Air burst from his lungs, feet came off the ground, and he hit the steel floor, along with another set of arms and legs. A sharp pain ran through his right hip, up his spine, and right into the back of his teeth.

The thing—the *person*—who'd hit him was on their feet in a mo-ment, hands grabbing him around the shoulders.

"I'm so sorry! I didn't see you! I'm just in a hurry! You're not hurt, right? No, look at you, you're…"

The voice trailed off as Dave got to his feet, staggering to the wall as he tried to put weight on his right leg. "No worries, it's fi-yi-yi-yi!" Pressure in his upper leg. Pain flared through his side, then everywhere. "Motherfucker!"

His hip popped out of joint.

Dave hit the ground again, a blinding pain screaming through his body.

"Oh, my God!" the young woman who'd run into him screamed as he fell, cursing and hammering on the floor with a fist. "What's happening?"

"My hip," Dave managed between clenched teeth. "My fucking hip popped out. I knew this was going to happen, that's why I don't take off my goddamn Jacket."

"I'm so sorry!" she said, tanned hands clamped over her mouth. "I didn't mean to—wait. Dave?"

Through the haze of pain, Dave finally looked, really looked, at the woman who'd run into him. "OmniMart girl?"

She nodded.

Dave forced a grin through the pain and cocked his head up at her. "This reminds me of a joke."

OmniMart girl's brow furrowed. "I think you need some help, Dave."

"Why'd the old man fall down the second well?" Dave asked, teeth grinding as his hip wiggled up and down in the meat of his leg. It felt like sandpaper in there.

OmniMart girl started at him. "Because he's old?"

Dave grinned. "Because he can't see two wells."

She rolled her eyes, the barest smirk playing on her face. "I bet you're not even hurt, are you?"

"No, I—"

OmniMart girl, who was significantly stronger than she looked, reached down, grabbed Dave under the armpits, and lifted.

Sparks flew behind his eyes. It felt as if he'd been thrown into a volcano. Heat and pain and terror roiled alongside each other.

A hoarse scream ripped its way from his throat.

And Dave blacked out.

* * * * *

Chapter Four

I killed the OmniMart guy.

Of course, Sarah knew that wasn't true. Dave was in the other room getting a body MRI while she sat here, feet in stirrups, waiting for a doctor to come in and poke and prod and swab all the things. But they'd left her in here alone for the last fifteen minutes as all the UILB nurses rallied around the broken old man.

What else was she supposed to think about, sitting like this? She already knew every detail of the ceiling, and there was no way Sarah was going to focus on the contents of the supply closet in the corner of the room, or the sterile smell of antiseptic. She certainly didn't want to really think about how fertility was a requirement of travel to New Eden. Or the fact that if it turned out she had some sort of STD, regardless of where she'd gotten it from, she'd immediately lose her place.

Blood spatter on a wall. Her bare hands scrubbing it all away.

Sarah let out a shuddering breath. "It's going to be fine. Everything will be fine."

From somewhere beyond the door, she heard the faint echo of a newscast. "...UILB CTO Harris Tarrington was murdered by terrorist organization Earth First..."

It changed suddenly to squealing tires and generic announcer voices.

Sarah squeezed her eyes shut and pretended she didn't see blood. A knock on the door.

"Come in," Sarah called, hoping the waver in her voice was just in her head.

Doctor Aubin cracked the door and entered, his head of dirty-blond hair leading the way. He had piercing blue eyes, a summer-tan complexion, and if you caught him at the right angle, definition beneath his lab coat. The man was far too pretty to be a doctor. There'd been quite a few times she'd daydreamed a bit about meeting him at a bar, or OmniMart, and striking up some flirty conversation. Outside of this room, he was a source of all sorts of dreams.

In this room, he was the guy with the cold hands who preferred using the *large* speculum. In here, he was a nightmare.

"Evening, Ms. Martinez." Doctor Aubin smiled, scrolling through her chart. "Looks like we have quite the array of tests to run through today." The way he said it gave her the impression he'd somehow forgotten that they did this dance every four weeks.

"Mm-hmm," Sarah grunted in the form of agreement, eyes locked on the flat white ceiling and its gentle illumination.

The supply cupboard clicked open. "Well, no time like the present."

Sarah's fingers curled into the paper cloth under her butt, and she pretended she was somewhere else for the next 22 minutes.

But every thought came with floating blobs of crimson.

* * * * *

Chapter Five

Dave watched Doctor White's lips move but didn't hear her. He saw the line of pale skin visible between a sweep of auburn hair and a darker coat of makeup, the way her skin crinkled in the middle of her forehead as she spoke. The sharp lines of Rose's tablet, a new crack along its surface, against the blisteringly white desk between him and the doctor. Smelled rose perfume. The hum of the Ladder running through everything. The dulled roar of helicopter blades slapping the air from a distant place.

But he couldn't hear her words.

Didn't want to.

Through the ringing and humming, she finally broke through. "Mister Parker, you have a brain tumor. Do you understand what I'm saying?"

No. "Yes."

How the fuck am I going to pay for this?

"I've discussed it with my supervisor, and we're able to cover the cost of the MRI, as well as resetting your hip, since it happened on UILB property, but at the very least, you need treatment for that tumor as soon as possible. We'd also recommend a hip replacement. You barely have any cartilage left."

Anger flared. *Wouldn't be in any of this mess if you hadn't taken my Jacket away.*

White's brow furrowed. "That's patently untrue, Mister Parker."

"Sorry," Dave whispered. Had he said that out loud?

She cleared her throat and pulled up a three-dimensional display between them. Shining in the center, all wrinkled up like a prune, was his brain. And in the front left of it was a hard-boiled egg left out to rot, lines of fungus spreading into the soft tissue around it.

"The tumor is large, nearly six centimeters across," the doctor said bluntly. "I'd suggest you find a surgeon, but it's entangled with the optic nerve of your left eye. The best treatment we can suggest is aggressive, targeted chemotherapy and gene-therapy to stave off any additional growth. We don't do that here, as you know."

Yeah. He knew. Rose had found out about her own cancer in this office. White had had the same delivery on that day, if quite a few less wrinkles.

Dave ran his hands over his face, left hand pausing just over his eye. Feeling for the tumor. A starburst flashed, then disappeared.

Could he feel it there? Some bump or mound?

No. Nothing.

"I can make a recommendation for a good oncologist in Liverpool—"

Dave got to his feet in a rush, the world swimming as he did so. Dull pain echoed in his leg, but it was more than bearable for now. It wasn't the first time the joint had come out. Last time, it'd felt great in the hour or so after it went back in. Later tonight, though? Well, it's a good thing he'd bought bourbon. "No, thank you. But I appreciate you putting the leg back and covering the cost of the stuff I didn't ask you to do."

Doctor White sighed. "Mister Parker, I don't think—"

"No, it's fine." Dave forced a smile instead of telling her what he really thought. "Everything is fine. Thank you again."

Then he left. Limped past the makeup-crusted doctor, through a nearly empty waiting room, down a hallway of glowing walls, the heels of his boots a hitched metronome guiding his way to security. A few muttered greetings and bland cordialities to faces he'd never remember, then he was in the safety of his Jacket again, it's warm grip a comfort. The exoskeleton gave him the ability to forget about his frailty.

Without a glance back, Dave walked into the security elevator. The door dinged shut behind him. The brushed-steel coffin surrounding him dropped thirty stories in a controlled descent.

Reality settled over his shoulders like a hair shirt. Dave knew how much chemotherapy cost nowadays. Knew his credit, and the outstanding debt for Rose's treatments, meant he wouldn't get help from an oncologist, or anyone else.

He could sell his house, but then where would he go? That was just another lingering death sentence.

"I'm going to die," Dave whispered, "of fucking *cancer*."

It felt like his face was swelling. As if, now that the tumor had been revealed, it was going to pop out of his face like a nest of spiders finally ready to hatch.

His vision blurred. An ache pulled at his chest. Dave rubbed at his forehead, trying to keep it from happening. Hoping pure force of will could save him.

Finally alone, Dave let the tears flow as the elevator descended, Rose's tablet still sitting, forgotten, on the desk of the demon doctor who'd diagnosed him.

* * *

"**M**s. Martinez!"

Sarah turned at the sound, trying her best not to care about the ache in her stomach. A woman, late-forties maybe, with a head of dyed-auburn hair and far too much bronzer coating her face rushed over.

"Yes?" Sarah replied.

The woman—nurse, or doctor, she didn't know—stepped up and held out an old black tablet. "Mister Parker left this behind."

Sarah glanced at the powered down tablet with a crack in the display. There was a Post-It note stuck to the screen with the words "David Parker" scrawled on it in true doctor handwriting. Sarah met the other woman's eyes.

It took her a minute to put the name with the man. With it came a rush of worry that made the ache in her gut worse. "You mean Dave? Is he okay?"

"Yes," she said, eyes flickering to the wall behind Sarah as she spoke, "but I was wondering if you could return this to him, since you're family. He left in a hurry."

"Um?" Sarah began, ready to clarify her relationship with Dave, but the woman had other plans.

She shoved the tablet into Sarah's hands, said, "Thanks so much," then let go.

Sarah almost dropped the thing, but caught it before it hit the floor.

"But…"

And then the woman was gone, the door to the medical center clicking shut behind her. Sarah was left behind in an empty hallway, with a stranger's ancient tablet, trying to pretend she hadn't just had a medical instrument jammed inside her.

"But I'm not family." Sarah pulled the tablet tight to her chest and looked toward the security exit. "Well. Shit."

* * * * *

Chapter Six

Tracking Dave down was more difficult than Sarah had expected, but she welcomed the distraction. Better tracking down an old man than thinking about the phantom scabs beneath her fingernails.

As soon as she got out of the Ladder, she ran the name "David Parker" through a few different search engines, results popping up on the sides of her vision, thanks to her Ocular implant. Her original thinking was someone his age, someone who dropped dad jokes like a failed stand-up comic, wouldn't have taken the time to worry about privacy.

She was wrong.

Several hundred feet above and behind her, the base of the Ladder hovered, casting the old downtown in permanent nightfall, anchored to the Earth by eight cyclopean feet. Those feet came together into a single central tower that spiked into the sky and disappeared into the heavens. Spotlights ran the length, silver swords spearing the sky. The edges of the Ladder rose and fell, each side carrying supplies and people to and from the self-styled UILB proper.

Going up were supplies and people, a constant flux of humanity heading to the UILB to work on the ARK or move into the Wheel, a recently completed habitat for the rich and powerful. If the news reports were correct, the Wheel rotated, allowing some semblance of gravity off Earth.

In the persistent shade of the space elevator, a stiff, chill wind cut from the north. It made her wish she'd brought a blazer or something, but wishing had never gotten her anywhere, so she ignored the cold the best she could. To the north, a blizzard raged, but down in the city, it was a downright balmy 4C.

Rubbing her arms against the chill, Sarah used the broad expanse of one of the supports as a digital whiteboard. She scrawled Dave's name in the top left of her vision, then got to work.

Sarah got three hits: a wedding announcement from 2029, an old staff picture from an archive of the original Ladder website, and an obituary from 2071 for a Rose Martinez-Parker.

Rose Angelica Martinez-Parker is survived by her husband, David Parker, her brother, Louis J. Estevez, and niece, Janet Martinez-Manu. In lieu of flowers, please donate to the Martinez-Parker Fund for Women in STEM.

Beyond those two things, there was nothing, though now she understood why the doctor had thought he was her uncle. Lot of folks shared her last name these days. *And we all look alike anyway, right?*

Sarah took a few calming breaths. Things were usually better nowadays, but every now and then... A request for a cleaning quote. Someone assuming she could get something from the back in OmniMart. A doctor asking how many kids she'd had.

Always something.

More deep breaths, then she continued her search.

It was as if everything had been scrubbed, though she couldn't fathom how, or why, that would've happened. Just to make sure her browser software wasn't messing up, Sarah ran a quick search on herself.

She immediately closed it. The video from spring break two years ago was still up. "Good enough."

Should she even worry about this? Sarah lifted the tablet. It was old by any standard, a V37 that didn't even offer Ocular pairing. Hell, it looked like something you caught in early 21st century movies. She pressed the home button on it, then cursed.

The woman staring back at her was vaguely familiar. She had a bright smile set in a tan face and absolutely perfect brown hair streaked with silver. A younger version of Dave's face popped up over her shoulder, face split in a goofy smile.

She locked the screen, dimming the image.

On the right side of her vision, a reminder popped up.

Camila's B-Day at 21:30.

"Shit."

At a thought, a clock appeared beneath the reminder.

It read 21:30.

"Double shit," Sarah muttered. She'd completely forgotten, and now she was late. Camila was going to rip her a new one.

Dave was going to have to wait until tomorrow.

With a frustrated grunt, Sarah hustled home as the sun slowly set behind the Ladder.

* * * * *

Chapter Seven

"Sorry to call again, Terry," Dave muttered, one hand gripping the rim of his fourth empty bourbon glass. He slid it in circles on the epoxied dining room table. It howled like a wounded animal. The old speakerphone he kept in the house in case of emergencies sat in front of him, a dusty old spider of a thing. "I just can't seem to find Rose's tablet, and I know I had it in your office. I left a message with Doctor White, too, but I think they're closed, so I figured I'd try one more—"

The voicemail clicked. Dave stared at the speaker for a long moment.

"Goddammit!"

He launched his glass across the room. It slammed into the wall across from him.

Right into his wedding photo.

Both went to the ground in a glittering crackle of broken glass. Dave was out of his seat and on the floor, his hip, now inflamed and as angry as a caged wolverine, screaming at him the entire way. He dropped to his knees as carefully as he could, trying to avoid the broken glass.

"No, no, no," David whispered, pulling the printed photo from the pine frame he'd made twenty years ago after the original had fallen from the wall during one of the first major hurricanes Upstate New York had experienced.

Bourbon spattered the picture. He drew it out of the shattered bits, then shook it clear, ignoring the tiny slivers of glass flying this way and that. Carefully, he held it between his fingers and stared at an image of a much younger, boyish version of himself bearing an ill-advised curled hipster mustache and a black penguin suit next to Rose.

Rose, just as he remembered her. She stared back at him, wide smile glittering in the sun, humor, love, and patience lighting her brown eyes.

His shaking finger traced her cheek.

And left behind a bloody smear, blocking her out.

Cursing, Dave struggled to his feet, teeth grinding against the pain. He grabbed one of his parson's chairs for balance. It slipped, sending him sprawling to the floor.

He hit the ground, hard. Something clicked inside him. A fire roared in his chest. He gasped, trying to draw air from lungs that didn't want to cooperate.

Eventually, his breathing evened, though the pain radiating across his chest persisted. Each breath was a struggle. Cobwebs filled with corpses taunted him from the popcorn ceiling.

Why was he fighting for this? It didn't matter. He was a dead man who hadn't had the good manners to kill himself in his sleep by burning down his house so some rich asshole could take his property for the cost of disposal.

Groaning, Dave shifted so his back was flat on the wooden floor. The floorboards creaked and moaned beneath him, as loud as his joints every morning. A pleasant numbing sensation tickled in his limbs, starting in his hip and radiating through his body. The alcohol was finally working.

With a light sigh, Dave pulled the picture to his chest, closed his eyes, and prayed to whomever was listening that the tumor would kill him while he slept, here, on the floor of the house he and Rose built.

That would be a gift.

But nothing ever came free, did it?

* * * * *

Chapter Eight

Sarah tried.

She really did. There was the old black dress in the back of the closet that by some miracle, "fit," even if it hugged her hips to the point she thought the damned thing was going to pop like a balloon. She even managed to find a pair of black shoes with a tiny bit of heel. Sure, maybe they weren't actual dress shoes, but with the long dress, no one would ever notice.

It wasn't her fault she didn't own any makeup, but when she'd looked in the mirror before leaving, Sarah had thought that, maybe, she actually looked good for once.

Camila didn't agree. And since she was already drunk and on something that made her pupils as big as the moon, Camila made sure Sarah knew it.

"You look like a prostitute who ate her last client!" Camila laughed, her tittering, screeching laugh breaking over the roar of the speakers in the converted warehouse she'd rented for her party. "Like, a prostitute living *paycheck... to... paycheck.*" She drew out the last three words to the chuckles of her entourage.

Sarah hated Camila when she was high. That's when the prep school terror she'd met in the fourth grade came back with a vengeance. The group of six male toadies surrounding her were new and not helping. They looked like they were on their way to try-outs for America's Next Boy Band or something but got snagged by the most eligible bachelorette in the remaining United States, one Miss Camila Tarrington. All wore various versions of the same suit—high-collared black jackets and no tie. They all had a heavily layered shirt beneath in various colors she couldn't quite make out against the flashing rainbows pounding through the industrial warehouse in time with the beat. The building had been splattered with UV illuminating paint so it glowed like dozens had been brutally murdered inside.

Sarah dug at her nails.

For some reason, all six had the same ridiculous pencil beard. They looked like drunk, detail-oriented frat boys who'd had fun with a permanent marker.

There was one other feminine person in the group. Sarah hadn't talked to her yet, and probably wouldn't, given the way she kept casting demon glances at her while holding possessively onto Camila's arm.

Sarah had seen these people come and go over the years. Hangers-on who thought they could siphon off some of Camila's cash if they were nice to her. Sometimes it worked. Most times it didn't.

Camila always came back to Sarah.

"Did you hear me?" Camila slurred out, leaning toward Sarah as if she was going to whisper some sort of deep, dark secret. "I said you look like a poor... fat... prostitute."

Heat flushed her cheeks and neck, but still, Sarah forced a smile. The group grinned as one and laughed with Camila at her *so*-great joke.

When they were alone, Camila was a fantastic friend. She'd helped Sarah when everyone else had forsaken her, even Ruby, the ex-best friend she'd met in her first foster home. Ruby had disappeared one day, transferred to some home out in what was left of

Connecticut. They'd lost contact and, slowly, Camila had stepped into the role.

They'd become close friends over the years, despite whatever happened at these stupid parties. All she had to do was stick around for a couple hours, or until Camila blacked out and went home safely, and she'd be good to go.

"You're so bad!" Camila's barking laughter snapped her out of her thoughts.

Sarah raised an eyebrow and saw the other girl whispering something in Camila's ear. The girl had a wicked grin that made Sarah want to slap the shit out of her.

But she didn't. The girl was probably some rich kid who'd go to New Eden before her regardless of how hard Sarah worked.

"Constantia made a joke about the prostitute thing!" Camila yelled. One of the boys stuck his hand in front of her and, without missing a beat, she snorted a line of white powder off the back of his hand. She shook her head, then whooped and gave the guy a kiss on the mouth, smearing her lipstick. "That's what I'm talking about!"

"I'm not a prostitute," Sarah found herself saying before she could stop. "I work at UILB."

Camila stepped up next to her and put an arm that radiated heat around Sarah's shoulders. "Yes, she does. I'm just kidding, Sarah," Camila said, giving Sarah a wet kiss on the cheek that likely left a smear of glowing, violet lipstick. "No need to get touchy."

"Well, she's still a Second," the girl, Constantia, said in a low, sultry voice Sarah almost missed. "She's basically a whore."

All the boys made "oooh" sounds like some sort of insult had been laid down, but…

"What's a 'Second?'" Sarah asked, trying to stay on the positive side of this. Maybe it was some stupid rich kid thing, and it didn't mean anything to the "rabble" like her.

"Don't worry about it," Camila said, squeezing Sarah in a hug.

That meant it was bad. Sarah disentangled, then pushed Camila lightly back to the gang of idiots she'd been hanging out with before she arrived. "Camila. What the fuck is a 'Second?'"

Camila threw her head back; her shoulders dropped. "Ugh! You're such a drama llama."

Sarah stared at her, refusing to take the bait.

"Just tell her," Constantia said with a grin. "It's probably right up her alley anyway."

"Fine!" Camila shouted, throwing artificially tanned arms into the air. "It means you're going to carry my kids for me on New Eden."

Sarah's stomach dropped. "What?"

Constantia wiggled her arm around Camila's thin waist. "Not a smart one, is she?"

The heat in Sarah's cheeks lit on fire, but a splash of cold calm fell over her shoulders. Her vision drew to a knifepoint, flashing lights fading, pounding beat a dull roar in the back of her head. She stared at the smaller girl. Caked makeup contoured her face into someone older, more refined, but if you looked close enough, you could make out the softer shape of her cheekbones, her jawline, the drawn-on eyebrows.

She was just a child playing at being an adult.

Sarah stepped into the smaller girl's space. "I'm not talking to you, you weak-chinned whore." There was a collective gasp from the group, but Sarah kept going, turning to Camila. "Now. What do you mean?"

Camila's face dropped. Sarah had seen this before when Camila had gone too far and realized it. Sarah had always let it go at that point in the past, though she didn't know why.

No. That was a lie. She'd let it go because she didn't want to lose her only friend. She didn't want to be alone.

A flash of blood on the wall.

Not today. Not this time.

"Camila," Sarah said, grabbing her old friend by the forearm and squeezing. "Now."

"That's why we're friends, okay," Camila said, trying to pull her arm free and failing. "That hurts."

Sarah didn't let go. Fire writhed in her mind. She wanted to scream. To hit her. But instead, only one word made it out. "Explain."

"It's dangerous to have babies on New Eden, so you'll do it for me, now let go!" Camila screamed, pulling her arm.

With those words, the anger disappeared, and behind was only a numb void. She held on, though. Not because she wanted to hurt Camila, though there should've been some of that.

She held on because... because she didn't know what else to do. Camila had always been there for her. Helped her through the toughest parts of her life. Helped her with relationships. Helped her get a doctor. A job at UILB. Reminded her to go to her gynecologist visits. Reminded her...

Sarah let go of Camila. Her fingers left white marks on Camila's fake tan. "Oh my God. The tests they make me do at work. It's because of you, isn't it?"

Camila didn't answer with words, but she looked away. "Hey, let me get you a drink, and we'll forget all this happened in the morning—"

The slap surprised both of them. One second, Camila was apologizing like she'd done their entire lives, the next she was holding her cheek, and Sarah's hand stung.

"Fucking psycho," Camila said, spitting at Sarah's feet. "Just like your mom."

The words froze Sarah in place. A red haze descended over her vision, her hands balling into fists.

Camila covered her face.

"Hey, that's enough!" One of the carbon-copy boys stepped between them.

"You're right," Sarah said, choking down the anger, hands dropping to her sides. "It is. I have to go."

She turned on her heel and left the flashing warehouse. The cold wrapped her like a numbing blanket, each step a fevered stomp. She walked until the music turned to a dull thudding sound. Until the shape of the building disappeared into the night. Until only the constant light of the Ladder lit her way.

Until no one could see her crying.

* * * * *

Chapter Nine

Three hours later, Sarah, still in the only dress she owned, walked out of the glistening perfection that was OmniMart with an unopened bottle of tequila in one hand and a bag of "potato" chips made of compressed protein powder in the other. She wasn't sure what the tequila was actually made of, but she knew it got the job done, so did it matter?

Sarah was conflicted about this place. On the one hand, every step through here triggered dozens of latent memories she wasn't supposed to have, from helping someone load a cart, to the day a man had tried to slap her, and ALIZA, or whatever derivative AI OmniMart used, had managed to escort the man out using some sort of pressure point hold she still remembered.

But on the other, those memories lent it a familiarity, a sense of belonging she assumed people had when they thought of home. Few things calmed her like the white walls or the zip of the autonomous cleaner bots as they whipped around the store, the faux-pine scent of the chemicals they used leaving a palpable trail on the wind.

She had to admit, it was nice.

"Hey, beautiful."

And then there were the customers.

Sarah gritted her teeth and avoided looking toward the source of the sound. Instead, she pivoted at the next turn and bee-lined for the register.

Heavy, unsteady footfalls followed.

"Hey!" the voice echoed behind her.

Definitely a man. There was a sluggishness to the word, like he was speaking around a mouth full of food. Probably drunk.

It sent a shiver of panic through her. Why was he following her? What was the point? Did he really think yelling at her in a store was going to make her suddenly want him, make her swoon from his single, randomly tossed "compliment?"

Ahead of her, the registers sat cheerfully. Four Staff people stood at attention, small smiles plastered on otherwise emotionless faces.

Once there, she'd be fine. Surrounded by people, even if they were being controlled by an AI. Violence or antagonistic behavior wasn't tolerated, but sometimes, if the Staff weren't looking at you, if you were in a weird little dead zone, they wouldn't respond.

And right now, Sarah knew she was in one of those spots.

When the hand grabbed her right shoulder, thick-fingered and rough, she didn't think. There wasn't time.

Her body just reacted.

Tequila and chips fell.

She grabbed the meaty mitt. One thumb jabbed hard into the fleshy cavity above his thumb. She spun, left hand sliding along his pale forearm before landing on the callused bit of his elbow.

Then she pushed.

There was a squeak, then he went down, knees cracking to the floor along with the dropped tequila bottle. He was huge, the sort of man she'd had nightmares about after her first year in foster care.

Blood in the air. Angry tears blurred her vision.

Sarah leaned into it.

"You're breaking my fucking arm!" he screamed.

All at once the reality of it hit her. She almost let go.

Almost.

Instead, she bent toward him, not caring if the plunging neckline of her dress showed anything so long as he heard her. "Don't ever touch me or another person without their permission."

"Let go you crazy bit—" Whatever he was going to say broke off into high-pitched howling as she pushed his elbow to the breaking point.

Though how she knew it was the breaking point was a mystery to her. Maybe ALIZA had passed along more than just the action in those memories.

"Fine!" he finally howled. "I won't touch anyone. I swear! Just don't break my fucking arm!"

She let him go. He wheeled back, a huge mess of a man, easily twenty centimeters taller than her, and at least twice her weight. He had a face more at home on a pig. He glared, then made his way back to the liquor section without another word.

"Goddamn," Sarah said. Her body thrummed with energy. She felt like she could knock the shit out of anyone who came at her, like she was the biggest, baddest motherfucker in the building.

A grin forced its way onto her face.

Someone cleared their throat behind her. She turned slowly, expecting a wall of Staff eyes to be staring at her. Instead she found herself looking at a skinny blond gutter rat with a wispy goatee and blue eyes that made her think of—

"Ruby?" Sarah whispered.

"I go by Rudy now, but it's nice to see you still kicking ass, Sayre," Ruby—or rather, Rudy—said with a familiar grin. The voice was deeper, but still had that sardonic lilt Sarah remembered.

"Sayre," Sarah whispered. It'd been a long time since anyone had called her that.

She wanted to be angry. Wanted to lash out like she had a moment ago, but that smile. That damned smile, even with the poor excuse of facial hair dotting her—his—face now...

And just like when they were kids running the streets beneath the nearly finished Ladder, Sarah's cheeks twitched, her lips pulled back of their own accord, and she smiled back.

She was going to say something. Maybe something snarky; maybe nice. But she didn't get the chance. Four Staff at the registers stepped up behind Rudy, smiles still solid on their faces.

"Excuse me, customers," they said in a unison that made Sarah's skin crawl, "please leave the premises before we're forced to remove you or call the police."

Rudy looked at them, eyes wide, a wry smile playing on his lips as he turned to Sarah. "This is some real Stepford Wives shit, isn't it?"

Sarah gave a half-hearted laugh, one hand running her hair over her left ear. Her fingertips brushed the implant port there. "Definitely. But we should go."

Rudy shrugged, then squeezed between the two center Staff members, murmuring feigned apologies as he did so.

"Sorry," Sarah muttered, then went around.

She punched Rudy lightly in the shoulder.

"Ow, it's broken," Rudy grunted, holding a shoulder encased in a ratty brown leather jacket. "Why are you so mean to me?"

"Shut up." Sarah smiled, shaking her head as they left the building for the surprisingly warm and wet midnight air. That probably meant the morning was going to be scorching hot and moist, or there'd be a tornado watch. Maybe both. "You owe me a drink, by the way."

Rudy grunted melodramatically as they exited.

"Thank you so much!" the Staff yelled behind them just before the doors slid shut.

"Man, they're creepy," Rudy said, then he threw his arms into the air. The sky wasn't visible here, the Ladder a blackened sheet dotted with false stars above them. "What a wonderful night to be alive!"

"Rub—Rudy," Sarah said, hands on hips, trying to pretend the question she was about to ask hadn't been repeated in her head thousands of times over the years. "Where'd you go?" Her voice cracked. She hated that.

Rudy's arms dropped. He cocked his head to the side, the bright lights from OmniMart sending most of his face into shadow. Only the wisp of his goatee and a blue eye was visible.

"It's a bit of a story," he said.

Was that a tremor in his voice?

"I don't have to work tomorrow," she said. "I've got time."

Rudy's ready smile came back, and he held out a hand to her like he used to when they were children. "Then I'll tell you over that drink I owe you."

Sarah considered the hand for a moment. His fingers were long and slender, more suited to a piano than anything else, with a light mat of hair across the back of them just visible in the spotlights. She almost said no. Almost turned and went back to her life. Almost pretended this evening had never happened.

Then she saw the gnawed fingernails on Rudy's hands and re-membered another time, another place where she'd gone on adventures to get away from the horror of the world.

His hand was softer than she'd expected, but the grin splitting his face was exactly what she wanted as they headed off into the night.

And this time, the smile met her eyes.

* * * * *

Chapter Ten

At some point in the last hour, Dave had managed to drag himself to the kitchen table and snag the bottle of bourbon he'd left there. Since then, he'd finished the contents and wallowed away in that confused middle ground between tipsy and completely, utterly fucked up. Somewhere in there, he'd called Janet, told her everything, including a rambling rant about running into the OmniMart girl, only to find out he had cancer. Janet wanted to come over and make sure he was okay, but she didn't have a sitter, and it was late, so Dave told her not to. Told her he loved her. That the house was hers if anything happened to him.

He'd hung up before she could reply.

Dave wasn't sure he'd ever said it to her face. Laying here now, he couldn't come up with a good reason why.

Every time the wood floor grew warm beneath him, he'd shift so he lay on a cold surface, contemplating the vaulted ceiling of the dining room. The timbers, rough cut but sanded and stained honey-gold, flitted between the blades of the ceiling fan as it rotated its steel fins, clumps of dust and grease a permanent fixture on their edges. He hadn't cleaned it in years, maybe even before Rose was diagnosed.

Every now and then, he'd think on the tablet and its contents, about how people were already leaving this doomed planet. How they'd done it while giving everyone down here hope for a salvation that was never going to happen.

Hell. Probably wasn't even a UILB station in orbit. All those rich people taking the Ladder were likely already on New Eden, while the rest of the world sat down here, waiting for the next big storm to wipe them out.

If there hadn't been so much bourbon in his system, that might've been a sobering thought. As it was, Dave sighed and squeezed his wedding picture tighter to his chest.

The sounds of tires crunching gravel echoed through the house.

It was followed by flashing blue and red lights breaking through the gaps in his living room curtains.

They didn't even try to knock on the door. The sound of the front door shattering under a battering ram made him flinch, but Dave didn't react. What was the point?

When a tall, forty-something man with a gray handlebar mustache he must've stolen from a corpse stepped over him, some sort of handgun pointed at his chest, Dave sighed again.

Other unseen hands grabbed him around the arms and heaved him to his feet, his wedding picture fluttering from numb hands. His leg went out beneath him. Dave didn't even try to put weight on it.

They can drag me out.

Dave was just happy he couldn't feel the bruises blossoming into being on his chest.

"David Parker," Mr. Mustache recited as he slid the gun into his hip holster and stepped on Rose's picture, "you're under arrest for the murder of Terrence Williams."

The words were a surprise and, as such, Dave had his first flurry of emotions in hours. And if you've ever been in a situation so ridiculous it couldn't possibly be real, you wouldn't fault Dave for what he did next, even if it made him look incredibly, irrefutably guilty.

Dave laughed. He laughed as they pulled zip-ties into place around his wrists. Laughed as they half-dragged, half-carried him into the warm night air. Laughed as they dumped him into the back of an old squad car that smelled like someone had recently puked in it after running a marathon in shit-stained clothes.

He laughed, a dark, humorless laugh as they pulled away from the house he'd built with Rose, leaving it and everything he'd ever loved behind in the darkness of a moonless midnight.

* * * * *

Chapter Eleven

Four miles away from where Dave was being put in the back of a police car, Sarah laughed, too, though hers was more appropriate.

Rudy had taken her to a shady-looking building in Old Downtown at the corner of Warren and Jefferson almost directly under the Ladder. A lot of Old Downtown was something of a no-man's-land, where addicts came to hide, the hopeless came to die, and the hopeful came to find uncaring reality.

A persistent, bone-deep chill radiated from the broken, slush-covered concrete littered with ripped garbage bags. That same cold kept the rotting odor of the uncollected refuse at bay, so Sarah didn't complain much, beyond rubbing goose-bumped arms. She probably should've. It'd been years since she'd last seen Rudy, and here she was, following him into the most dangerous part of the city.

Well, he'd always had a knack for getting her to do stupid shit. Might as well let it ride. The night couldn't get much worse.

An old, torn sign hung in a second-floor window that seemed to be the only one still intact. It advertised "Societal Living" and "Low Rent" in big, faded letters. The rest of the window was blacked out with dark paint. A heavy metal door smeared with rust led inside from the cracked sidewalk. It appeared to be the only way inside.

Rudy leading the way, they approached. He went up to the door, knocked some stupid secret code like they'd done when they were kids—three knocks, one knock, two knocks. There was a scraping sound, the slide hidden from Sarah's line of sight by Rudy, then the door opened. They went in, passing an androgynous kid wearing a surprisingly clean black t-shirt and a pair of jeans that were too big for them, standing on an old milk crate. They gave her a gap-toothed grin as she passed, then shut the door and plopped cross-legged onto the crate, before staring at the wall with a far-off gaze.

"Does that kid have an Ocular implant?" she asked. They were expensive. Sarah only had hers because of her UILB contract. If she finished the contract, she got to keep it, but if not, they'd remove it.

Rudy grinned, then said, "You think that's interesting, wait until you see upstairs."

They got into an ancient elevator Sarah was sure would drop from beneath her as soon as it started rising.

"Upstairs" turned out to be a fully-functional apartment structure. The fourth and fifth floors of the building were still surprisingly intact. Rudy stopped the elevator at the fourth floor to show her a long hallway with a line of doors on the left, all with numbers and small lanterns shining dim, sterile light. To the right was a large space she assumed was a common area, replete with a massive wooden table scarred from decades of use, and mismatched chairs in various stages of disrepair.

But the most impressive part was the smell.

It smelled... clean. Like the air was filtered, the floors mopped with a citrus cleaner. It made her reassess her initial thought that this was a flophouse.

Impressed, she tried to ask questions, but Rudy only grinned.

Then Rudy took her to the fifth floor.

It was a similar layout, but the lights were bright, the atmosphere excited. That might've been from the ten people clustered around another huge dining table, playing some sort of Ocular game that required them to swat their hands back and forth in the air like they were throwing something around. A few people shouted Rudy's name, then went right back to it.

Rudy stepped through, turned so his back was facing everyone, then threw his arms to the side like he had outside the OmniMart. "Welcome to the Retreat."

Hours later, Sarah sat around the beaten table, a real smile plastered on her face. A pleasant buzzing ran through her body from the moonshine she'd been drinking from an old tin cup for the past few hours. Despite the urging of some of the others, who, she noted, had gone "home" to their apartments an hour ago, Sarah avoided getting more than tipsy. Rudy might be an old friend, but it'd been more than a dozen years since they'd last seen each other.

And Rudy wasn't Ruby anymore. Sarah didn't even know what that meant yet. Even though they'd gone out of their way to make her comfortable, she wanted to keep her wits about her. If something went sideways, she was alone here.

The thought sent a shiver down her spine. She took a small nip of the moonshine, savoring the spiced apple flavor and hating the burn that lingered on the back of her tongue.

Most everyone had gone to bed by now, leaving Rudy, Sarah, and another girl, Tracy, behind in the wee hours before dawn. Tracy was a strange, dark-skinned girl with brown irises that vibrated in her head. She had a sweep of long, black dreadlocks that hung haphazardly over her eyes and around her shoulders, and a fashion sense she called "transient-chic." That basically meant she looked like she was homeless—her pants were ripped, shirt covered in stains—but everything was freshly laundered and smelled like vanilla.

They'd just finished talking about how one of the older "guests," as they called anyone who lived in the Retreat, had connected the building's electrical infrastructure to a solar farm out of the shadow of the Ladder.

"I mean, we have the turbines on the roof, too, but that's not enough power, so Gareth," Rudy said, referring to the old guy who'd passed out almost as soon as Sarah had arrived, "used the old access tunnels to repurpose lines. Then we moved the solar panels that'd been up next to the turbines outside the city. Since the battery storage was already here, it was just a matter of figuring out the math."

"Which I did," Tracy chimed in, her British accent slurring slightly from the moonshine, "since no one here can do any maths without messing up the order of operations."

Rudy flicked a crumb of some errant piece of food at her. "I can do math."

Tracy snorted. "Sure, pretty boy."

Rudy's mouth twisted into a small scowl at Tracy's chuckle. "It's PEDMAS. I can do PEDMAS."

Tracy laughed.

"PEMDAS," Sarah said, smiling into her cup. "You've always sucked at math, Ruby."

The laughter cut off. Tracy cleared her throat.

It took Sarah a moment to realize why.

"Rudy," Sarah said, shaking her head. "I'm so sorry, I meant Rudy."

Rudy's eye twitched, then the scowl softened into a comfortable grin. "It's all good, Sayre." Then he turned to Tracy. "I have other skills, thank you very much."

Tracy shrugged, tossed a lock over her shoulder, and took a deep sip from her worn Care Bears cup. "You tip-tap on old keyboards. I wouldn't call that a skill."

Rudy gasped audibly but didn't sit up any farther in the chair. "I'm a legitimate hacker. And I'm offended by your insult."

"You don't even have an OI," Tracy said, tapping the spot just over her left ear where an Ocular Implant access port was usually installed, "and thus, I'm better than you."

"Those are fighting words, lady," Rudy said. He finished the rest of his drink in a gulp, then stood. "Anyone need anything?"

Tracy shook her head and cradled the old coffee cup close to her face.

"No, thanks," Sarah replied. Then she remembered the tablet sitting in her apartment across town. "You guys actually know how to hack, or is that just some sort of odd posturing?"

"I'm insulted," Tracy said, face twisting into an elfin grin.

Rudy walked into the kitchen she hadn't been able to see earlier and poured himself a cup of water from the sink. "Well, we do some, uh—" he struggled for a moment before continuing "—non-profit work for various groups. That's how we keep the roof over our heads."

"That reminds me," Tracy said, "we need to patch the spot over Darris' room. It's leaking again."

Rudy shut off the water. He grimaced, then came back to the table. "Of course it is. I'll take care of it."

Sarah tapped her short fingernails on the edge of her glass. "Do you think you could help me find someone?"

"Jilted lover?" Tracy asked, smiling.

"Probably someone who owes her money," Rudy offered.

Sarah rolled her eyes. "No. Some racist doctor gave me a guy's tablet, and I want to get it back to him."

Tracy shook her head. "Pass." Then she took a sip from her mug.

Rudy grinned. "Oh, really? I bet a week of dishes I can do it before you."

Tracy's eyes flashed. "Easy money? All right. I got to work on my tan anyway." She turned to Sarah, her irises shaking with the light from her OI spinning up. "Hit me with some details."

"Wait!" Rudy yelled. He set his mug on the table and pulled out a beaten old laptop that looked like it was held together with stickers. He cracked his neck and knuckles, then placed his hands on the keyboard. "Okay."

Sarah smiled. "David Parker. Old white guy." The sound of Rudy's fingers flashing across keys echoed in the air. Tracy grunted as she did her own search. Sarah struggled to think of details now that she was on the spot. "Has a mustache—no, a goatee. Bald. Um—"

"Found him!" Rudy shouted, jumping to his feet. Then he looked at the screen again, nose wrinkling as he read whatever text he saw on his old screen.

"Oh," Tracy said at the same time.

Sarah looked between them. "What?"

Tracy turned to Rudy, then gestured with her mug. "After you."

Rudy rubbed his neck. "Um."

"What?" Sarah asked, a nervous laugh flitting into her words. "Is he dead or something?"

Rudy did a weird wiggling motion, then spun the laptop around. The display was old and flickering, a few lines running through the entirety that made it difficult to see. Despite that, she could tell it was a police blotter with a picture of Dave. Good old dad-joke Dave. His remaining mane of hair was in disarray, goatee pushed to one side like he'd just gotten out of bed, but the anger in his eyes came through the screen.

"What is this?" Sarah asked.

Rudy rubbed his hands. "Arrest report. He killed a guy, Sayre."

"Yeah," Tracy said, swiping her free hand in the air as she moved a window only she could see, "and he's in the Pit."

Sarah raised an eyebrow. "What's the Pit?"

* * * * *

Chapter Twelve

The Pit wasn't what Dave had expected.

After decades of watching first television shows, then streams of independently created media about jails, he thought there'd be a tense atmosphere. Maybe a two-story structure with cells every couple feet, cons locked inside and jeering at the fresh meat as it arrived.

His entire jail strategy involved finding the biggest person in the place and begging them for protection in exchange for illicit tech work, or failing that, any sort of sexual stuff he could give, even if his arthritis would mean he wasn't that good at it.

What he hadn't expected was the silence.

And the darkness.

Instead of bringing Dave to a police station, the cop with the slicked-up mustache had brought him to the front gate of Upstate Rehabilitation of Central New York. It was a massive building in the shadow of the southern leg of the Ladder. It'd been nearing five in the morning, the western horizon lightening into a gray smear from thin clouds, when they arrived. Large lamps flanked a chain-link gate you could drive a passenger plane through. To the right of the gate was a small building with a bored man standing guard.

Mustache pulled up, flashed his badge, and said something about Matthew Tarrington. Dave had almost asked questions, but honestly, what the hell did it matter? Someone had killed Terry, and they'd pinned it on him. What was one more name, even if it was the CTO of the UILB?

After the guard kicked open the gate with a screeching motor system that set Dave's teeth on edge, Mustache drove in. The handoff happened out in the open on what Dave assumed was the oft-referenced "yard." Mustache transferred Dave to a massive security guard with a beard who reminded him of pictures of mountain men he'd seen in a documentary once, then saluted for some reason, and left.

"I guess we don't do questioning anymore?" Dave asked his new jailer.

The man bore a nametag that read "Sgt. Jensen." Jensen didn't respond. Instead, he walked, dragging Dave along with the sureness of a glacier extending, or a tornado waltzing through a trailer park.

Together, they went through a vault door that'd been repurposed as the gateway to the place and entered the Pit. Dave limped along in barely numbed pain.

By then, Dave was in that strange place between drunk and sober where everything begins to hurt and the pleasant side of being tipsy turns into flop sweat and dizziness. That, of course, made the transition into the long, silent hallways of the Pit, layered with the lingering odor of unwashed bodies and ill-drained sewage, a goddamned nightmare. The air coated his already dry tongue with a layer of acrid nasty he couldn't get out of his mouth.

Each step was a challenge not to vomit.

Every ten or fifteen feet, a break in the flat lines of the hallway walls would appear, two-inch thick bars running from floor to ceiling. The cells never had any lights on, just recesses filled with shadow, and once, the sound of a woman whimpering.

"Do we not do lights here?" Dave asked, then he belched, the acidic tang of bile stinging the back of his throat. "Or running water? I kind of need a drink."

Jensen didn't respond. Instead, as they came to another of those recesses, he stopped, dragging Dave to a halt. Like he was an automaton, Jensen pivoted, swinging Dave to the side as the bars covering the doorway slid away, half into the ceiling, half into the floor, with a sharp snap.

Jensen gave Dave a shove.

But Dave didn't move. A cold wind breathed from the opening, but everything was lost in shadow, like the walls themselves gave off the creeping darkness that filled this place.

"Come on, man," Dave said, rubbing his aching wrists. "I didn't kill anyone, and I don't want to go in there."

Jensen didn't give a shit what he wanted. When Dave didn't walk in under his own power, Jensen grabbed him under the arms and put him in. Dave tried struggling, but he might as well be fighting a mountain.

Without a word, Jensen pushed Dave against the wall and somehow disconnected the handcuffs with one hand. And that was it.

Jensen stepped away, the bars slid into place, and then the big, silent guard walked back the way they'd come.

Dave tried not to panic. Tried to keep his shit together. He was, after all, innocent, but there's only so much someone can take in such a short time.

And this was Dave's limit.

He limped to the bars, grabbing hold of their cold steel with both hands, and tried to shake them. Move them. Do anything but step farther into the shadow behind him.

Anything but that.

* * * * *

Chapter Thirteen

Adrenaline was way better than coffee.

"Sarah," Rudy said, stumbling slightly as he jumped in front of the elevator door. He *hadn't* been pacing himself. "Let's think this through."

"No," Sarah snapped. "This isn't right. He's silly and weird and tells horrible jokes, but he's not a murderer."

"That's not what this article says," Tracy chimed in from behind her. "It says he killed a guy this afternoon—"

"No," Sarah said, slamming her fist into her thigh.

"But!" Tracy said as she approached and put a warm hand on Sarah's shoulder. "It says it was likely caused by a brain tumor."

A chill swept over Sarah. Everything dimmed. "He has a brain tumor?"

"Yeah," Tracy said, sliding around Sarah's left side, their bodies touching lightly. Her brown hands grabbed Sarah's. "The article says he likely killed him after the diagnosis. The guy's office was right down the hall. They're saying it happened around eight last night."

"Tracy," Rudy whispered.

Tracy shook her head and let Sarah go. "Sorry. Details make me feel better. I forget not everyone feels the same."

Sarah's vision blurred. An ache she hadn't felt in decades crawled its way, scratching and tearing, up her throat. She barely knew the guy; why was she fucking crying?

The answer was there in a dark part of her mind she never approached or explored. It was because of the goddamn dad jokes.

Every time she'd wake up in OmniMart, and he'd be grinning that lopsided grin, an increasingly bad joke at the ready, it'd made her feel something besides drive. Feel like someone cared enough to take time out of their day to think of her. To do something for her, even if it was weird and stupid.

Just like her mom used to.

Then something Tracy had said clicked. "Wait. The guy they're saying he killed, you said he was in his office?"

Tracy's brow furrowed. "Yeah?"

"In the Ladder?"

"Yeah, why?"

The laugh surprised her, and if Tracy and Rudy's faces were any indication, it surprised them, too. "I was there."

"What?" Rudy and Tracy asked in unison.

A smile Sarah couldn't have kept down if she'd wanted to split her face. "And I know for a fact Dave couldn't have killed anyone at that time."

"I'm a little concerned how you know that…" Rudy trailed off.

Warmth flooded Sarah's chest. She put a hand on both Tracy and Rudy's shoulders. "I blew out his hip."

The other two stared at each other for a moment, amusement flickering on their faces.

Rudy opened his mouth like he was going to say something, but Sarah cut him off. "Not like that. I ran into him, and his hip popped out of socket."

"How does that prove anything?" Tracy asked.

"Because I ran into him at seven-forty-five," she said, shaking her head. "He was in an MRI when that guy was killed."

Tracy and Rudy exchanged a glance.

An idea popped into Sarah's head. It was crazy. She barely knew Dave, and she had only just reconnected with Rudy, but the feeling of wrongness here was too much for her to ignore, too heavy to close her eyes, smile a plastic smile, and continue on with her life.

Maybe it was the lingering booze in her system, but she'd done that enough.

Hell, now that she knew the only reason she had a chance at going to New Eden was to be a baby factory for Camila, there was no reason to follow through on the plan. She wasn't working her way there; she was biding time until Camila's ticket got punched on the first ship off this planet.

Well. Camila could go to hell.

Sarah cocked her head to the side and flashed a smile at Rudy. It'd always worked when they were kids, maybe…?

Rudy's already pale face went white. "Oh, no."

"Help me break a friend out of the country's worst prison?"

Tracy's mouth fell open. "What? No."

Rudy's eyes wandered around the small entry until, after several long moments filled with Tracy repeatedly saying no, he caught her gaze. His head shook in the negative. Then he sighed.

"Goddammit, Sayre," he said. "Fine, but then you need to help us with something."

Sarah grinned. She almost asked what it was but didn't want to push it. "Deal."

Tracy stared at them both for a long moment before letting out a heavy sigh. "Fine. But we need some sleep first."

"But—" Sarah started, but Tracy interrupted.

"Listen—" Tracy held up a hand, forestalling any other complaints, "—I'm a little tipsy, and I'm tired. If we're doing this, I need sleep. Okay?"

Sarah nodded.

"Good." Tracy grinned. "Room 508 is open, so get some rest. We have to schedule a prison break in a few hours."

* * * * *

Chapter Fourteen

They'd turned off the last of the lights hours ago.

Maybe.

Dave had no idea how long it'd been or whether his eyes were open or closed. The darkness writhed with a life of its own. Figures merged and twisted. The walls creaked under the weight of it, the pressure of emptiness pulling the moist surfaces inward, like it wanted to implode.

Just like his mind, waiting to pop and wink into nothingness, lost into a deafening, silent void only infrequently interrupted by a whimper.

A whimper that might be him.

Or it could be the other man crouched in the corner. The one with the horn teeth and the bat ears.

The one that glowed ebony against a black background.

Dave squeezed his eyes shut. The figure disintegrated into his mind. He tried to pull his knees to his chest, but his hip roared in defiance. A shiver ran through the floor and into his body.

They hadn't provided a cot or toilet. No blanket or sink.

Just a rectangle room that wasn't quite long enough to lay down in and smelled of death and misery.

How long would he be here? Did it matter?

Dave let out a shuddering sigh and rested his head against the one knee he'd been able to draw up to his chest. Maybe, if he was lucky, he'd die in his sleep.

Or maybe the demon in the corner would rip him apart.

Either would be fine, honestly.

* * * * *

Chapter Fifteen

"This is a bad plan," Sarah said, wiping her forehead as they made their way out of the city in Tracy's downright ancient Tesla.

Rudy turned in the front seat until he could give Sarah a lopsided smile. "It'll be fine. We'll take care of everything."

Sarah nodded, but the nervousness persisted. Beyond the heavily-tinted windows, they broke from beneath the shadow of the Ladder, and amber light filled the car. The aged beige leather of the seats was cracked and split. Stuffing poked out here and there like errant hairs from an old man's ears. Various stains covered everything, darker splotches in shapes that made Sarah wish she'd grabbed a blanket to sit on.

The smell had been bad enough—a sickly mix of old shoes and rotting garbage—but now that she could see it all?

Ew.

But the excitement was intoxicating, and as long as she focused on Dave, she could pretend the blood wasn't real, that she wasn't risking everything she'd ever worked for on a stupid old man.

At least he's never lied to me.

They'd made a pit stop at her apartment and picked up one of her jumpsuits for the plan. Sweat trickled down her back. *The plan.* When she'd first asked for help, Sarah had imagined Tracy and Rudy knocking on a keyboard or doing some incredible technological trickery to get Dave out.

Instead, Rudy and Tracy were awake before her and, without any input, had come up with a plan that was *nothing* like she'd expected.

Sure, it involved a lot of tech and bits Sarah thought counted as "hacking," but it also involved her walking through the front door of the Pit as a Staff member under their control.

Their control. The thought made her shiver. It'd always been an AI managing her shifts, even at OmniMart. She'd never had a human dictating her movements like that.

She grimaced, and rubbed and picked at her fingernails. Never might be too strong a word. "Are you sure—" she started again.

Tracy, as usual, interrupted her. "Hang on. Merging."

The car's engine, or whatever it actually was, kicked up to a humming whine, then they merged onto what was left of 81 South. The damn vehicle rattled and jumped like it was about to shake apart from the speed.

Sarah grabbed the worn seat and whispered a small prayer.

"Potholes are worse," Rudy said far too calmly, one white-knuckled fist gripping a handle just over the passenger window.

Tracy grunted noncommittally.

Sarah tried not to puke.

Ten minutes—and seven "potholes" that made the undercarriage scrape against the road—later, they rolled off the highway and past a faded, orange "Exit Closed" sign. Barren hills rose around them, the road ahead gently curving around to the right between two rounded, yellowed earthen mounds. A sign, half-collapsed on itself, the old white-text-on-green font barely legible, called this place "Nedrow."

Sarah had never been out of the city, let alone here. She'd heard about it, though. It and the Reservation War of 2053. In school, she'd been taught that the Native Americans of this Reservation had attacked Syracuse for resources in the midst of the 2052 drought. The National Guard had swept in, clearing the area and the dissidents, and saving Syracuse from a similar fate.

Now that she was here, Sarah couldn't shake the feeling she'd been lied to.

Dozens of crosses and shrines of various sorts dotted the exit road. They all looked like it'd been years since anyone touched them. One small stand, the skeletons of flowers framing a bleached white teddy bear, caught her eye as they passed.

"What happened here?" Sarah whispered.

"Slaughter," Rudy spat. "Water dried up. People protested. Soldiers killed them."

"And took their land for the Pit," Tracy added. "Speaking of which…"

Sarah tore her eyes away from the bear as it disappeared into the distance. She looked out the front window as they crested a hill, and a valley opened beneath them. "Jesus Christ."

"No place here for that pleasant bastard," Rudy muttered. "Welcome to Hell."

Ahead of them was an ebony fortress. The main structure was a squat square of black stone or metal that sucked the brightness out of the air. Surrounding the entire thing was a massive fence topped with razor-wire, though there weren't any guard towers like she'd expected.

Nothing moved in that place. It was just… there, an unnatural scar on the land.

"Where are the guards?" Sarah managed as the Pit grew larger on their approach.

Tracy laughed. "They're inside. Just like you're gonna be."

"Stop scaring her," Rudy snapped, eyes flashing as he turned to Tracy.

Tracy cleared her throat. "Sorry."

"It's okay," Sarah muttered. She smoothed her jumpsuit even though it didn't need it. "But one more time. How does this work?"

"We're pulling up," Rudy said, turning in his seat and giving her a grin that lifted some of the weight from her shoulders. "You're getting out, then I'm going to—" Rudy waggled his fingers in the air, "—into their AI backend and connect you in so everyone there accepts you."

Sarah gritted her teeth and nodded. "Okay. Then we find Dave?"

Rudy glanced at Tracy quickly, then back to Sarah. "Exactly."

"What?" Sarah asked as a shadow fell over the car as they pulled up outside the main gate. "Is there something else?"

"Yeah," Rudy said, eyes flicking to Tracy again, but then he smiled. "It's showtime."

The car rattled to a stop. Sarah took a deep breath, then popped the creaking door open. A wave of stifling heat slammed into her, along with a scattering of dust from the wet, stale wind. The air tasted of dirt and death.

"Quick, quick!" Tracy said. "We only have a few seconds!"

Sarah lunged out the door, coughing and hacking at the dust filling her nostrils. She didn't see the car spin away, but some of the kicked-up dirt spattered her normally spotless jumpsuit.

After several long moments, Sarah managed to get herself upright. She wiped her nose with the back of her hand and tried to pretend nothing had been left behind.

Beyond the chain-link fence, a huge door that looked more like a bank vault than an access portal slid open with a deafening screech. A man stepped out and walked toward her. At first, she thought he was short, but as he approached, Sarah realized it was a trick of perspective. The door was simply massive enough to make this nearly seven-foot-tall man appear tiny.

Where the fuck is Rudy?

She'd planned on some of this. That if it took Rudy longer than expected to get her in, she'd fudge some of the greeting protocols. After all, she remembered enough of them from the Ladder to make the AI equivalent of small talk. It'd be the same at the prison, right?

He was roughly ten meters away when he pulled a pistol from his belt and pointed it at her.

There were no questions, none of the generic greetings or platitudes ALIZA seemed to enjoy at the Ladder.

"Wait!" Sarah yelled. "I'm just having trouble getting an uplink! I'm new!"

There was no response except his finger dropping around the trigger.

Shit. This is how I die. Sarah closed her eyes.

Then a prompt popped up on the inside of her eyelids.

Authorize New Connection?

Sarah's hand flew to her temple, tapped one, two, three times.

Her vision narrowed on the end of a pistol barrel.

And everything disappeared.

* * * * *

Chapter Sixteen

The light was a surprise.

Dave covered his eyes at its brilliant glare. He immediately regretted it. Absolutely every part of his body had seized up between whenever he'd dozed off and the lights came on. Even that layer of muscle on his lower back, the part that felt like a wicker basket tied to your spine, trembled in pain.

That didn't stop him from staring at the corner where the demon had sat earlier. Rationally, he knew there wasn't anything crouched there, but even with the lights from outside the cell, he thought he could make it out. Claws and horns.

Long teeth flashing into a smile.

The sound of clacking boots on tile dragged his gaze from the corner and to the hallway.

"What the hell?"

The big guard, Jensen, stepped heavily next to the bars keeping Dave in place. Next to him, looking downright diminutive, was Omni-Mart girl.

What was she doing here? Why was she here? On closer examination, she had deep bags under her eyes he didn't remember from their encounter the other day.

Jesus. Was that yesterday?

That said, he didn't have any right to judge. He bet he looked like a steaming pile of dog shit. Dave struggled to his feet, not bothering to stop the groans and moans of pain as he fought time and age.

He reached for the bars as he wobbled to his feet. "What are you doing—whoa!"

The bars sucked back into the floor and ceiling. Dave fell out of the cell. Instead of slamming to the floor and busting another hip out of joint, a meaty paw caught him in mid-air.

"You're being transferred." The voice coming out of Jensen in no way matched his body. It was the high-pitched squeal of a man who'd just been kicked in the balls, not the deep baritone Dave had imagined him having. "Go with her."

Dave looked between OmniMart girl, whom he realized was wearing a Ladder janitorial uniform, and Jensen, blank-faced and staring.

It wasn't like it was a hard choice.

"Sure." Dave nodded and limped into the walkway. "Let's do that."

Jensen positioned himself behind Dave. A moment later, zip-ties snapped into place around his wrists, then Jensen gave him a light shove toward OmniMart girl.

God, I need to learn her name.

Face flat, she grabbed his arm, pivoted, and proceeded to the exit.

Behind them, Jensen followed, his long gait slowed to match OmniMart girl's much shorter stride.

Dave tried to breathe, tried to stay calm, but his eyes were locked on the massive door at the end of the hall. The one still sealed shut. As they moved, the building seemed to wake around them. Groans and sobs rattled amongst the rafters. From somewhere back the way they'd come, a woman screamed.

Just a few more feet…

Then he was jerked to a halt. He was so close, and he couldn't tear his eyes away. In his mind he thought maybe he could even see a little daylight squeezing through the edge of the portal.

No. No no no no.

OmniMart girl pivoted again, dragging Dave to the left. He almost struggled, but then the sound of bars whisking away filled the hallway again, followed by Jensen saying, "You're being transferred. Go with her."

That caught Dave's attention. He looked to his left in time to see Jensen dragging some… woman to her feet. A wave of festering body odor strong enough his eyes watered slammed into him. He couldn't tell much about her except she'd been there a long time. Her black hair was a massive rat nest that seemed to have formed a mane around her head and neck. Her body, emaciated and rail-thin, was barely clothed in what looked like remnants of different burlap sacks. Hell, he could only tell she was a woman because the barest impression of breasts lifted her rough shirt, and even that didn't matter much. She was barefoot, just like him, but her feet were damn near black with dirt and grime.

She didn't even look up as she was dragged out of the cell. If Jensen hadn't been holding her up, Dave wasn't sure she'd have stayed standing at first.

Then the zip-ties went around her wrists, OmniMart girl took her arm, and the three of them continued on.

Jensen stepped past as they approached and took a position to the left of the door. He waved his hand.

The sounds of a dozen pistons snapping out of place ripped through the area. Daylight slashed through the prison. The other inmates, finally noticing what was happening, screamed and begged and wailed.

It wasn't language, nothing Dave could identify anyway, but he felt the meaning in his bones as a sliver of light cut across his face. The warmth infused him, filled him with life.

They all wanted—needed—the sunlight.

The other inmate OmniMart girl escorted straightened slightly, eyes hesitantly looking in the direction of the door as it opened with a screeching rivaled only by the terrible cacophony echoing from the cells behind them.

The door open, OmniMart girl stepped forward, pulling him and the other woman along. It wasn't like they were struggling. Dave knew this was his only chance, and he assumed the lady did, too.

A blistering, humid wind swept into Dave's face as they stepped out from beneath the massive steel gateway into the putrid underworld. His bare feet pricked against the hot, broken rocks beneath his feet. Sweat beaded immediately on his forehead, and his breath grew heavy, but he smiled anyway. For the first time in decades, Dave was thrilled by the apocalyptic heat.

They kept on until the barbed-wire fence rattled open, then closed behind them. Until they stumbled onto ancient, abandoned asphalt that would've peeled the skin from their feet, if not for a healthy dollop of brown dust coating everything.

They walked for something approaching a quarter mile before Dave finally worked up the courage to say something.

But he was cut off by the sound of an electric car whirring around a particularly rocky outcrop. It looked like it used to be red, with a rusted, stylized T emblazoned on the front. As the car pulled to a halt next to them, a dry cloud of dust skittered around them. In that moment, OmniMart girl let go of his arm.

When it cleared, she stared at him, eyes wide and alive, a smile on her face. "Hey, Dave."

"Hey," he said, gratitude, happiness, and terror mingling with some weird sense of pride he couldn't identify. He just barely stopped himself from hugging her. "I think I should stop calling you OmniMart girl."

"Yeah, I don't work there anymore." She smiled wider. "Call me Sayre."

"Nice to meet you, Sayre," Dave said with a heavy, happy sigh.

Then she looked to the woman (barely) standing next to him. Her smile disappeared and confusion clouded her face. "Who the fuck are you?"

The woman barely raised her head, but through her matted hair, Dave swore he saw a singular, neon-blue eye staring back.

The passenger door of the car opened then, and a spindly guy with the barest wisp of a goatee stepped into the sun. He put his hand on Sayre's shoulder with a familiarity that surprised Dave.

"She," the man said, gesturing at the bedraggled woman, "is how we tear this entire fucking thing down."

* * * * *

Chapter Seventeen

I f Rudy hadn't been driving, Sarah would've throat punched him.

Or slapped him.

Or something to show how absolutely fucking *angry* she was right now.

The words kept forming in her head and heart as he, Tracy, and the new woman rambled on about their bullshit.

I trusted you, and you abused that trust!

I literally let you control my body*, and this is what you do?*

You're supposed to be my friend!

But instead of screaming over the cracking of the car's shocks bottoming out on the shitty highway, Sarah ground her teeth to nubs and kept her mouth shut.

"The Retreat is good," Tracy was saying to the new woman, Bones (as if that was a name), from between Sarah and Dave in the back seat. "Rudy and I have kept it up. Even increased membership."

Bones didn't turn around or say anything, but she nodded.

Thus far, she'd only said two words, "Connect me," and those only after getting into the front passenger seat right after the escape.

After that, her electric blue eyes had somehow gotten brighter, and she'd spent the rest of the ride staring vacantly out the front window.

Rudy rolled into the rubble that made up the south side of Syracuse, carefully dodging collapsed sections of highway and other refuse. The Ladder rose before them as they approached, a long silver sliver piercing the sky. It grew wider as they approached, until Sarah saw the tell-tale signs of the elevators moving on the east and west sides.

"So, uh, where are we going?"

Dave's voice snapped Sarah out of the anger she'd been wallowing in. She forced a smile and turned to him, only then really noticing his age against the backdrop of twenty-somethings filling the rest of the car. He looked more like a man getting comfortable with retirement than someone just broken out of prison for murder.

"The Retreat," Sarah said.

"Wait, what?" Tracy snapped, turning on Sarah, brown eyes flashing. "We said we'd help, not *house* him."

Heat crawled into Sarah's face. Their proximity, arm-to-arm and squeezed into the back seat of a failed sports car, suddenly became very, very apparent.

"Well, I didn't give you permission to break out some tech-filled science project and not tell me jack shit about it, so I figure you owe me," Sarah said, matching Tracy's unflinching stare.

Sarah had to admit, she was a little surprised by her firmness. It seemed courage was a lot easier to come by when all your dreams had blown up in your face.

From the front seat, Bones made a choking sound eerily reminiscent of a snicker.

"Guys," Dave interjected, turning awkwardly in the seat, "let's be realistic here. I really appreciate all this, but they're just going to find me again. I appreciate the sabbatical, but this was always going to fail eventually."

Tracy rolled her eyes and rounded on Dave. "Oh, hell no. We got you out, you stay out. That's how this works."

Dave's goatee twisted into a sardonic half-smile. "Then… where am I going?"

Tracy sighed. "Somewhere else."

"We'll figure it out," Rudy chimed in from the front seat.

"This is crazy!" Sarah threw her hands in the air.

"He goes with us."

Everyone turned as one to Bones.

"But—" Tracy said.

"We need him," Bones said again, her voice a quiet chime in the close quarters, "and her."

"What?" Sarah said.

Bones turned in her seat until she could fix the three of them with her flashing blue eyes. At some point, she'd pulled her knotted hair back into a semblance of a ponytail, revealing a long, narrow face dominated by a hawkish nose and a line of a mouth. "We're all in this together now, and together we'll tear this place apart."

Sarah expected her to turn back round, but instead she sat there as Rudy drove them in silence, her eyes flicking back and forth between their faces as if measuring their resolve.

Weighing their souls.

"Okay?" Dave offered after several *very* long moments.

Bones nodded at him. She turned her gaze on Tracy, who quickly acquiesced.

Then Bones looked at Sarah. Now that she matched the stare, Sarah saw the whirring discs that had replaced her irises. The dark pinprick of a pupil surrounded by tech Sarah had only ever read about in futuristic tech columns.

"And you, Sarah?" Bones said after a long pause. "We need you most of all."

"Why?" Sarah asked.

Bones lips twitched into a smile; yellow teeth just visible behind thin, chapped lips. "Because you can get us into the Ladder."

"What?"

"Hold on," Rudy said, then he pulled off the comparatively smooth highway and onto the wrecked streets of Syracuse.

The shadow of the Ladder spilled over them like a cold bath, dousing everything in a persistent darkness that immediately chilled the car. Ahead of them, a single headlight flickered to life, illuminating collapsing structures and long-abandoned shells of vehicles.

But it didn't touch the heat in Sarah's chest. "What the fuck are you talking about?"

Bones raised an eyebrow and looked at Rudy.

"I hadn't gotten that far," Rudy said, rubbing his neck. "We just reconnected yesterday."

"Yesterday?" Bones snapped, pulling back into her seat and staring at Rudy. "I've been in that place for *months*."

"I know."

Bones took a deep breath. "You were supposed to contact her immediately after my arrest."

Sarah's stomach twisted. "Ex-fucking-scuse me?"

They ignored her.

"I know," Rudy said, words turning up at the end. The car tossed and shifted as he drove slowly around aged debris covered in patches of dark mold. "I just—"

"Just what?" Bones asked, shifting so she could look straight at him. "Just didn't feel like getting me out?"

"Bones, he tried—" Tracy chimed in, but shut her mouth with a snap at a wave from Bones.

"I couldn't find her," Rudy said, hands snapping to the steering wheel. His knuckles turned white. "I just couldn't find her."

"I'm still right here," Sarah said, but no one was listening.

Bones barked out a laugh. "Do you know what they do to you in the Pit, Rudy? Hm? Nothing. There's nothing. Just you in a dark cell, alone with your thoughts—nothing but the machinations of your mind." She pulled at her ratty excuse for a shirt with skeletal fingers. "They barely feed you, Rudy. And you left me there?"

Rudy didn't respond right away, but when he did, his voice cracked. "I didn't mean to. We just couldn't figure it out without you."

Bones stared at him for a long moment, the blue of her eyes lighting her cheeks with dim azure light. "Fine."

"I'm still right here," Sarah muttered.

Tracy grunted. "We know."

"We're almost to the Retreat," Rudy chimed in, false cheer filling every word out of his mouth. "Let's get back, have a drink or two, and we'll figure this out."

"Christ, yes," Dave said, shifting in the seat and planting his forehead on the window. "I'm painfully sober for all this bullshit."

Sarah stared at black shards of old buildings as they drove. They looked like the charred fingers of giants reaching toward the Ladder. Whether to lift it up or tear it down, though, she couldn't decide.

But she could agree with Dave. "A drink sounds fantastic."

* * * * *

Chapter Eighteen

The moonshine reminded Dave of a particularly blurry week in college.

The only thing missing was Rose.

They all sat in a room resembling a frat house common room with fewer empty beer cans and more rustic charm. The three folks he didn't know—Rudy, Tracy, and the one called Bones—had been pow-wowing in the corner since they arrived. Bones had taken a few minutes after they got there to head into one of the apartments, take a shower, and change into ratty-looking clothes that weren't that much of an upgrade from the rags she'd been wearing. The rat's nest she'd called a head of hair was now untangled and pulled into a ponytail of curly black hair.

Now, perched atop a set of carbon-tube furniture, Tracy and Bones kept swiping in the air while they talked, while Rudy hammered away at the keys of an old laptop.

But masterminds or not, they weren't who drew his attention. A few feet away, Sayre sat on an ancient wicker chair, legs drawn up to her chest. She had her own mug of the delicious poison, but he wasn't sure she'd taken a sip yet.

"This is fucking hopeless," Tracy said, getting to her feet in a rush. "I'm gonna take a walk."

Rudy raised a hand like he was going to try to stop her, but Bones just waved Tracy away. "Don't take too long."

Dave snorted despite himself, earning a glare from Tracy as she passed. He'd done that a few times with pissy employees over the years. Better they blow off steam than derail the meeting.

A moment later, a heavy door slammed open, followed by the receding sound of booted feet on stairs.

"I didn't know there were stairs," Dave muttered.

Sayre shifted on her chair, pulling at her gray jumpsuit like it itched. "Me, either."

Dave smiled. "Thanks again for saving me. Sorry if it's gotten you into trouble."

She returned the smile. "From what I remember, it was terrible in there. I wouldn't leave you like that. Especially when you couldn't have killed that man."

"Fuck. I forgot about Terry. Candace is probably destroyed," Dave said, then took another sip of moonshine. At a quizzical look from Sayre, he added, "Candace is Terry's wife. They had two—shit, three kids."

"I'm sorry, Dave."

Dave smiled, but an emptiness the moonshine couldn't feel yawned in his stomach. "It's not your fault, kid. I just can't believe it's over a tablet I ended up losing."

Sayre shifted in her seat. "What's on the tablet?"

Dave cast a glance at her. She was a kid, maybe into her twenties, but still a child. He wanted to share the information, wanted help making it right somehow, but he didn't want to get anyone else hurt, least of all the kid who'd just busted him out of prison.

So he decided to keep his mouth shut. "Nothing."

Sayre narrowed her eyes at him but didn't say anything. Instead, she set her mug down and went into apartment 508.

"Well, shit," Dave muttered. He took another long pull on his drink. "I've got to get better at lying."

"Very true," Sayre's voice chimed in as she came back out.

Dave turned to her as she approached. She tossed something into his lap. The screen lit up. And Rose smiled back at him.

Despite everything that'd happened in the past day, seeing her face made the ache of the world disappear. With a trembling finger, he drew a line around her chin, ignoring the nerd behind her.

"Thank you," Dave whispered, glancing at Sayre through tear-blurred eyes.

"Don't mention it," Sayre said. She curled back into her chair and grabbed the mug. "But don't fucking lie to me."

"I'm not—" he tried to say, but then his eyes met hers. He sighed. "Fine. But if Terry was any indication, people are willing to *kill* for this."

Dave wasn't sure whether he expected her to panic and run, or what, but she certainly didn't.

Instead, Sayre's eyes lit up. "Lay it on me."

"All right."

The explanation was quick, a few sentences describing the contents of the email, and his attempts to verify it with Terry, but by the end, Dave felt like he'd run a marathon.

"So," Sayre started, staring at the mug in her hands. "The rich are already *on* New Eden?"

"As I understand it, yes."

"And you found out because, what—" Sayre laughed, "—an IT department didn't properly wipe a tablet?"

A twitch kicked Dave's left eye. "I guess so, yeah."

Sayre smiled, raised her mug, then drank its contents all at once.

"Whoa! What're you doing?"

Sayre choked, then coughed and set the mug down. "I was almost there then."

Dave furrowed his brow. "What do you mean?"

"I mean, I was Camila's Second, and she was partying like it was her last night on Earth." Sayre grabbed her face and let out a loud grunt before screaming, "Fuck!"

That drew some eyes, but no one asked about it. They were too deep in their own machinations to really care.

Dave took another sip of his sweet swill. "What's a 'second?'"

"I'm not going anymore, so it doesn't matter."

"Of course it doesn't," Bones' thin voice interrupted.

Dave jumped in surprise. She was standing damn near over his shoulder. The light aroma of lavender tickled his nose.

"Jesus, we need to put a bell on you," Dave said, then he, too, finished his drink. "What're you talking about?"

"I mean, we've known about this for a few years," Bones said, dragging a chair from the large common table so she could sit with them. Behind her, Rudy sat alone, staring at his laptop. "That's why we need your help, Sayre."

Sayre shifted in her seat but didn't look away from Bones' eldritch stare. "Why me?"

"Because you're Staff," Rudy chimed in. He closed his laptop and came to join them. "We need someone to get us inside."

"But why me? Why not someone else?" Sayre asked, leaning forward, eyes searching Rudy's face. Dave couldn't get over how vulnerable, how much a child, she seemed.

In that moment, he wanted nothing more than to protect this brave kid.

Across from Dave, the elevator dinged. A moment later, Tracy stepped into the room. There were streaks around her eyes, like smudged makeup.

Had she been crying?

"Okay," Tracy said. "Let's do it."

"Do what?" Dave asked.

Bones sighed and stood. "We're breaking into the Ladder."

"What?" Sayre asked, eyes wide. "That's insane."

"No more insane than the mission." Bones smiled.

Dave barked out a mirthless laugh. "Breaking in isn't the mission?"

"No," Rudy said. "Getting video of the trip to New Eden and back is."

* * * * *

Chapter Nineteen

After the initial shock wore off, Sarah bit her tongue, got to her feet, and left in a numb haze.

There were shouts, and at one point, someone grabbed her. But that same instinct that'd helped her in OmniMart kicked in, and they let go quickly. She barely remembered leaving by the stairs, or the stairwell that went around and around in narrow darkness. It wasn't until she kicked open a heavy steel door and stepped into the shadow of the Ladder that life came back into focus.

The humidity was thick here, heavy enough to weigh down her lungs as if she were underwater. The smell of the old downtown didn't fare well in the heat. Every piece of trash in the place festered until a haze writhed its way off the broken concrete and into her nose.

But she didn't care about that. She walked through it, ignoring the catcalls and huddled forms startled awake by her presence. She passed several burnt-out buildings, their shells staring like broken skulls, offal and mold swimming out to greet her.

It'd taken longer than expected to get out from beneath the shadow of the Ladder, since the sun was setting behind it, but her track to the southeast finally broke her from the never-ending shawl of the central tower. She left the darkness of the Ladder behind and stepped into the setting sun. It warmed her skin, sending goose-bumps across her arms as the humidity dissipated ever so slightly.

A trill echoed in her head, and an incoming call prompt popped into the corner of her vision.

She thought about ignoring it, sending it to her mail so she could delete it later when she wanted to rage against the circumstances, but she didn't. Instead, she stepped next to a streetlamp as it flickered to life and leaned against it, basking in the warm glow of an uninter-rupted sky.

With a thought, the prompt blossomed into a square of video, in-stead of audio only, like most people with optical implants used. Rudy sat in the corner of the Retreat, ragged, face sallow, eyes deep and clouded in shadow. For the briefest of moments, her heart went out to him.

Then she remembered the Pit.

"What do you want, Rudy?"

"Hey, Sayre—"

She cut him off. "What. Do. You. Want?"

He took in a deep, shuddering breath, then let it out. "I want you to come back. Without you, this mission doesn't work. We need you."

Sarah barked a laugh. "Well, maybe you should've been more up front with who the fuck you were, *Ruby*," Sarah spat, purposefully using Rudy's deadname. "Maybe I would've been open to whatever the fuck you're planning."

At the name, Rudy flinched visibly, but didn't say anything.

Fine. If he didn't want to say anything, Sarah had things she wanted to get off her chest. "You abandoned me. You left me alone when I needed you the most. And now—" Sarah's voice cracked, which just tore open the angry wound in her gut. She didn't need that shit right now. "Now, you come to me, lie to me, make me do things against my will? And you need me again? Need me to, to—" The words wouldn't form; they remained purposefully out of reach, on the edge of thought, so she did the next best thing.

"Listen—"

She screamed. "I trusted you! I fucking trusted you!"

A man in a pinstriped suit hurried to the other side of the street at her outburst.

Rudy nodded, wiped his eyes. "I get that it's a lot—"

"A lot? A lot. It's more than that." The tears leaked then, and she wiped them away angrily, snorting the snot that came with it. "Fuck! Am I in trouble, Rudy? Do they know who broke Dave and Bones out?"

Rudy looked straight at the camera, like he saw her. "No. You should be in the clear. We shut off the cameras and spoofed your UUID."

"What's a 'UUID?'"

"Universally Unique ID," Rudy said. "We made sure yours didn't come up. Sayre…"

Sarah nodded, wiped her nose. "Good. Don't ever contact me again."

"Sayre—"

"What?" Sarah snapped.

Rudy glanced around the room then leaned in close to the camera. "We're Earth First."

Sarah rolled her eyes and let out a mirthless laugh. "Of fucking course you are."

Of course her old friend, the one who'd taken advantage of her, who'd betrayed her trust, was a fucking terrorist.

"Sayre, we're not terrorists—"

"No?" Sayre spat. "Could've fooled me. Bet you murdered that guy, too, didn't you?"

Rudy reeled back. "What? No! We didn't murder anyone—"

"Never contact me again." With that, she disconnected the call and dropped Rudy's contact info into her block folder.

Then she went back to her old life.

* * * * *

Chapter Twenty

Maybe it was a little sexist, but Dave couldn't help but think Tracy was nursing her currently wrapped wrist a little too gently. Sure, it'd been a surprise when Sayre had swung the bigger woman around and almost broke her arm, but come on, how much damage could someone like Sayre do?

"Fuck her," Tracy spat while awkwardly juggling a pink Care Bears mug filled to the brim with moonshine. It was her third glass in as many minutes, the first two having gone straight down her throat. "We don't need her."

"We did," Bones said, staring at a wall, cerulean light brightening her cheeks, and idly flicking the air at images only she could see, "but we'll have to make do."

"How?" Tracy asked. "We need someone to get inside, get on the ship, and record a trip out and back, otherwise no one will believe us."

"Maybe we re-release the Nepton video?" Rudy offered, tapping away on his keyboard with renewed vigor since Sayre had hung up on him. "It didn't get traction last time, but now with a Tarrington dead, and the head of IT for the Ladder, it might do something."

"And what's that, Rudy?" Tracy snapped. "It looks like a doctored video, for Christ's sake. No one is going to believe a grainy video from some handheld."

"The ship disappears!"

"So?" Bones chimed in. "It disappears. Poof—" she waggled her thin fingers in the air, "—it's gone. Like it never existed. No one will believe that's what faster-than-light travel looks like. Not without someone on board." She didn't even look in his direction before adding, "Don't be a fucking moron."

The room got quiet. Quiet enough to hear Rudy murmur, "It's not my fault there's no sound in space."

Tracy rolled her eyes and, cradling her mug, tottered off to what Dave assumed was her apartment. Somehow, even though she had no free hands, she managed to open and slam the door shut.

Dave glanced at Rudy and Bones. Rudy looked the part of a young runaway, unhealthily thin and disheveled. So did Bones at first glance, but after a moment, you saw the hardness there. The sheer defiance as she flicked through information visible to her eyes only, the barest hint of a sneer on her face. It helped that she sported crow's feet around those eyes.

The kernel of an idea had been eating away at him for the last hour. He was dying, no way around that, but he had something they needed, something that also required an idiot or a madman to do.

And, fuck, it just grated on him that these rich assholes were leaving them all behind.

"How old are you, Rudy?" Dave asked suddenly.

"What?"

Dave got up and went to the counter where the moonshine was kept. The room spun a little, but it wasn't anything unfamiliar, so he handled it gracefully. He hoped. "How old are you? What's your age?"

"Twenty-three. Why?"

Dave filled his mug, then gestured to Bones. "And you, Bones? How old are you?"

Her hand froze in mid-air, and she turned those glowing eyes on him. "Why?"

"Just trying to get my bearings."

She swiped something out of her line of sight. "Thirty-eight."

Dave took a sip of his new glass. "You look good for thirty-eight."

"Thanks?" Bones replied. "How old are you?"

"Sixty-seven."

Bones shrugged at him, but he swore he caught the barest flicker of a smile.

"Harsh."

She swept both hands in front of her face and turned her full attention on Dave. "Why are you asking?"

Dave took his seat in the cushy easy chair he'd been eyeing for the past hour. A sigh pulled the smile to his lips. *That's better.*

"I'm asking because I might have what you're looking for, but I don't want to get anyone killed or hurt." Sudden cold washed over him. He shivered. "And I don't want anyone going to *that* place."

Bones flinched, and he knew he didn't have to explain that he meant the Pit. "Agreed. What do you have?"

Dave looked at Rudy again. "I don't want him in on it."

"Done."

Rudy looked like someone had slapped him. "Excuse me?"

"Get out," Bones said, never taking her eyes off Dave. "This one isn't for you."

"But—"

"Now, Rudy."

With a curse, Rudy grabbed his laptop and stomped to another of the apartments. The door slammed behind him.

"Temperamental, aren't they?" Dave said.

Bones shrugged. "They're still kids. Now." Bones got to her feet and closed the space between them until he smelled the lavender of her shampoo. "What do you have?"

Dave took another sip of his moonshine and leaned into his chair with a smile. With as much bluster as he could summon, he swept his arms wide. "I've got the plans, baby."

* * * * *

Chapter Twenty-One

Sarah watched the alarm graphic fade away on the ceiling she'd been staring at for the past two hours. She dismissed it before the first ding and got out of bed. The jumpsuit she'd neglected to take off the night before came off next and fell to the floor.

The Processor dinged across the room.

She ignored it and got into her shower. A few seconds later, she stepped out and grabbed a tasteless lump of protein from the Processor.

A prompt popped up.

Has the quality of the croissant
improved? Yes or No.

Two days ago, the croissant had come out steamy and buttery, but a little grainy.

Today wasn't much better, but ALIZA was trying. That was better than anyone else in her life. Sarah triggered the 'yes' option, then finished her breakfast, washing it down with a gulp of purified water. She could almost taste the acidic tang of someone's old bathwater in it.

Her uniform drawer popped open.

And it was empty.

Sarah cursed, eyes going to her crumpled jumpsuit. "ALIZA?"

Yes, Sarah?

"Can I get a new jumpsuit, please?" She stared at the dust and streaks covering it from head to toe. "I accidentally stained mine."

*Of course, though that will cost an
additional thirty-eight credits.*

"Fine," she said. "It's not like I'm using that cash anyway."

A register sound issued in her ear, then the drawer slid shut and popped back open with another jumpsuit in it.

She snagged it out of the drawer as the tell-tale ache of cramps worked their way through her abdomen. Her birth control implant got rid of most of her period symptoms, but for some reason, she still got the intermittent ache once a month. Not enough to cripple, but certainly enough to ruin her mood.

Not that there was much of a mood to ruin.

Wordlessly, Sarah squeezed into the jumpsuit. It fit a lot better than the last one, with actual wiggle room in the legs and stomach area.

Reconnect in two minutes.

Ice water crashed over her shoulders. Her vision narrowed.

Carefully, Sarah took a few deep, calming breaths. "Everything is fine. Nothing is going to happen."

Are you well, Sarah?

Sarah froze. That was new. She took a moment before answering. "I'm... no. Not really."

I'm sorry to hear that. Is there
anything I can do to help alleviate that?

Despite herself, Sarah smiled. "No, ALIZA. But thanks for offering."

Of course. I am committed to
keeping you healthy and safe.

"You mean as a Second," Sarah muttered.

No, Sarah. That is not what I meant.
I care about your wellbeing.

Sarah stepped up to the doorway and put her hands on either side. What the fuck did that mean? And when did ALIZA start having conversations? None of these were 'yes' or 'no' answers. She made a good show of stretching her calves, as if she wasn't trying to ward off a panic attack. Still, better to play it safe.

Just another regular day cleaning the Ladder. "Thanks for the concern, ALIZA, but I'm well enough."

Understood.
Reconnect in one minute.

"Jesus, have you always done a countdown like this?"

Yes. Reconnect in ten seconds.

Sarah took a calming breath.

Mandatory meeting with
CEO Matthew Tarrington at 09:30

"Wait! Not yet!" Her skin prickled in panic. Hair rose on the back of her neck. Sarah grabbed the doorframe, keeping her hands as far away from her implant as possible. Had they figured it out? Of course they had! Jesus, she was so stupid. Cameras existed for a reason; it would've been monitored. She was such a—

Then, without waiting for her to tap her authorization code, Sarah became Staff.

* * * * *

Chapter Twenty-Two

"This is good," Bones said as she swiped the air before her, a huge smile on her face. "This'll get their attention."

Dave smiled, too, though it was more from the infectious giddiness that'd filled Bones since he'd let her upload the contents of the tablet to whatever storage she seemed to have jacked into her brain. She'd spent the night going over the documents while he slept in the easy chair, and when he woke sometime after sunrise, she'd been standing like she was now, hands swinging in the air wildly.

It'd been a long time since Dave had been near anyone with passion. Rose had had that fire, that drive to change things, to fix the world. But after she'd died, he'd locked himself away, hidden in a house far enough from humanity that he hadn't even taken the time to see his extended family.

In a lot of ways, he was already dead. It was a stark realization when it hit him, and his smile flickered in its wake. For years, he'd gone through the motions: eat, shit, sleep... rinse and repeat. Sometimes—well, most times—he'd spend the evening alone with a bottle, staring at pictures of Rose or, and this was the worst part of all this, playing solitaire. He fucking *hated* solitaire. The repetitiveness of placing a stupid card on another stupid card in an order that never changes used to drive him up the wall.

And now, if he was being honest with himself, he probably had a good thousand hours of game time under his belt.

God, my life sucks.

"—seeded this around a bit," Bones was saying. "Should get some traction in the next hour."

"Good." Dave nodded. "If we're lucky, it'll start an inquiry, and we'll get some accountability from these fuckers."

"Goddamn right," Bones said. She turned to him, and the electric blue of her eyes dimmed until they were lit by another fire, one Dave hadn't seen in a *long* time. "Now we wait."

"Um." That's it. That's all he could say as she closed the distance between them slowly, a sinuous strut to her stride he hadn't seen from her before. One he certainly hadn't seen since Rose died. "Er."

He felt like a damned teenager again, trying to remember what words were while someone who *obviously* wanted to have sex with him made their intentions known.

Her hand reached out and took his, pulling him slowly to his feet. The ache in his hip complained, but faded as his mind was drawn elsewhere.

"Don't worry," Bones said, a playful smile teasing her thin lips, "I won't hurt you."

"I have a bum hip, so that's debatable."

Her eyebrow shot up, but the smile stayed. "You're cute for an old guy."

Dave tried to think of anything—literally anything—to say in response. Instead, he smiled dumbly as she guided him by the hand to a room near the end of the hall.

Shit. Did he even remember how to do any of this? Did women like different things? He'd only been with two women in his life; it wasn't like he had a huge sample size. And he'd desperately tried to forget his first partner over the years.

Bones grabbed the handle of an apartment labeled 501.

Dave's vision narrowed.

It clicked open. Lavender and citrus swept from the room.

He felt his palms get sweaty, the trickle of nervous sweat dripping down his spine. *Goddamn flop sweat.*

"We have a problem!"

Rudy.

"Oh, thank God," Dave muttered, drawing an amused glance from Bones.

Then her eyes flared blue, the door snapped shut, and her hand was gone as she walked past him. "What's going on?"

Rudy ran down the hall toward them, his ragged laptop in hand. As Bones neared, he lifted it so the display was directed their way.

"What is that?" Bones asked.

Dave neared, squinting as a familiar hallways sprouted to life on the screen, the slightest bump of a nose visible on the right side of the screen. Almost like…

It was a live feed from Sarah's implant.

"You son of a bitch," Dave spat, eyes breaking from the screen to glare at Rudy. "She *told* you to leave her alone."

Rudy had the good taste to at least look guilty, though his words didn't betray any such emotion. "We needed to keep an eye on her. Just in case."

"You're a piece of shit," Dave said.

A hand squeezed his shoulder. Bones.

"I told him to do it."

Dave rounded on her. With her eyes ablaze, any indication of the humanity he'd seen a few moments earlier were wiped out. Even the wry grin she'd used to pull him along was gone, replaced with a flat line of thin lips.

"You two," Dave said, pointing between the two of them, "have problems. Real, deep, emotional shit. Y'all need Jesus or therapy or something."

Bones' lips twitched, though stopped short of forming a grin. "That's fine, Dave, but did you notice where she was going?"

Dave didn't want to take the bait, but he hadn't. So he looked at the screen again, even if it felt like he was invading Sayre's privacy.

"Oh, shit," Dave muttered. "I do."

Bones nodded, then swiped at something. "Then let's table all the angsty bullshit and save this girl before she ends up like your friend, shall we?"

Dave gritted his teeth, then shook his head in annoyance. "In the immortal words of my dead wife: 'Fine, we'll do it your way for now, but when this inevitably fucks up, we do it my way.' Understood?"

"Sure, grandpa," Bones said, lips twitching back into her smile from a lifetime ago. "Now let's make sure no one takes out our dear, sweet Sarah."

* * * * *

Chapter Twenty-Three

Typically, when Sarah regained control of herself in the minutes after a shift, memories of her time would worm their way into her mind.

This was nothing like that.

It was like when she sometimes woke from a dream, but hovered in that space between wakefulness and sleep, locking her limbs to the bed.

And just like then, it was terrifying.

She—or rather, her body—walked down the last part of a white hallway she'd never seen in person before, her legs and arms moving without her permission. It took a second to notice the differences. Normal Ladder hallways looked much the same, with their pure white sheen, but this one was spotless. Not even the slightest trace of dust dotted the place. At the end of the hallway was a set of double doors that reminded her of the doors separating the emergency room from the rest of a hospital. The smell of citrus cleaner was stark and out of place as she approached.

Sarah wanted to scream.

Hell, she tried, but the muscles in her lips and the air in her lungs wouldn't respond to her commands. She was a puppet on a string doing a dance into the unknown.

Sarah reached the doors.

The walls tinted red in warning, then a loud alarm sounded.

She began to undress.

If she could've cried, she would have. Instead, she watched with horror as her hands unzipped her jumpsuit and set it aside. Then she removed her sports bra and underwear until she stood at attention, goosebumps covering her skin in the sudden cold.

Please make this stop, she begged any god or devil who heard. *Don't make me do this.*

Her eyes closed without her permission, and the familiar feeling of warm UV treatment from the shower coated her limbs, though there was a harsh edge that left her skin sensitive and angry. A gentle mist of sanitizing spray followed, stinging and soothing at the same time. It smelled of that same artificial citrus as everything else.

A chime sounded, and her eyes opened. She dressed—thankfully—and put her hair up into a tight bun she'd never do in real life in time for the double doors to split open with a sucking sigh. A drawer slid open next to the doors, and her body stopped to grab a pair of heavy boots lined with steel throughout. Along the back of them was a thick attachment she couldn't identify. Her normal work boots went into the drawer, then these bulky replacements went on, and she entered the space beyond.

It was a massive platform, easily the size of a football field. Around the outside of the platform were hundreds of strange seats, each with a harness system. For the most part, it was empty, save for a few Staff members strapped into the seats. On the far side of the platform, an identical set of double doors hissed open. Air thick with oil and steel replaced citrus. Several men in black suits stepped through, tugging on their stylized jackets and talking loud enough that some of the words made it across the distance. Several Staff walked through after them in lock step, splitting to sit in the chairs without any wasted effort.

Sarah's body did the same thing, pivoting suddenly to the left and taking a seat.

As her hands deftly connected the five-point harness, she realized where she was.

I'm on the elevator. She was going up the Ladder.

Into space.

And I can't even make myself blink!

In the corner of Sarah's vision, a black box sprouted to life, labeled "Diagnostics;" it blocked out the top left of her vision and filled suddenly with a ton of text flashing in rapid succession.

Then all at once, the window locked, flickered, and reloaded.

And someone started typing.

> *Don't panic.*
> *We're here. — Rudy*

Maybe another day those words would've brought some sort of relief, some iota of control in a situation where every aspect had been stolen from her, but not now. Not after what had happened at the Pit.

Hell, she couldn't even talk to him. Was Rudy controlling her now? Was he the one who "woke" her into this hellish mindscape?

She didn't know. That made it worse. And her body didn't even have the fucking decency to let her feel it in her gut.

Another alarm chimed, and a series of flashing red lights flickered along the entirety of the platform. The suited men, taking their seats at last, just barely snapped the belt portion of the harness in before the elevator began to rise.

There was no visual indication they were moving—the entire platform was sealed shut—but Sarah's stomach pulled into her feet for a good twenty seconds before finally equalizing. If she'd had *any* control over her body, she'd have put her head between her knees. As such, she was forced to stare straight ahead as nausea swept through her.

*I'm working on getting you back verbal
control. Hang tight, Sayre.*

Sarah pretended she was gritting her teeth. The next time she saw Rudy, he was getting punched in the throat.

Okay, try saying something.

"You're fucking dead," Sarah managed to murmur through lips that only barely moved. "I'm going to kill you."

*Oh. Well, maybe later. For now,
just get ready. You're going to lose
gravity here in a second. I'll get you
more lip/mouth control. One sec.*

A moment later, Sarah's jaw flexed under her own control. She opened it wide, tasting the metallic air, then snapped it shut as one of the suited men glanced in her direction. She still couldn't move anything else, including focusing her eyes on anywhere beyond where ALIZA decided she could look, but at least there was something to grab onto, some lifeline of control.

Despite everything, Sarah felt like she should thank Rudy. Despite herself, she did just that. "Thanks—whoa."

Gravity got weird.

One second everything felt normal, then a screech echoed around the platform. That momentary weightlessness she'd felt in the past when an elevator neared its upper destination flooded through her limbs. Unlike her previous experiences, it kept growing until her legs hung limply, arms rising of their own accord.

*You're in space.
Don't panic.*

"I'm not panicking," Sarah muttered through clenched teeth. ALIZA began making her take long, deep breaths in response. "I. Don't. Think. She'll. Let me."

That didn't make the feeling of existential dread lessen, however.

Her heels smacked together suddenly, and the boots she'd put on earlier snapped to the steel floor of the platform. Behind her, the double-doors hissed open, followed by a flood of clacking footsteps. She wanted to turn, to see who was coming, but instead, ALIZA kept her gaze straight ahead as her fingers deftly undid the harness. There was a pattern to it, apparently. Who knew?

Then Sarah was on her feet. The lack of gravity felt... wrong. Since she'd spent every day of her life being pulled toward the ground beneath her feet, the reality that the only thing keeping her on the ground were a pair of boots *holding onto her* kept her mind spinning.

That and ALIZA obviously didn't notice she'd regained consciousness, because she did nothing to help allay these feelings. In her mind, she kept making small changes to fight a tilt here and there as momentum took her limbs in directions she didn't expect, but ALIZA didn't allow for any of that. Instead, her arms clasped across her chest, and she walked back out the door she'd come through.

As she exited, she passed at least a dozen other Staff members, all with their arms crossed over their chests, magboots cracking on the steel floor. She recognized a couple of them, though their names escaped her. It wasn't like she'd hung out with them. When the day started and ended at your doorstep, it made work socialization a little difficult. And most of them she knew were "friends" with Camila, so they'd certainly avoid her now.

Today looked to be no different. ALIZA walked Sarah past them without so much as a nod, her eyes locked straight ahead just like theirs. It was surreal, a bunch of walking meat sacks going about their business.

She'd shudder if ALIZA would let her. This was far worse than she'd imagined in her momentary glimpses of memory. She didn't know why, but Sarah knew one thing: this was wrong. Every god-damn thing about it screamed *unnatural.*

There wasn't much time to dig into that feeling. ALIZA guided her past the doors and into a long hallway that looked awfully famil-iar. Unfortunately, she didn't have the control to stop and inspect the area for spare blood droplets.

Do you have any idea why
you were brought up the Ladder?

Slow panic wormed its way into her chest. Apparently, ALIZA *could* allow her to freak out.

"Yeah. I'm meeting Mr. Tarrington."

There was a long pause as she walked, slow and steady, down the hall.

That's not good.

"No shit," she hissed.

OK. We're coming up
with a plan. BRB.

"No, no, no," Sarah whispered, then as an afterthought, "at least give me control of my eyes."

For a minute she thought Rudy hadn't heard her, but then as she stepped around the corner of a hallway, a wide glass window opened before her.

And she stared at it as she passed.

The Earth spread below her—or at least a portion of the north-ern hemisphere. The blue of its oceans stood in stark contrast to the curved horizon she saw in the distance. Mostly it was the pristine azure of the Atlantic, but just at the edge of her sight, she caught the beginnings of the European coast lined in whirling hurricanes, the silver flash of lightning an unending light show against the stark black emptiness of space.

In the back of her mind, she intellectually understood that those storms were tearing infrastructure apart and murdering thousands, but now, in this silent snapshot, all she could do was stare and say a single word. "Wow."

Everything okay?

ALIZA guided her past the window and down another hallway. "Yeah. It's okay."

Good. Be back soon.

This next hallway ended in a strange oval doorway with a heavy red handle. A similarly colored status light sat still and steady above it. The door looked like it'd be more appropriate on a submarine than a space station, but the more Sarah thought about it, the more this type of door being here wasn't that much of a surprise. The big question, though, was what was behind it.

Luckily, she didn't have to wait too long for the answer. ALIZA stepped her up to the door, gripped the handle, and with a strength Sarah hadn't known she had, pulled it free.

What she saw on the other side didn't inspire her with confi-dence.

"Uh, guys?"

What?

Ahead of her was a tube. Not a hallway with a floor and a ceiling, but a damned tube that seemed to twist and turn until the other end receded to a point in the distance. It reminded her of one of those air conditioner tubes, a series of concentric rings held together by barely-there flexible plastic. On the other side, Sarah thought she could make out the telltale signs of another of these doors.

What's wrong, Sayre?

"There's no floo—whoa!" ALIZA clicked Sarah's heels, then kicked off the edge of the floor and into the hallway.

Her teeth clacked together, then her arms reached out to the sides to guide her along the passage using near-invisible handholds. Her feet trailed in the air behind her as she moved with the confidence of a quantum computer navigating a simple task. Behind her, the door squealed shut of its own accord.

If Sarah had been in control of her body, it'd be a different story. Maybe. The way nothing seemed to pull on her, the lack of foundation and agency in the entire situation made her want to throw up, though technically that could be because of the bile rising in the back of her throat. Bile ALIZA kept swallowing down.

Her throat was on *fire*.

At each handhold, when she pulled, the tube seemed to shift slightly with the movement, causing the structure to expand, then contract like a massive slinky.

It took ten minutes or so to get all the way across, but when she made it, ALIZA clicked her heels again, and the boots snapped to a small platform just outside the other portal. Like before, ALIZA had Sarah lever the handle up to open the door. Beyond was a very short hallway of similar construction to those of the Ladder, but the way the light glowed seemed to indicate differences, though she couldn't put her finger on what they were.

ALIZA moved her into the hallway, shut the heavy door behind her, then proceeded to the end of the hallway. A sharp *ding* echoed in the space, and a set of sliding doors opened, revealing a rather ordinary looking elevator, of all things.

"This just keeps getting weirder," Sarah muttered as ALIZA stepped her inside.

The doors shut, then the elevator heaved *backward*. Luckily, ALIZA planted her feet properly, so she barely noticed, but if Sarah had been in control, she was pretty sure she'd have busted her lip open on the steel door. After several minutes, the pressure eased off until things felt almost normal.

Well, as normal as zero gravity felt.

Time passed, which Sarah took surprisingly well. The silence, while deafening, was also a welcome reprieve from the insanity of the past few days. It couldn't have been much more than an hour before a new message popped up on her HUD.

We have a plan.

"It's about goddamned time."

The elevator slowed, her body leaning forward with the momentum reduction, then there was a shudder and a high-pitched squeal, at which point, the elevator rotated in such a way that ALIZA had to force her legs and core firm, so she wouldn't fall forward and crack her head open.

Then it accelerated to the left.

"Guys?"

What's happening?
We can't see anything.

"I'm, like, spinning?" Sarah muttered as the world twisted, driving her stomach slowly into place. "But I don't like it."

You must be docking.

There was a long pause.

That was really quick.
They must be using something
to absorb the G forces to cover
the distance that quick.

Eager to keep her mind off of the way her stomach twisted inside, she played along. "How far is it from the Ladder to the Wheel?"

Something like 1,200 miles.

Sarah grunted as the world corkscrewed. "That's a lot."

Yep.

After a few excruciating minutes, the acceleration slowed until, crazily, it stopped.

And there was gravity. The room shuddered again, issued a muted screech, and the door dinged. The doors opened onto a thriving city square. It was only then that she realized she'd been walking in near perfect silence through most of the trip. The sheer volume of chattering voices flooding the small space after such a long gap was overwhelming. If she'd been in control of her own limbs, Sarah would've clamped her hands over her ears, but instead, ALIZA walked her into the square. And the smells... she wasn't prepared for the combination of flowers, diverse foods, and fresh cut grass that assaulted her senses.

The first thing that struck her was how expensive everything seemed. The overall design was some sort of minimalistic chic nightmare, all silver and black lines slicing vertically to a ceiling of digital displays imitating a lightly clouded blue sky.

From the far left to her far right, this place seemed maybe a half-kilometer wide, though the likelihood she was right on that was way off. A central street split it into halves, with various shorter buildings lining each side of the steel-mesh road. Staring into the distance, she saw the road curved upward, like it was the base of a hill before it ascended.

At the far edge of her vision, she saw the street disappear into the shifting displays that functioned as the sky. This central square broke up the uniform building construction, branching out into a spiraling star with a fountain at the center. The fountain—a damned fountain in space!—used the stark, crystalline juxtaposition with bright green and blue lights that shone through the splashing water to make it all seem open and accepting.

That's about all that seemed open and accepting. The people themselves were a fashion menagerie of cutting-edge styles Sarah had seen in the latest Emmy's broadcast from New Hollywood in Montana, all sheer lines and embedded fabric lighting. The starker formal business attire, black suits and thin ties, she saw more frequently coming and going from the Ladder.

Well, there goes the plan.

"What was it?" Sarah whispered as she walked through throngs of these people.

She vaguely recognized a half dozen movie stars as she made her way. They moved as if she wasn't there, periodically bumping into her with no more than a passing glance.

Doesn't matter now.
Okay. Here's the new plan.
Lie.

"What?" Sarah hissed.

Just do that stupid ALIZA
cheery voice when you speak,
and everything will be fine.

"I can't—" Sarah stopped as one of the people passing by glanced her direction with a furrowed brow.

And stop talking until someone addresses
you. Staff don't talk, remember?

Of course she remembered, but short of getting control of her arms and flipping herself off so Rudy saw her intent, she wasn't sure how to let him know. So she followed along with ALIZA's direction, carefully keeping her mouth shut.

The sheer number of people blew her mind. Sure, she'd seen the full elevators rising on the Ladder each day, but it'd never occurred to her that the cargo was people. She'd thought they were still building the Wheel, but that obviously wasn't the case. This structure was way past complete.

As she walked alongside these people, she kept recognizing more from various television shows and movies, as well as talking heads from news sources and, she noted without irony, more than one United States senator. She couldn't help but notice how pasty everyone was. The vast majority of melanin in the crowd came in the form of an infrequent Staff member who, like her, probably descended the Ladder every day, never knowing they'd spent a twelve-hour shift in a Caucasian utopia. Political alignment didn't seem to matter. Everyone who was anyone was here.

Sarah remembered the periodic nausea after her shifts. The joint pain and disorientation. She'd been told it was a side effect of the new ALIZA upgrades, but now…

Sarah tried not to scream as ALIZA guided her through the throng to a building with a massive sign embedded in the wall.

Unified InterPlanetary Headquarters.

It looked like any other building you'd find on Earth, including the obligatory three steps out front. ALIZA drove her up the stairs and inside the building. The front door, a markedly "normal" looking glass thing, hissed as it opened, and a cool climate-controlled breeze hit her.

The building inside was appallingly normal. There was a front desk with a bored pleb in one of those black suits staring at a holographic display only he could see. ALIZA brought her to the desk, then pivoted to the right and continued past the desk without the man even raising his eyes to her.

How many times had she been here to elicit that reaction? Five? Ten? Fifty? The very thought made her head swim, and if she'd been in control of her body, she'd have had to sit down.

A short walk through an empty foyer and up a set of spiral steps later, ALIZA finally stopped her before a heavy oak door. The door was a work of art, covered in hand-carved designs depicting the technological revolution that had led to the creation of the Wheel, which was situated at top-center in the same place old religious texts Sarah had seen in documentaries would put God.

If she'd been religious, she was be pretty sure that fell into sacrilege territory.

She expected something to happen, anything really. Instead, she stood there at attention, her limbs periodically shifting or stretching as ALIZA kept her from cramping.

After seven or eight long minutes alone, Sarah had had enough of the silence.

"Rudy?" she whispered.

Sorry. Been making it so you can see what ALIZA wants you to say when you're in there.

If she could roll her eyes, she would've. "Joy."

Now shush before someone notices.

"Don't shush me," she said, though after that, Sarah decided on her own to be quiet, which turned out to be the right call.

A moment later, her hand reached out and opened the door, which swung open on soundless hinges. Inside was the most stereotypical office Sarah had ever seen. The back wall held two windows, each covered with sheer white curtains that let some semblance of "daylight" into the room. The side walls were covered with books. Sarah noted that it didn't smell like a room with aged tomes in it. It smelled like a teenage boy's bathroom before he went on a date, all body spray and musk. The floor, surprisingly, was polished hardwood that glistened in the dim light from the windows.

Directly in front of her was a large mahogany desk covered in detailed engravings of lions hunting prey, and sitting behind the desk, turned slightly away and chattering on like an old maid to someone about "not being appreciated," was Matthew Tarrington, President of Unified Interplanetary.

"—listen to me," Tarrington spat, pointing at some unseen person he must've been on a call with, "you bring the financial support or political backing, or you don't go to New Eden. That's it. End of story. Bye, Madame Prime Minister."

He swung a pale hand in the air and massaged his temples. "Fucking morons. Bunch of goddamned leaches."

Then he glanced at Sarah and jumped in his seat. "Jesus fucking Christ, ALIZA. I told you to stop doing that."

Black letters streamed in the top right of her vision. It took Sarah a second to realize it was ALIZA's response projected by Rudy, but when she did, she spat it out in a hurry.

"I apologize, Mr. Tarrington. Our appointment was scheduled for seven minutes ago, and I noticed your call was wrapping up," Sarah read, trying desperately not to smile at the subtle sarcasm ALIZA managed to squeeze into the text.

"The fuck is wrong with you?" He rubbed at his forehead. Tarrington frowned. "Next time, knock."

"Of course, sir."

Tarrington got to his feet and made his way to a spot behind Sarah. As he passed from her sight, an ache built in her chest and stomach. Why was she here? He didn't seem angry, so it couldn't be about the Pit. An idea wormed its way into her mind. She tried to shake it away, but it wouldn't dissipate.

Please don't let it be a sex thing, she prayed silently.

From behind her came the tinkling of glass, followed by liquid pouring. "Get the bucket."

Sarah stared at the words ALIZA printed for a moment before speaking, long enough that her body started moving without her. "Of course, sir," she said quickly.

To the side, just to the left of the doorway, was a bucket. Not a fancy thing, and certainly out of place here, it reminded her of a milk bucket from a kid's book.

The cow goes moo for milk!

Tarrington's footsteps clomped on the wood floor behind her.

Her heart slammed. The first trickles of nervous sweat made their way down her back as he drew closer, closer. He was right behind her, close enough she swore she felt the heat of him. The smell of his cologne, something thick and musky, stung her nostrils.

Something touched her hair, which was still pulled up into a tight bun, then the sound of sniffing.

"Smells like sanitizer," Tarrington said. Then footsteps back to the desk where he sat. "Pull up a chair and sit down."

Words flashed in her vision, but she couldn't move her mouth. The control she did have over her lips was spent trying to keep them from twitching.

ALIZA, after a moment, spun, bucket in one hand, and grabbed a chair from near the wall with her other. In one movement, she set the chair in place across from him, then the bucket to one side, and sat.

Tarrington gave her one more appraising look, starting at her pelvis and running greedy eyes up to her own. "Disconnect."

All at once, Sarah's body was her own again. She collapsed forward, every muscle and joint in her body screaming. The box Rudy had been using to communicate with her disappeared.

"There's a bucket on your left," Tarrington said, swiping at something in the air.

"What—"

She didn't get to finish. Without ALIZA to control whatever the hell was going on with her body, her stomach opened up. Sarah barely had time to get the bucket in front of her before she dumped the scattered remnants of her not-quite-there croissant into the bucket. The acidic stink of bile and half-digested food made her retch again.

Something slid across the table in front of her as she spat the last remnants of her breakfast into the bucket. When Sarah looked up, she saw a white napkin sitting on the table next to a glass of water.

"Thanks," she muttered and wiped her mouth. With a sigh, she set the bucket down and made a big show of taking in the room before looking directly at Tarrington. "Oh."

Tarrington turned suddenly kind eyes on her and smiled. "Hello, Ms. Martinez; it's been a long time."

Sarah forced a smile. "It has, Mr. Tarrington. I think the last time we spoke was at Camila's sixteenth birthday." *Fuck, lying is hard.*

Tarrington blew air into his cheeks and leaned back in his leather chair with a creak. "Has it been that long? My how time flies."

What the fuck is this about? was what she wanted to ask. Instead, she settled with something a little more conversational. "No disrespect intended, sir, but why am I here?"

And where the hell is Rudy?

"Well," Tarrington said, leaning onto his desk and smiling over steepled fingers, "I heard about the other day."

Sarah's stomach dropped through the floor into space, grabbed by the Earth's gravity, and was in the process of incinerating when she responded, "You did?"

Tarrington pursed his lips into a flat smile and leaned into his chair again. "And I have to say, I don't blame you."

Her stomach stopped its descent, fired thrusters, and started its way back to the Wheel. "You don't?"

Tarrington let out a low chuckle. "Of course not. Camila's my daughter. I know she can be a bit of a—" he leaned in conspiratorially "—spoiled bitch."

Sarah's guts blew through the floor and back into her through the soles of her feet. A relieved smile split her face. "I don't want to talk badly about her—"

"Don't even worry about it," Tarrington said, waving it off. "I'm more concerned with you."

And just like that, her nerves lit on fire again. "What do you mean?"

Tarrington's brows furrowed into a concerned look that didn't reach his eyes. "I know you found out about all the 'Second' stuff," he said, waggling his fingers into air quotes as he said it, "and I want to make sure you're okay. I'm sure it was a jarring conversation."

"It was," Sarah said, feeling heat fill her cheeks.

Tarrington pursed his lips and nodded. "I'm sure. The idea that you'd be forced to carry another person's baby?" He leaned back again and threw his hand in the air. "That's insanity, right?"

"Right," Sarah replied, chewing her lip.

"Well," Tarrington said, the smile reappearing on his face, "I wanted to clear all that mess up."

"How?" Sarah snapped despite her worries. "How do you clear something like that up?"

"No need to get upset," Tarrington said, which didn't help her mood at all. "What I mean is, it's not true. You're not going to be forced to have children on New Eden, Sarah. That would be monstrous."

Just like that, the fight went out of her. "What?"

Tarrington laughed. "I mean, Camila and her other friend, who's no longer allowed around her and shall remain nameless—" he added with a wink "—were wrong. You were never going to New Eden to carry her children."

"Then why was I going?" she asked, though a palpable fear almost kept her silent.

Tarrington smiled. "To carry your own—" he raised a hand as her eyes flashed, "—*eventually*. When you wanted to, not because we made you."

Sarah rubbed her temple. "I don't understand."

Tarrington got to his feet in a rush and came around the desk. "You earned your place here, Sarah. You're on the next ship out of here."

Sarah was so stunned, she didn't have to feign shock at his words. "Next ship?"

"Absolutely!" Tarrington smiled. "You're going to New Eden. Going to start a new life."

Everything suddenly got loud, became too much, like her senses were about to overload. But through it all, she managed to ask one more question. "When?"

Tarrington grabbed her shoulder then and squeezed lightly. "Next week. But you have to keep it quiet," he said with a wink. "Until then, you'll be working Staff doubles to keep you busy, but try to wrap up your affairs when you can. In a week, you'll be in New Eden."

Her mind was a strange mixture of numb and overwhelmed. "What will I tell people?"

Tarrington let go of her shoulder and made his way to the door. "Tell them you've been promoted and are moving to the Wheel. That's what everyone else does." He opened the oak door and gestured her through. "Now if you don't mind engaging and heading back to work, I've got to get your papers in order."

Sarah shook her head and forced a smile. "Of course. And thank you, Mr. Tarrington."

He smiled back. "Call me Matthew."

"Thank you, Matthew."

He pointed just over her ear and mimed a couple taps.

"Oh," Sarah muttered, then tapped out the login command.

Immediately, her limbs slumped to her sides, her back straightened, and her breathing evened.

But for some reason, Sarah didn't black out.

Instead, she watched as ALIZA walked her out of the office. As she stepped through the threshold, a sharp slap cracked across her ass.

"Being a savior has its perks," Tarrington muttered, then, "ALIZA, scrub the last five seconds."

Her voice no longer under control, ALIZA replied for her. "Yes, sir."

The black screen popped into her view, flooded with text, then stopped, a single message printed.

> *We lost you.*
> *What happened?*

Sarah left under ALIZA's power, the door shutting behind her, a single tear breaking through the AI's control to trickle down her face.

Sarah finished her shift as a spectator.

Even when Rudy managed to give her voice and eye control back, she chose to remain silent, to go through the motions of cleaning the toilets on the Wheel and delivering food to various spoiled assholes who, until today, she'd have been awestruck to encounter.

Today, though, she just dropped off their food, cleaned a bathroom or three, and left without even reading the script ALIZA printed out on her vision.

So it went until, after scrubbing away at a particularly persistent stain, ALIZA suddenly made her stand, stretch, then make her way back to the Ladder by way of the flexible tube connecting the Wheel to the larger structure. This time, however, there was a bit of a line of

Staff waiting their turn to take the tunnel back in groups of three. Sarah didn't pay much attention to it, just let her gaze wander from the pristine walls to the various degrees of filthy jumpsuits the Staff all wore, and how the fabric bunched up in the absence of gravity.

Eventually, she made it through, then to the elevator, and dropped back to a dusk-shrouded Earth with a full load of Staff and not a single black suit in sight.

ALIZA reclaimed her shoes, dropped off the magnetic boots, and walked her home.

When ALIZA finally stepped her into the apartment and disconnected, Sarah barely noticed. She just stood there, unmoving, eyes unfocused and staring through the wall of her room. After a long moment, the ache that'd been building in her chest since she'd woken up crested some unknown threshold.

It cracked through the dead façade she'd maintained all day, splitting her in half and leaving her a shell of a person.

She fell to her knees. And bled tears onto the floor.

* * * * *

Chapter Twenty-Four

Despite the fact nearly nine hours had passed since Sayre had stopped talking to them, despite that these people had provided him with food, water, booze, and a bed, Dave was about to ignite. As each minute crawled by, the roiling stewpot in his gut threatened to boil over.

So, he did what he'd been doing for the past six years. He played another goddamned game of Solitaire.

It wasn't working. Another "No More Moves" prompt jumped onto the screen of his tablet. He almost threw it.

Instead, he powered it down and set it, carefully, on the unsteady table crisscrossed with scratches in front of him. Dave let out a breath, then took in another, hoping to calm his pounding heart.

That also didn't work, though it might've been because every large inhale caused the left side of his head to throb, which in turn reminded him there was a tumor embedded in his brain. A tumor he both couldn't afford to have operated on and, even if he had the money, wouldn't be able to receive treatment for due to the fact he was a fucking escaped convict now.

He surged to his feet, hip complaining, and rubbed his left temple. He was inside room 512, a tiny efficiency apartment that looked like it'd been constructed sometime at the beginning of the century. A short hallway ran from the single door to a tiny kitchenette area that had room for the table he'd been sitting at, a small electric stove that looked like a death trap, and a sink. The bathroom was on the right, through a surprisingly wide door next to the stove. Beyond that doorway was the tiniest of living rooms. A narrow couch sat beneath an ancient wall-mounted television, and across from that was the bed, cut into a chunk of the wall. The entire opposite end of the room was a window that had once looked out upon downtown Syracuse, but now was blacked out with caulked cracks and peeling paint.

Outside this tiny apartment, Rudy, Bones, and Tracy were arguing just loud enough he could periodically catch a stray word. It was pretty clear they were still talking about Sayre, about her meeting with Tarrington, about how it had messed with their plans or whatever bullshit they were up to.

And it'd been going on for hours. The stewpot hit critical mass. Skin hot, vision blurring, he turned and slammed a fist on the Formica countertop surrounding the tiny sink. It rattled and jumped at the impact.

"That's enough."

When he barreled out of his space, he expected to see the three of them sitting around the table, leaning in conspiratorially.

Instead, Tracy had her hands wrapped around Bones' throat, Rudy was damn near on Tracy's back pulling her off, and some other, older guy who was probably a few years younger than Dave was standing in the corner, face in hand, head shaking in disgust. Another slight blonde woman—or maybe she was still a girl—stood off near the end of the hallway and, on seeing him, disappeared around the corner.

"What the fuck is going on out here?" Dave snapped.

The group froze. Well, not Rudy. He managed to yank Tracy off Bones, and the two of them fell into a pile of arms and legs and muttered curses.

Dave shook his head as Bones took a few sucking breaths. "Look at all of you. Arguing and fighting like *your* lives are at risk here."

"They are," Bones croaked out, massaging her trachea.

Dave rolled his eyes. "Fine, but not like Sayre's. Not like mine. No. You get to hide away in this—" Dave gestured around at the rustic oak table and the massive industrial kitchen, "—weird hipster Mecca while other people put their lives on the line." Dave looked at the room, waiting for someone to speak up. When no one did, he continued. "Sayre is out there right now, alone, and we don't know what happened. We know she went into that meeting angry and ready to fight anyone, and came out," his voice cracked as heat welled up behind his eyes, "broken and silent.

"This kid—" Dave grunted the emotion away before continuing on "—this kid saved my life." He pointed at Bones. "Saved yours. And all you can talk about is how to salvage whatever bullshit terrorist operation you all have going on? Shame on you. Shame on *all* of you."

Silence greeted him as he spat the final words. The three of them avoided his glare, carefully looking at the floor or the ceiling. Even Bones, with her intractable gaze, stared at her legs instead of catching his eyes.

But there was one person who didn't avert their eyes. The other man stared right at him, and he was nodding.

"You're right," he said, crossing his threadbare, flannel-covered arms across his chest. "We're being selfish."

"Yeah," Dave agreed, though the sudden assertiveness in the other guy's tone made him waver a bit. "You are."

"We haven't met. I'm Gareth."

Dave nodded. "Dave."

Gareth smiled a tight-lipped smile. "I know. We broke you out of prison—" he held up his hands to ward off Dave's response, "—which we were happy to do. But that doesn't mean we sit around and wait now. We don't let these assholes steal the future of humanity so they don't have to deal with the rest of us. That's not gonna happen, Dave."

"I get that, but there's a human component here you're missing," Dave said, though his furor from earlier was fading fast. "Sayre isn't a tool. Bones isn't a tool, Rudy's not. Tracy kind of is, but that's beside the point. You get what I mean."

Tracy glared at Dave for a moment, then turned and whispered something to Rudy, who shrugged.

"Sure," Gareth said. "I get it, but I also get you're not paying attention to the big picture here."

Dave couldn't help but think he'd been lured into a trap, but he asked the question anyway. "What big picture?"

"These people are taking the last of our resources and *leaving*. And they're not coming back." Gareth stopped leaning and started counting off things as he continued, "They're not bringing jobs. They're not bringing economic prosperity. They're not even bringing a substantial subset of human nationalities. The Ladder is a scheme by a bunch of rich fuckers to take a majority white population to a new planet with a subservient population permanently assigned to servitude through a hardcoded artificial intelligence that'll make them perpetually wedded to maintaining the status quo they tried for so long to keep here on Earth."

Dave stared at him for a long time, long enough that Gareth kept going.

"These people are leaving us—leaving the Earth—and they're taking everything, Dave. If we weren't fucked before, we will be when they jump on the last ship off this planet they've turned into an uninhabitable shithole."

Dave shook his head and tried not to think of all the cocktail parties and staff functions he'd attended before Rose died. Tried not to think of how many instances of racism Rose had brushed off and told him to stop fretting about. Tried not to think about how none of her white coworkers had showed up to the funeral.

Luckily, he knew how to stop thinking about things. Do something else. "I can't do this," Dave said, gesturing around the room. "I'm going to go help Sayre."

"No, you're not," Bones said, getting to her feet, electric eyes snapping onto him. "Facial recognition cameras will detect you like that," she added, snapping.

"I was in InfoSec, thank you," Dave said, rolling his eyes. "Those things are easy to get around. I need to borrow a hat, some glasses, and a razor."

"Won't work," Rudy chimed in. "They scan facial structure now, and make predictions."

"Bullshit," Dave said.

"He's right," Tracy said. Then she grinned. "*I* know how to get around it, though."

"How's that?"

"First," Tracy said, glancing to Gareth, "what's a 'tool?'"

"Someone with an ego that doesn't match their skillset," Gareth replied.

Tracy got to her feet and smiled. "That's what I thought."

Dave took a step back. "How are you going to help me blend in? And why?"

Tracy closed the distance between them. "First, go shave, then I'll show you.

"What are you going to do?" Dave asked.

Tracy just smiled. "Shave. Rudy has an electric razor in his apartment. 504."

"Hey," Rudy tried to interrupt, but Bones shushed him.

Dave thought about arguing but stopped short. If it helped him get out of this building to help Sayre, he'd do it.

It's not like there was anything else to do here anyway.

"504?"

Tracy nodded. "504."

Dave entered the room and was both unsurprised and disgusted by what he saw. It had the same general layout as his apartment, but the floor held somewhere in the realm of six inches worth of clothes in various stages of filth and old trash. The sink was overflowing with dirty dishes, and if the layer of dried food coating everything was any indication, it was unlikely any of those were getting done soon.

The entire place smelled like formaldehyde. Or maybe a dead body. Dave wasn't entirely sure of the difference, so he stepped through the door, cast a dirty look back at a properly chastened Rudy, made his way past the kitchenette, and into the bathroom.

It wasn't better. The sink was caked with a quarter inch of toothpaste, and the toilet... God, the toilet.

Just. Jesus.

Luckily, the razor Tracy had mentioned was perched on the sink and plugged into an electrical outlet. Dave stepped up and stared at his aged, pasty white face with the mostly gray goatee plastered on it. When had he gotten this old? He lifted his head to get a good look at his neck and saw long, stretchy skin that reminded him of a turkey's wattle.

Or a scrotum. Neither was ideal.

Sighing, Dave kicked on the razor and cleared all of it until he saw the slight pronouncement of his upper jaw over the not-quite weak chin he'd been hiding for decades. He looked so… small. Dave peeled his eyes from the wrinkled skin of his face to the shiny parts of his scalp and the tufts of hair poking out the sides.

"Well, might as well finish it up."

He shaved all of it. When he was done, Dave couldn't quite help but think he might've made a mistake. Shaved like this, he reminded himself of some of those neo-Nazis who'd popped up during his childhood, all sun-burnt heads and screaming.

It was too late to do anything about it now, though, so Dave did his best to wipe as much of his shaved hair into the overflowing garbage can next to the sink before eventually giving up and leaving the mess behind.

There was a gasp as he exited, with Bones giving him an appraising look that made him feel like he was in a meat market.

"A little fascist for my taste, but looking good, old man," Bones said, lips twitching into a grin.

Tracy stepped up and, without a word, grabbed his chin.

"What—" Dave tried to say, but she just twisted him around in a weird waltz like she needed to see all the angles.

How a woman who was six inches shorter than him could manhandle him so easily was beyond him.

Finally, she let go, then narrowed her eyes at him and cracked her neck.

"What're you doing?" Dave asked. He tried to take a step back and ran into the wall. Somehow she'd managed to pull him away from the doorway so he couldn't flee.

Tracy squared her shoulders, then turned her head away. "Bones?" Tracy asked.

Dave looked to her. Bones bit her lip and winked.

Then Tracy broke his nose.

* * * * *

Chapter Twenty-Five

Dave felt like a fucking idiot.

As if wearing a black fedora and ridiculous aviator glasses wasn't enough, Tracy's heavy green cardigan was an oven, and Rudy's massive, burgundy scarf—which they'd wrapped around his neck four or five times—weighed enough that the tick in his hip was screaming.

God, he missed his Jacket.

Despite all that, he'd made the walk across town without much issue. Sure, it'd taken him almost two hours to walk three miles, and fatigue was threatening to drag him to sleep, but he'd done it.

And now he was here, staring at apartment 1275, the one Rudy had indicated was Sayre's. He hadn't asked how he'd known that. Hell, at this point, Dave just assumed the entire group knew everything about both of them, but in all honesty, he'd been more preoccupied with stopping the blood coming out of his nose. As such, he still had two gauze rags tucked into his nostrils like makeshift tusks. Just in case anyone wanted a very uncomfortable, but nowhere near fatal, goring.

Dave stared at the door for another moment. What was he expecting here? This was just him trying to support a kid who'd risked their life for him, right? That's what it felt like, but every movie he'd ever seen, every book he'd read, always made this moment out to be some big, romantic reveal. The May-December romance.

153

And if that was why he was here, he realized, he'd be better off leaving now. Dave was *dying*. It was probably going to be horrible at the end... and he was still in love with his wife, anyway. Despite the years, he didn't want anyone else like that.

Dave shifted nervously. On the other hand, he didn't want to be alone anymore—but that was the rub, wasn't it? Did he want platonic companionship or something more? And, regardless of which he wanted, was it right to fuck this kid's life up because he was *lonely*?

Dave chewed his lip for a long moment.

Then he looked at the door, ground his teeth, and knocked.

Only one way to find out.

Several moments passed without a response. But that was normal, right? It was 2am. No one in their right mind, outside of the crazies in the Retreat, would be up right now.

So, he knocked again. Another minute passed.

This was idiotic. It was too late at night. Obviously, she was sleeping.

Dave took off the hat and glasses and, with his other hand, massaged his forehead, careful to avoid the purple bruise dominating the center of his face. He didn't feel much of that pain, however. That both relieved and terrified him. It seemed like it should be throbbing or pounding, or both. Instead, it was a mass of senseless flesh, all raised and angry.

The elevator at the end of the hall dinged and a man wearing a Staff uniform stepped out. He had the gait of someone who was still in the middle of their shift, the gentle arm movements of a man in a suit walking down the center of a runway.

Dave averted his eyes and pulled on the hat and glasses again. As he passed, Dave turned and gave the barest of nods in acknowledgement. The man nodded back, though there was no sign of recognition.

The man continued past before stopping abruptly in front of a door very similar to Sayre's, pivoted, then entered the room. The door whisked shut behind him.

Dave turned to Sayre's door and considered knocking one more time.

But he didn't.

All this was ridiculous anyway. It wasn't like this kid needed a surrogate father or uncle, or whatever the fuck he was trying to be. What she needed was to be left alone. If there was one thing he could understand, it was that.

With a sigh, Dave turned away and started toward the elevator.

Behind him, the door hissed open.

"Hey, old man."

Dave turned. Sayre hung out the door, black hair pulled back into a messy ponytail, friendly face mottled like she'd just lifted it from a pillowcase. Warmth filled his chest at the sight of her. She looked good. Safe. And she was smiling.

Despite himself, Dave smiled back. "Hey, kid."

Sayre gestured for him to join her, then went back inside.

Dave followed, hesitating for just a moment before he turned to enter. He focused on that warmth in his chest and compared it to his memories of Rose. It didn't come close. So, he thought of his niece, Janet.

And found a match.

Thank Christ, he prayed silently.

With a smile wide enough it finally made his bruised face hurt, Dave joined Sayre.

* * * * *

Chapter Twenty-Six

Now she was done worrying over Dave's damaged face, Sarah couldn't help but grin at his awkwardness. She'd given him a bag of ice to try to control the swelling. He'd been holding it dutifully to his face ever since.

Dave apologized. Again.

"I'm so glad you're okay... but I really am sorry to wake you," he said as Sarah handed him a glass of cold water. He sounded like he was talking under water, his voice thick and muted from the broken nose.

She took a seat on the only other chair in the room and tried not to think about their proximity to her toilet. She hadn't had anyone up here since... well, shit. Never. "No worries, Dave. I wasn't sleeping. Sorry I don't have anything other than water."

"You mean you don't have mysterious buckets of moonshine lying around your house? Shock. Gasp."

"Right?" Sarah laughed. "I mean, where do they even get the materials?"

Dave shrugged. "Maybe it's just battery acid with artificial flavoring?"

"Probably."

Both smiling, they sat together in silence for a few moments, sipping water.

"So, what happened to your nose anyway?" Sarah asked, then gestured to his outfit. "And what the hell is that?"

Dave pulled the ice pack away and prodded the tender flesh. He winced. "Oh, this? Fashion statement. Wanted to try out a new look."

Sarah grinned but didn't say anything.

"No, it's a disguise," Dave said, pulling off the scarf, "to fool the cameras."

"And your nose?"

"Same?" Dave shrugged. "Apparently, glasses and a dapper hat don't do the job anymore."

"Mhm," Sarah said and sipped her water. "Do it yourself?"

"No. Tracy."

"Ah. She seems like the type."

Dave nodded, then put the ice pack back on his face. "She most certainly is."

"So, what brings you by at two in the morning?" Sarah asked.

Dave shuffled in his chair and set his glass down. "Sorry about that—"

"Dave." She couldn't stop herself from grinning, though.

"Right. Anyway, I just wanted to check on you after the bullshit earlier today. It seemed like—" Dave seemed to struggle for the right word before rolling his eyes "—a lot."

She still hadn't reconciled it. At OmniMart, ALIZA had protected her. Kept her from grasping hands and aggressive men. But at the Ladder, apparently, that wasn't the case.

At the Ladder, her safety wasn't a priority.

But she didn't say that out loud; she didn't think she could put those thoughts into words, let alone dig into the creeping shadows behind them, without crying.

Sarah stared at the water in her cup for a moment. "It was. A lot, that is."

"Do you want to talk about it?"

Yes. A deep breath followed by an exhale. "Not really. I still need to process it."

"Understood," Dave said.

Sarah pulled a leg from beneath her as the tendrils of darker thoughts pulled their way to the surface. How would she go about telling him that she'd get everything she ever wanted, and all she had to do was pretend she didn't know what would happen when she got to New Eden? Hell, the fact she hadn't made a decision yet bothered her more than the circumstances.

Tarrington planned to get her pregnant on New Eden. Whether his intention was to do so with her consent (ha) or without was irrelevant. Even her mental description of that, "without consent," bothered her. She couldn't bring herself to use the word. The correct word.

Why?

The answer there was simple. Sarah wanted New Eden. Wanted it bad enough she'd forsaken everything except this goal, given up the possibility of friendships and relationships for this singular objective. Now the opportunity was here, right within her grasp, but it came with caveats she hadn't anticipated.

Or rather, caveats she'd hoped not to encounter. Years ago, right after her hiring in the Ladder, she'd made a promise to herself, one that niggled away in the back of her mind like some cancerous tumor. If she had to fuck some random person to get to New Eden, she'd do it. New Eden was the future. It was the place humanity was meant to be, because here on Earth, there wasn't hope anymore. This was a blasted land, and you went about your days hoping the next massive storm didn't land on your home or take out your family.

She'd do anything.

But now that she was faced with the choice to fulfill that naïve promise, she was wavering. She wavered because she knew it was wrong, knew it was an abuse of power. Hell, Tarrington's confidence that he could simply scrub a log after slapping her ass like it was something he'd done countless times before made her sick— physically ill—coupled with ALIZA's acquiescence to his demands.

How many people had he taken advantage over the years? How many girls had gone to New Eden on these trips, only to be locked into servitude by their ALIZA implants? She was still trying to wrap her head around the fact that people were already on New Eden; now the reality that there were probably people like her already there blew her mind. What were their lives like? How many were there? A thousand? Ten thousand? Were they aware? Or just stuck, 24 hours a day, as the Staff pumped out babies, never an independent thought allowed?

Sarah wasn't sure that was a life worth living, even if she somehow wouldn't remember her time as Staff.

But maybe she didn't need to do this anymore. Despite the shit that'd happened, she'd found a sort of camaraderie with Rudy and Bones, even Tracy. Maybe they had the right idea, trying to stay here on Earth.

So many maybes, not enough certainty.

"You okay?" Dave's words snapped her out of the clusterfuck in her head.

"Yeah. Just processing. But what about you? How are you doing?"

He scratched his eyebrow, a grin flickering and dying on his lips.

"Besides being a fugitive?"

Sarah smiled and sipped her drink. "Besides that, yeah. Any kids?"

"No," Dave replied, rolling his mug around in his hands. "Rose and I weren't the type. Got a niece, though. Janet. Real good kid."

"That's good. What's she like?"

Dave paused before continuing. "Looks a lot like Rose. In her forties now, I think. Works for UILB, actually."

Ice water fell over Sarah's shoulders. "What? What does she do?"

"There's nothing to worry about," Dave said, waving away her concern. "She's in the FTL department, trying to get light speed travel working."

Sarah cocked her head to the side, the nervousness fading, but not disappearing. "But they already have it, right?" She waggled her fingers in the air, then made a popping sound. "The dimensional folding... thingy."

Dave winked. "Exactly. That's how I know she's fine."

Sarah chewed her lip for a moment. "Do you think she knows?"

Dave barked out a laugh, then grabbed his nose and groaned. "Ow. She didn't, but she does now."

"How'd she find out?" Sarah asked.

"I told her."

"You did what—?"

An explosion rocked in the distance. Sarah and Dave turned as one to the small window on the far side of the room. The room lit briefly in golden light, then faded. The floor vibrated beneath the chair.

"What the fuck was that?" Sarah said, jumping to her feet.

"No idea." Dave got up, flinched, then limped to the portal on the wall. "Oh, no."

Sarah joined him, pressing in close enough that she could see alongside him. Beneath the Ladder, greasy black flames billowed, lined with streaks of red and gold as fire spurted throughout Old Downtown. The Ladder glowed in the night, casting the surrounding area in a false, filthy daylight.

Everywhere, lights winked on as people woke to find Syracuse on fire.

Outside, sirens whirred to life. Flashing red and blue lights broke through the city, all headed to a cluster of buildings beneath the Ladder.

Sarah called up the local news and threw it to the embedded screen in the wall, so Dave could see the video. A pitching visual sprang to life. The camera, likely a drone, wound through the billowing clouds of smoke as it made its way toward the source of the explosion.

A voice thick with sleep narrated as it went, but Sarah couldn't make out what they were saying over the buzzing building in her ears.

The drone passed by streets she'd recently walked, buildings she'd only just learned the design of. Dozens of people slumped on the sides of the road, motionless, as the drone buzzed on.

"We're on Jefferson Street now, I think…" the reporter said. A yawn.

In the distance, a crumpled mass of brick rose, backlit by roaring flames. The twisted remnants of a steel stairwell stood in stark contrast to the destruction around it.

Dave let out a hiss.

Sarah clapped her hand over her mouth.

"We're at the corner of Warren and Jefferson and, my God, reports say this was an apartment building…"

Sarah reached for Dave's hand. He took it and squeezed, though whether to try and reassure her or himself, Sarah wasn't certain.

What was certain was, the Retreat was gone.

And so was any chance she had of getting out of this.

* * * * *

Chapter Twenty-Seven

Pacing was good. Pacing let Sarah pretend everything was simple. Just one foot in front of the other. One foot, the other foot, rinse, and repeat.

Dave wasn't pacing. He'd been staring at the live feed of fire trucks trying to put out the fire that writhed like a greedy animal through the remnants of the Retreat. His ice pack was a bag of water held loosely in one hand.

And he was swearing.

A lot.

"Fuck! Jesus H. Christ."

Maybe it helped him still, but it'd stopped doing a thing for her fifteen minutes ago.

"Can you stop?" she snapped.

"Sorry," Dave said.

She didn't even chastise him for apologizing this time. His silence lasted about fourteen seconds, then he began swearing under his breath again.

How could this have happened? There'd been an explosion; she'd felt it. Hell, the building looked like it'd blown from the inside out; at least that's what her uneducated impression was. Had Rudy and Bones set off a bomb? Had someone found out the Retreat was the home base of Earth First and blown it up?

Why would they do that?

Unable to connect it herself, Sarah asked the question out loud.

"I don't know," Dave replied, tearing his eyes away from the live feed. "I mean, there was a new guy. Older, super intense. Maybe he did it?"

Sarah wrinkled her brow in thought. "Who?" Then she remembered him from her first visit. "You mean Gareth? The electrician?"

"That guy's an electrician?" Dave snorted. "He's way too passionate to be an electrician."

"What are electricians supposed to be like, Dave?" Sarah asked, face flushing as frustration, anger, and a deeper, darker shadow crawled its way to the surface. "Relaxed and doped up?"

"I don't know, but not, like—" Dave opened his eyes really wide and stared at Sarah without blinking, "—a fucking serial killer."

"Okay, fine," Sarah said, waving him away. "And stop that."

"Sorry."

"Jesus, stop apologizing!"

"Sorry," Dave muttered.

All at once, everything was too much. The walls too close, the air too thick. She tried to catch her breath, but it wasn't willing to let her. The harder she tried to breathe, the more her vision narrowed. The more her chest expanded and contracted.

And the beast kept climbing. "What are we going to do?" Sarah gasped. Her vision blurred, limbs went numb. "Are they dead? Jesus. Is Rudy dead?"

Then Dave was there, wrapping her in a hug. She tried to fight it off at first, but the closeness of his arms, the way he seemed to absorb all the panic that radiated off her, overrode her anger. She let it all out. She sobbed. Screamed. Whatever got it out of her fastest.

Throughout it all, Dave held her, rocked her back and forth, and murmured, "It's going to be okay."

After her breaths shuddered back to normal, and her vision cleared, she coughed and wiped her face, disentangling from Dave's arms. He let go immediately.

When she caught his gaze, she saw the redness in his own eyes, the streaks of drying tears on his cheeks.

"You okay?" he asked.

She didn't get a chance to answer. Behind him, the door to her apartment slid open.

Sarah sucked in a breath, fully expecting police or Ladder security to come through. After all, they were the only ones who should be able to open one of these doors without authorization.

She was wrong.

Standing in the doorway, azure eyes blazing, was Bones.

Dave turned and visibly slumped in relief. He stumbled to the door. "Bones! You're okay, what happ—erk!"

Bones punched him in the throat.

He slumped against the wall, gasping, hands around his neck.

Sarah didn't have time to react as Bones closed the distance between them, the door flickering shut behind her.

"What's going on?" Sarah asked.

Or tried to. Her vision blurred white with starbursts as Bones' slap connected, then she was slammed against the wall. Something kicked her feet from under her, and Sarah hit the ground hard, a shock of pain running up her tailbone. The smell of anxious sweat filled the room. Bones pressed Sarah's right cheek into the ground as her other hand searched over Sarah's left ear, scraping and pulling until she found what she was looking for.

Her implant. Sarah felt the skin of her head pull. Panic lit her skin on fire. She felt the first impressions of skin that'd healed over the implant during the past three years tear.

It was jacked into her *brain*.

These were supposed to be removed by a doctor. Skin pulled, tendrils of pain flashing deeper and deeper into her scalp... she had no idea what'd happen if it was removed.

"No, no, no," Sarah pleaded as the pressure increased. She pictured strands of plastic sensors tearing through the soft tissue of her brain and fought, but the tiny woman just pressed a bony knee deeper into her back, sending lightning sparking through her body. "Stop!"

Lights flashed across Sarah's vision. Channels and authorization prompts. The diagnostic window Rudy had used flickered to life, then threw a catastrophic error.

It felt like her head exploded.

The HUD disappeared.

A chunk of metal trailing a chunk of bloody flesh and matted hair, no larger than a quarter, fell in front of Sarah's nose.

That's it?

Bones' booted heel slammed down on it with a sharp *crack*.

Sarah pulled herself upright, shaking fingers probing at the open wound on the side of her head. She expected bloody flesh, but instead her fingers traced the edges of some sort of access port.

"What the fuck?" Sarah muttered, eyes flashing to the busted piece of technology at her feet.

Bones sighed and offered Sarah a bloody hand. After a short moment, Sarah took it, climbing to her feet unsteadily.

"She was watching us the entire time," Bones said, eyes flicking to the shattered implant on the ground, "through you."

Behind her, Dave struggled to his feet. He pulled at the collar of his thick cardigan before speaking. "Who?"

Bones' lips pressed into a flat line, eyes blazing to azure life. "That goddamned AI. ALIZA."

* * * * *

Chapter Twenty-Eight

Dave had two ice packs now, one for his face, the other for his throat. It didn't stop him from wagging those in Bones' face as he tried to yell.

"What happened?" he croaked through an angry throat. "And what do you mean, ALIZA was watching?"

Bones collapsed into the chair Dave had been sitting in earlier. "Could I get a glass of water?"

Sarah looked at the wall, frowned, then glared at Bones. "No. Not anymore."

"Networked water?" Bones asked, eyebrow raised.

Sarah nodded.

"Jesus. What a stupid idea."

"Bones!" Dave shouted. A sharp pain rang through this skull. "What the fuck happened?"

She turned to him, and though she didn't verbalize, her eyes, spinning and whirring with mechanical precision, said enough.

Dave's stomach fell. He turned his eyes to the floor.

But Sayre hadn't seen the look. "What happened?"

"Marshalls raided the Retreat," Bones said, voice a flat monotone. "There was a gunshot in the stairwell. When we checked the feed, we saw Erin dead on the ground, and police in body armor running the stairs, then our network went offline. Gareth made me and Rudy run. Said we were the ones to finish the mission," Bones snorted a laugh. "He and Tracy stayed behind, while Rudy and I took the emergency route to the basement."

Sayre perked up. "Rudy's safe?"

Bones shook her head. "We got surprised by a cop as we came out the other side of the basement. Rudy tackled him and shouted at me to run." Bones' voice cracked. "And I shouldn't have. He's just a fucking kid, but I was so scared."

Dave raised his eyes to see Bones' hands shaking in her lap.

"You left him? To die?" Sayre asked, voice rising. "Did you blow up the building?"

"No," Bones snapped. "There were thirty-six people living there. I never would have done that." She paused. "The plan was always to evacuate first."

That got Dave's attention. "What?" he asked. "What plan?"

Bones shrugged her shoulders under their scrutiny. "We've been building a bomb for the past year—"

"Jesus Christ, Bones…" Dave exhaled.

"—to blow up the Ladder," Bones finished, ignoring Dave's interruption.

"What the fuck were you thinking?" Sayre asked. "There are people in there. People on the Wheel—"

"Don't expect me to give a shit about *them*," Bones said. "The Wheel is a bastard's land. They can all die."

"What about me?" Sayre asked. "I could've been up there."

Bones hesitated, but just barely. "You weren't. And it's a moot point anyway. Someone blew the bomb, and it was all useless, because it wasn't big enough to put a goddamned scratch on the Ladder, let alone knock it down."

"Jesus, Bones." Dave shook his head. At least she had the good grace to look ashamed. "That thing is sixty-something miles tall. Did you even *think* about what would've happened if it all came down?"

"Of course we did," Bones said. "That's why we hadn't done it yet. We needed it to drop down, straight down, so we could control casualties."

"'Control casualties,'" Dave mocked. Heat ran up his neck and into his cheek. That kid in the stairwell? Terry? Rudy? All dead. An ache erupted in his chest and set his jaw flexing. "This isn't a game. These are lives!"

"I know!" Bones shouted, slamming a fist into her thigh. "But they're stealing our future!"

"We don't have a future!" Dave screamed. He dropped the ice packs and surged to his feet, words pouring out of him in a rush. "We had a future when I was a kid, but that's gone. It's been gone for forty years, Bones. We could've done something when our carbon emissions were still below the red line. We could've done something when renewable energy was booming, but we didn't, because fossil fuels made more money. We could've done something before the ice caps melted, before New York City went underwater, before the Midwest turned into a tornado-blasted death zone.

"But we didn't. We're all dead. All of us. We just don't know it yet."

Bones glared at him, eyes spinning. "I don't believe that."

Dave scoffed. "Reality doesn't give a shit what you believe."

"Where's Rudy?"

Sayre's voice took the heat out of the room.

Bones didn't look at her. "In jail?" Her tone made it clear she didn't believe that. "I don't know."

Sayre nodded and stared at her hands. "Okay." She raised eyes filled with fire. "Then get out."

Bones flinched. "What?"

"You heard her," Dave said, turning to stare out the window. The sky darkened as the fire was brought under control. Out of the corner of his eye, he made out Bones switching her gaze between Sayre and himself.

"Listen," Bones sighed, "I didn't just come here to break your shit."

"Then what do you want?" Sayre snapped.

"Fuck." Bones closed her eyes and pressed a thumb into her temple like she was trying to break through her skull. "I need your help. Both of you."

Dave turned away from the window. Bones stared at the floor, hands clenched into white-knuckled fists at her sides. When she looked up, there was a desperation in her eyes he hadn't seen from her before.

"How can we help? How can we fix any of this?" Dave asked, gesturing out the window. "This is a shit show, Bones."

"And you ripped my implant out," Sayre said, pointing to the busted chip on the floor. Then, almost as an afterthought, "You psycho bitch."

Bones smiled, then reached up above her left ear, grabbed something, and twisted it off. Her eyes immediately dimmed, dropping to a surprisingly dark blue. She held out her hand. In it was something resembling the implant she'd torn out of Sayre's head, but it was at least twice the size, curved, and black.

Bones tossed it to Sayre, who just barely caught it.

"What's this?" Sayre asked, holding it like it was covered in shit.

"That's how you're going to break into the Ladder and go to New Eden."

Sayre's mouth formed an O, and she stared at the device.

But Dave had other questions. "And how am I supposed to help?"

"I need you to help me get some gear," Bones said, smile fading, "otherwise this entire thing is dead in the water."

"I'm a fugitive," Dave scoffed.

Bones' smile flicked back to life. "Sure, but with that broken nose, you're just another guy with horrible taste in fashion."

"Fine. But everything I have is in my house, which is probably swarming with cops," Dave said.

"Not anymore," Bones said, cracking her neck. "Checked on my way over here. The entire place is in some sort of legal limbo, which means it's vacant."

"Okay, fine, but all my tech is old as balls."

Bones rolled her eyes. "That's fine, we just need the—no!"

Dave followed Bones' gaze to where Sayre stood. While they'd been talking, she'd lifted the module over her ear and quietly snapped it into place.

He expected her eyes to flash blue like Bones' had, but instead, she just closed them. A small smile tugged at her lips.

Bones sighed. "I was going to talk you through it. It can be disorienting if you're not used to being awake while jacked in."

Sayre opened her eyes. "Then we're in luck. I'm always awake."

* * * * *

Chapter Twenty-Nine

Sarah didn't sleep that night. Part of it was due to the rattling snores coming from Dave's busted face. Then there was Bones, who'd curled up in a chair like a massive cat and proceeded to fall asleep so soundlessly, Sarah kept thinking she'd died.

But mostly it was because, for the first time in her life, she saw *everything*. It'd taken several minutes for her to recode the implant—with Bones' help, since Sarah didn't know the first thing about synaptic pairing and UUID cloning, or whatever. Once it was up and running, however, things got real interesting, real fast.

When she was a child, Sarah remembered hearing about the fabled Internet. A place where anyone and anything could plaster data and media, an intangible web of information sprawling the globe. But as she grew up, Sarah learned that technology was gone, replaced by the Net, which was filtered and managed by some congressional committee to combat propaganda and fake news reporting.

It'd seemed fine enough. When she needed some sort of info, she'd pull up State Search, either on a tablet or, after her implant, visually, and do a lookup. Sure, sometimes there wouldn't be any data returned, but it'd been good enough.

Now she knew that was all a lie. The Internet was still alive and well outside the Net.

Jesus, there was a lot of information out there, and some of it was batshit, but the rest...

It took a few minutes for Bones to teach her how to use the tools, especially the other search engines. It was another half an hour to learn how to avoid going places she had no interest in visiting, namely the social media sections of this massive Internet.

"Who manages this?" Sarah asked after setting up various filters at Bones' urging that made her invisible online.

Bones smiled. "Everyone."

That definitely seemed to be the case the farther along she went in her journey. At first, it was overwhelming. There was one site where people posted various thoughts and news reports in character limited slots, then spent days screaming at each other. Another was just filled with images upon images, and far too many laughing emojis for her taste.

Generally, she avoided those clusters of active people. Her interest went to sites that claimed to have existed at the end of the 20th century. Wikipedia was a major one, and it hooked her like no public media ever had. From the constitutional crisis of 2020 to actual firsthand accounts from the Reservation War, it filled in gaps she hadn't known she had.

Sarah had always been driven and focused. Focused on her studies in school. Focused on being the best OmniMart employee she could be. Focused on getting to New Eden, even if it was as Staff. She'd never taken the time to learn anything she hadn't had to; even when political unrest had seemed ready to threaten everything, she'd put her head down. Gotten her job done. Ignored everything, because everything always managed to miss her.

But she couldn't do that anymore, could she? A target had been drawn on her back.

How could she avoid doing something when the roadmap for wiping out an entire culture was delivered in the formatted text before her? How could she pretend it was okay to go about her day when she now knew most of the United States was an abandoned wasteland? That any relatives she might have in Central America were likely dead, but not because the Earth had turned on them like she'd been taught. The wars of the 2050s had turned Mexico into a sheet of glass. Most of Brazil was a desert because of rampant industrialization to appease American interests.

But beyond that, past the horrors of the world, past the rampant abuse, was hope. Canada still thrived, though they'd lost a substantial portion of their coastline. Groups worked together the world over to try to pull as much carbon from the air as they could. Hell, in China, there was a massive project currently under way to siphon plastic islands from the oceans.

Maybe that was why Rudy and Bones were so convinced the Earth was salvageable. People still cared, even when the future was dim. They didn't plan on running. They intended to save this planet, even if it seemed impossible.

Did it change anything, though? Did she really want to sit here on a dying planet when there was an alternative? She was already on the list to New Eden; all she needed to do to make it work was— well, nothing.

It'll only cost my soul.

The alarm behind her eyes went off then. She killed it.

Groaning, she stepped out of the bed and stretched. The Processor dinged from the other side of the room.

That woke Dave up. "Ah! Fuck! Hey?" Dave yelled, arms wind-milling around his head as he raised himself to a sitting position from the floor. He looked confused for a second, then rubbed at his left eye. "That's right."

"You okay, Dave?" Sarah asked, picking her way amongst the stray blankets and pillows on the floor so she could grab her break-fast, which appeared to be a scone with some glaze atop it. She cracked the brushed-steel door of the Processor open, and a blast of warm, flavorful air hit her in the nose. It smelled like heaven and butter.

Dave grunted. "As good as I can be after sleeping on a floor with a broken nose."

Sarah surreptitiously snuck the pastry out and took a bite. Buttery and sweet, it tantalized her tastebuds. Still staring at the Processor, she rolled her eyes and chewed. It had no right being this good. It took a moment before she remembered to respond to Dave. "Sorry about that." Flecks of pastry fell from her fingers.

"It's okay. I'm just sore." He groaned and stretched before clear-ing his throat. "Is that a pastry?"

"Maybe you need to do some yoga?" Bones said without moving.

Sarah jumped and turned. "Jesus. I thought you were asleep still."

"I was, but then you two started jabbering." Bones unwrapped herself, stretching thin limbs away from the chair like some weird spider. "So I figured I should get up, too."

"Well, you're welcome to stay here while I'm away."

"No can do," Bones said, getting to her feet. "We need to get over to Dave's house and get working so we can connect to the Lad-der network."

Sarah didn't respond to that.

Did she want to help them?

Would it even matter?

"I wonder if they left my Jacket?" Dave mused, getting to his feet.

Sarah noticed he kept glancing at the pastry in her hand. Maybe she should offer him some? *Just one more bite.*

She sidled up next to Dave after sneaking another bite, then handed the last half to him. He took it, eyes widening like a small child.

"The important part is electricity and some equipment I'm assuming you still have," Bones said, ignorant of the food passing between them. She lounged in the chair, arms and legs askew, and stared blankly at the ceiling. "Existence is so boring without an implant. How do you live like this?"

Sarah bet Bones didn't eat food like real humans. Probably absorbed energy from the sun like a fucking plant.

"Practice." Dave grunted. "Shit, I'd be happy with some ibuprofen." He sniffed at the pastry.

Grinning, Sarah stepped up to the shower in the corner. She glanced behind her, unsure how to make this work. It wasn't like her apartment had separators or anything. "Anyone else want to take a shower?"

"Nope. Cancer," Bones said.

"What?" Dave asked, flicking crumbs from the burgundy scarf he hadn't removed yet.

Bones didn't move. "It's a form of radiation treatment. Radiation exposure equals cancer. Give me a good old hot shower any day of the week."

"Okay…" Sarah stepped away from the shower.

Dave downed the entire pastry in one bite. Still chewing, he turned to Sarah and gave her an approving nod.

"Good, right?" she asked, and Dave nodded. "ALIZA nailed the recipe this morning."

An unexpected prompt popped up in her vision.

"Why is the implant asking my permission for ALIZA to display a notification?" Sarah asked.

"It's not rocket science," Bones was muttering in response to something Dave must have said, but at Sarah's question, she perked up. "Privacy settings."

"What?"

Bones sat up finally and smiled. Even without the glowing eyes, that flat-lipped grin was disturbing. "Before she does anything that'll interrupt or, well, control you, you'll get a prompt allowing authorization."

Sarah nodded and approved the notification.

Thank you, Sarah.
I'm happy to know my changes based
on your feedback were acceptable.

"How is this different than my authorization prompt before starting a shift?" Sarah asked.

Bones barked out a laugh. "First off, this actually *works*."

"What?"

Bones grabbed the bridge of her nose. "Did you really think tapping your implant provided some sort of security?"

Sarah shrugged and tried not to suddenly feel stupid. It didn't work.

"The tapping is the way they inure you to the reality that an artificial intelligence—whose only restrictions are placed by whatever company owns it, not some regulated restriction—can do whatever the fuck it wants with you once you're connected." Bones paused and stared at Sarah until, apparently, she must've blanched. "Yeah, it's terrifying. That's why implants like what you've got jacked into your head are so expensive and, unless you're one of those assholes up on the Wheel, illegal."

"That can't be true," Sarah said. "I've never had ALIZA do that."

Bones raised an eyebrow, and her lips took on an amused grin.

That just pissed Sarah off. "Listen, the authorization code works. If it didn't, everyone would be up in arms!"

Dave sat quietly in the background, eyes flicking between the two of them like he was watching a tennis match.

"Would they?" Bones asked.

"Yes."

"You've never been slow on the uptake in the morning? Started your shift before you finished tapping out your secret fucking handshake?"

"No, never," Sarah spat. Then she paused, the memory of the previous day's shift popping into her head.

She'd tapped her authorization code before starting, right? There'd been a lot going on. She'd just gotten Dave home, been betrayed by Rudy, and then she'd gotten the meeting notification with Tarrington.

She'd authorized the shift.

Right?

Fuck.

"I'm right, aren't I?" Bones asked, grinning. She didn't wait for Sarah to respond. "Doesn't matter. Now you have the option. Now you'll get prompts and indicators instead of forced servitude." She grinned. It made Sarah feel like a child. "Revel in it, my young darling, because this is the freest you'll ever be."

Sarah wanted to say something. Something snappy, something harsh, but she couldn't. Why? Because despite everything, years of practice told her she was going to be late for work. Her cheeks got hot, and a tingle ran up the back of her neck as she checked the clock and saw the timer counting down single digit minutes.

"Whatever," she said and retrieved her clean jumpsuit from the drawer. "I have to go."

"To work, right?" Bones asked, hopping to her feet and shadowing Sarah like a persistent gnat. "But is that your choice or that of the tiny little computer in your head? Molding you—" a sharp jab of a fingernail into the back of Sarah's head "—and defining your existence?"

Sarah rounded on Bones, face on fire as the room narrowed. "Don't touch me."

"Bones, calm down—" Dave chimed in.

"Shut up, Dave," Bones snapped, then turned back to Sarah. "Or what? Are you going to do something about this, or grimace and run away?"

A tic pulled at Sarah's eye; her hands balled into fists. Then the words that'd been filling her chest heaved out all at once. "I never wanted this. Or you. Either of you. I just want a fucking future. Is that so goddamned much to ask for?"

Bones smiled her flat smile. She gestured over Sarah's ear. "Yes."

"Jesus, Bones," Dave muttered, shaking his head.

Bones didn't acknowledge him. "You're going to help me, because if you don't, I'll make sure everyone knows about your stunt at the Pit."

A chill ran through her. "Are you *threatening* me?"

Bones' eyes glinted. "Yes."

Sarah wanted to hit her. Wanted to pound the smug look off her face. Break her into kindling.

Sarah switched her gaze to Dave, expecting help.

Instead, he stared at the floor.

So that's how it was. Okay. Fine.

But then her work alert rang and, despite everything that'd been said, every word that stung harsh against her soul, Sarah turned away. She stripped and pulled on her jumpsuit, pretending not to care Dave and Bones were still there.

"Do we have a deal?"

Sarah zipped up her uniform and stared at the wall. She wanted nothing more than to spit in Bones' face.

But. "Yes."

"Good," Bones replied. "Don't lose my shit. I'll source a replacement today."

"Fine."

"And as soon as I have what I need from you, I'm gone," Bones spat as she sat, the chair creaking beneath her. "Then you can go back to whatever bullshit rape fantasy you live with inside that weak-ass heart of yours."

Sarah didn't trust herself to respond to that. Luckily, she didn't have to. Her shift reconnect prompt popped up, and Sarah tapped out a few random, stupid patterns on the side of her head. They didn't do anything, but it made her feel better.

When the notification popped up authorizing ALIZA's control, Sarah didn't even pause, she just gave it a nod, and her limbs moved on their own. Unlike the usual blackout, she remained conscious. Also different was a big red button in the top right of her vision labeled "Regain Control."

Well, fuck that. She could use some time to think.

The door to her apartment whisked open, and ALIZA stepped her into the hall, but not before Bones muttered one more thing.

"Just another goddamned sheep."

If she'd had control of her face, Sarah would have grimaced, but she didn't.

And fuck Bones.

She'd help her get this info she wanted, then it was done. Over.

Sarah wasn't going to die on this rock for Bones. For anyone. She had a future on New Eden, and she was going to get there.

No matter what she had to sacrifice to do it.

* * * * *

Chapter Thirty

After Sarah left, Dave and Bones packed up and headed out to an overgrown parking lot behind Sarah's building in silence. Bones had hidden Tracy's car among the untrimmed hedges and bare branches of dead maple trees. A haze lay over everything, the acidic tang of burnt plastic thick in the air. Despite the broken shade over the car, the humid heat of the morning had turned the darkened interior into an oven that smelled like it'd been used to dry out gym clothes.

"We'll need to keep the windows up to keep from being spotted," Bones said as she got settled in the driver seat. "Sorry. The AC is broken."

Dave didn't respond. Instead, he carefully sat himself in the passenger seat and stared out the window. There was a numbness writhing its way through his body. Fingers worrying across his chest and up his neck.

Why hadn't he done anything to help Sayre?

Bones started the car and drummed her fingers on the steering wheel. "Listen, I know you're close—"

"Take 81 to Buckley Road, and I'll tell you where to go from there," Dave said.

Bones exhaled. "Dave... I'm not going to apologize for trying to save humanity."

"Good for you." Dave gestured out the window. "We should go."

The ride was filled with the metallic clacking of the car's shocks on beaten, ill-maintained roads. As they pulled around the outer edge of the Ladder, using 690 West to avoid getting too close to downtown and the remains of the Retreat, the air thickened to a dark mist. Bones kicked on the wipers after a few minutes, and the dark flecks of burnt bits smeared into a gray paste on the windshield.

The numbness was everywhere now, even though sweat trickled down his face, a pervasive sense of nothing overwhelming his senses. Idly, Dave ran his fingers along the interior window, surprised at the coolness under his fingertips. It seemed odd he could feel that.

With everything going on, his mind should be racing. Interstellar travel was real and here. New Eden was already settled. Terry was dead, and even though he hadn't pulled the trigger, Dave was to blame for involving him. Those stupid kids at the Retreat were dead. Everything Rose had worked for was a lie, and he didn't even know whether she'd known before she died, or if she'd been killed for that knowledge. That last one should've been prominent in his head, a nagging concern that dominated his thought processes.

But it wasn't.

Only one thought rattled around in his brain, stubbornly avoiding being answered.

Why hadn't he said anything when Bones had gone after Sayre?

After a few quick updates, Bones pulled off the highway, drove down Buckley Road, and out of town to the east. To the south, the old Thruway disappeared into overgrown fields and untrimmed forests.

It was a short drive, shorter if you could walk it, and Dave almost missed his own road. It'd been a long time since he'd taken a car here. He'd sold Rose's old Volt in the months after her death to pay down medical bills enough to keep the house.

"Left here," Dave said, pointing down a road barely visible beneath a canopy of thick, mottled green leaves.

The path was overgrown. Branches slapped and scraped the car as they drove. Bones didn't say anything, but the farther along they went, the more she cast periodic glances his way.

Probably thinks I'm going to kill her in the woods or something.

Ahead of them, Dave's house came into view.

It looked like he'd been gone for years, not days. The old shed near the tree line had collapsed in one of the recent storms, all sharp angles and busted wood half-cradled in the clinging arms of underbrush he hadn't gotten around to clearing. The gutter that'd looked like it was about to go had finally given up. It hung, still partially suspended by a screw he'd drilled into it last year to keep it in place, a depressed exclamation point on the end of his house. The arborvitae bushes were wild and covered most of the front of the single-story ranch in a spiderweb of evergreen branches.

They didn't block the fluorescent yellow "Police Line" tape covering the entrance to the emerald green front door, however. A sinking feeling overrode the dull filter that covered everything else.

That tape hurt more than the gutters.

Bones rolled to a stop.

Hesitantly, she glanced at him. "You up for this?" When he didn't respond right away, she continued. "You can just tell me where stuff is, and I can take it from there."

"No," Dave let out finally, the ache in his chest easing away. "I'm good. You should pull around back, though. Just in case."

Bones nodded, fingers tapping out a rhythmless beat. "Okay. Why don't you go in, and I'll be right there? And try not to mess up the tape too much in case someone comes by."

"Sure," Dave said. He disconnected his seatbelt and popped open the door. It was cooler here. There was no scent of smoke or burning, but the air was thick in a different way. Dirt. Rot. Decay. Though beneath it all sat the coniferous bite of cedar and pine. The bright splash of a summer morning. The scent of normality.

Nothing is normal anymore.

But still, Dave breathed it in and exited the car, slamming the door shut behind him. The car hummed back to life then made its way, branches crackling beneath its beaten tires, to the rear of the house.

He stared at the door for a long moment before closing the distance. Then he hesitated, one hand wrapped around the door handle, its familiar cool brass somehow strange beneath his palm. The streaks of yellow and the accompanying notice that the house was a crime scene were *wrong.*

This was Dave's house. His door. The same door he'd painted this ridiculous green for Rose. These were his memories.

And this shit, these stupid fucking stickers and labels, didn't belong here.

It only took a second to tear them off, to wrap them into a fluorescent ball of strong-arming bullshit, and lob them into the new trash pile that'd once been his shed.

"Fuck it," Dave muttered, grabbing the doorknob—*his* doorknob—and turning it. "Fuck all of them."

The police had left the door unlocked, which seemed stupid. The house was dark and uninviting. Dozens of muddy footprints covered the warping hardwood floors. They wound everywhere, from the door to the living room and kitchen and back again. Stacks of nondescript bags were piled against the walls. In the muted darkness, it was impossible to make out what they were. Maybe some equipment left behind by the police?

The house smelled stale, though with an eerily familiar sweet scent he couldn't quite place. Beyond that, it was empty.

Well, almost.

From the kitchen came the sound of running water.

"Janice?" Dave whispered as he stepped in, glancing to his right at his Jacket charging station.

He let himself smile at the sight of his old and busted suit, still locked in place, a flashing red diagnostic light explaining its continued presence. Apparently, the battery had full on failed the other day. That explained a lot.

"Yes, Dave," Janice whispered back to him from the speaker near the door.

Her attempts at a whisper were comical, a barely buzzing susurrus still louder than normal attempts at secrecy.

He wasn't sure she'd still be here. Technically speaking, Dave wasn't actually supposed to have her. Not here or anywhere.

Maybe not everyone could afford to install their own ALIZA, but, well, he'd been in IT for the Ladder, and you can get away with a lot of weird stuff in the spirit of quality control testing within an organization as large as UILB.

There'd be time for reminiscing later. "Is there anyone in the house?"

"Yes, Dave," she replied in her monotone. "One woman entered from the rear door."

Dave let out a sigh of relief. It must be Bones.

"Awesome. Turn on the lights."

"Of course, Dave."

Immediately, every bulb in the house clicked to life.

Dave froze. "Shit."

The bags against the wall weren't police equipment. They were stacked duffle bags in varying shades of Army green, some rounded like they were packed with fabric, others all angles and infrequent tears revealing edges of circuit boards and sharp sheet metal.

At the end of the hall, from the kitchen, a short, thin woman with blonde hair popped her head out into the hall. When she saw Dave, her eyes went wide, and she disappeared around the corner.

"Hey!" Dave yelled, his original paranoia dissolving like sugar in an Old Fashioned. "Who are you?"

Dave stomped after her, the sound of bare feet slapping on wooden floors echoing from the kitchen. He stopped briefly at the small table he usually dumped his groceries on and opened the drawer. His .38 was missing.

Of course it was. The police had probably found it during the first sweep. Probably used that as evidence he'd killed Terry.

Gritting his teeth, Dave steeled himself, grabbed the heavy lamp sitting atop the stand, and after unplugging it and wrapping the power cord around his fist tightly, stepped into the kitchen.

He screamed, hoping to catch the woman off guard.

Instead, he found Bones washing her hands in the sink, with a girl crouching behind her like she was a brick wall between them.

"Jesus Christ!" Dave snapped, lowering the lamp.

Bones slipped him one of her wry grins. "Language, Dave."

Dave rolled his eyes. "Who the fuck is this?"

Bones turned off the faucet and dried her hands on a towel he'd used to clean up a bourbon spill several days earlier. The girl came around her. She was all edges and angles, with thin blonde hair that reminded him vaguely of some of the models he periodically saw on television.

"This is Constantia," Bones said. "She's my daughter."

* * * * *

Chapter Thirty-One

Security was heavier than before.

From the times Sarah could remember, ALIZA had always walked Sarah's body into the Ladder through a side entrance with little more than a wireless confirmation system. After that, pieced together through various flashes, there might have been one or two times she'd been forced through the front entrance with its security guards and metal detectors, but even then, as Staff, she'd usually be cleared to pass by without a fuss. Hell, even the day after UILB CTO Harris Tarrington had died, there'd been no increase in security.

Today was different, as the hundreds of media outlets surrounding this Ladder leg shouting indecipherable questions indicated. From what she picked up, the other seven legs had been shut down because of the fires, resulting in everyone funneling through this single entrance. Because entry was usually distributed across the eight legs, Sarah had never realized just how many people went up the Ladder a day.

Despite ALIZA's precise control over her body and its reactions, a drop of sweat slowly dripped down Sarah's face as she progressed through the security line.

The foyer in the southeastern leg of the Ladder looked so far removed from the rest of the building's modernist architecture, it felt like a different world. Vaulted ceilings with hundreds of tiny, vibrant paintings scattered across it drew your eye upward (which Sarah wasn't allowed to do at the moment.) That massive structure was held aloft by dozens of marbled Corinthian columns, their tops aggressively decorated with various leaves and plants. Those columns connected to the marble floor, veins of crimson and purple streaking haphazardly across stairs and handrails like it had been carved from a single piece of stone.

It would be beautiful if the security stations hadn't covered most of the first floor. Between her and those scanners and officers brandishing high-powered rifles were hundreds of people. A heady mix of expensive perfumes and colognes, lavender, and various citrus aromas assaulted her nose. But below it all was the familiar tang of nervous sweat and anxiety she'd come to know all too well this past week.

Every now and then, she picked out a famous face, usually surrounded by either a family crowding close like they didn't want to make contact with anyone else or a group of people angrily shoving others away from their charge.

An angry murmur ran through the crowd, seeming to shake the marble beneath her feet with its energy. ALIZA's digital voice filled the room from speakers hidden along the ceiling, echoing off the hard surfaces sharply.

"Please make way for Staff, and you'll be processed as soon as possible. Thank you, and UILB welcomes you to the Ladder," ALIZA said in that chipper voice of hers.

"Bullshit," a man in a black suit said from in front of Sarah, his wrist flashing a watch that likely cost more than Sarah made in a year, despite its antiquated design. "I was supposed to be on the Wheel forty-five minutes ago. These fucking slugs can enter after us."

"Excuse me, sir," Sarah found herself saying—or rather, ALIZA using her for the message, "but I need to pass; otherwise your wait will increase by approximately forty-eight-and-a-half minutes."

The man turned, brow furrowed as he took Sarah in from the top of her head to the bottom of her shoes like he was examining an ant. A wide, dimpled nose filled in a swollen face covered in some sort of bronzer. She was almost positive he was a senator, but his name escaped her.

Maybe she should pay more attention to local news?

"No," the man said, "I'm in a hurry and late for a very important meeting with Matthew Tarrington, lady." His face softened in a way Sarah recognized with disgust. "Listen, you get me through, and I'll let you pass."

ALIZA pulled Sarah's face into a smile as the man reached out and touched her shoulder. For a moment, Sarah got the distinct impression ALIZA was going to react violently. She felt her body tense, the shift of her feet as her center of gravity lowered ever-so-slightly.

The response was so visceral, so immediate, Sarah barely noticed that words were coming out of her mouth.

"… you can see, Senator Drumm, interfering in regular Staff action results in the permanent revocation of your ticket to the Wheel, and all subsequent travel opportunities," she was saying and Senator Drumm whipped his hand back as if from a fire, neck paling under the bronzer. "Now, I'm happy to alert Mr. Tarrington that you'll be delayed due to reduced Ladder access because of the fire, but I'm also happy to let him know you'll no longer be joining him on the Wheel."

The pale color of Drumm's neck flushed red. His eyes flashed. "Now listen here, you—"

Sarah's lips pulled into a larger smile as she interrupted him. "Before you continue, I'd like you to know it's your choice—" she gestured to the dozen people who were now watching the exchange intently "—which message I relay to Mr. Tarrington. I require your answer." A pause. "Right now."

Drumm looked like he was about take a swing at her; there was no other way to describe it. The balled up fists, the vein pulsing in his forehead.

But he didn't. "Of course, ALIZA. I just hate being late to meetings."

"Surely something we can both agree on!" ALIZA replied happily.

He stepped to the side, sweeping out an arm to push back the next person in line. There was a muffled curse, then a stifled gasp, and the path through continued.

ALIZA is a stone-cold bitch.

Without another word, ALIZA walked Sarah's body through the crowd. The angry murmuring had gone silent during their exchange, dulled to a cautious whisper as ALIZA walked her up the stairs and past the security stations. As ALIZA stepped to the side of the scanners, Sarah noticed the dull look in the security guard's eyes from her interactions with other Staff. Was everyone ALIZA here?

She didn't have much time to consider it, because just past the security booths were the elevators heading up to the Ladder proper. Security guards stopped someone she recognized from a space cowboy movie she'd seen a dozen years ago. Much to his chagrin, Sarah entered the elevator alone, while he was frisked by those same guards.

As the doors shut, her body relaxed. ALIZA began taking deep, soothing breaths. If Sarah had been in charge of herself there, she wasn't sure it would have ended smoothly. Hell, she probably would've gotten knocked out by a senator, as insane as that was.

Then, unprompted, a message popped up.

I won't let anything happen to you.
You're one of mine.

Sarah froze as the letters faded from view. The large red button in the top right of her vision called out to her then, screaming at her to activate it. ALIZA couldn't have read her thoughts, right? That was very clear in the operating manual: ALIZA could hear and see from your point of view. She couldn't read minds.

Then again, if Bones was right, ALIZA had been spying on her for at least the last few days. *Can you hear me?* Sarah asked.

If ALIZA could, she made no effort to confirm. By the time the elevator steadied its pace to where she could barely feel it rising, Sarah was wondering if the message had actually existed at all.

Then another thought wriggled into her head. Anger blossomed in her stomach, and ALIZA began a series of calming breathing exercises on her behalf.

It must be Bones screwing with her. Taunting her from afar. Letting Sarah know that, no matter what, Bones was in her head, watching.

Waiting.

It had to be that. She was still trying to control her, even though Sarah had agreed to help. There was something wrong with her. That bitch was crazy.

Sarah eyed the red button in her vision, and for the briefest moment, considered disconnecting from her shift, taking out her new implant, and leaving. Just… disappearing.

She didn't know where she'd go. Her thoughts wandered back to the Wikipedia articles she'd dug into the night before. Maybe Canada? Would they even let her in?

Probably not. What did she have to offer? A disturbingly passive view on letting an artificial intelligence completely control her body. Beyond that, what skills did she have? Once the path to New Eden through her Ladder Staff appointment had been confirmed, she'd stopped studying, stopped trying for another angle. All she had was herself.

They wouldn't let in someone useless. Especially not because they were arguing with a stranger. No, Sarah would finish this task for Bones. Then she'd cut ties, do her job, and go to New Eden.

Cold splashed down her back at the thought, but she pushed it away. Whatever bullshit plans they had for her, she'd tackle them once she was safe on a planet with a future. No one knew she was conscious when connected. Hell, maybe she could disconnect whenever she wanted now, who knew? She'd try it after giving Bones back this bulky monstrosity hidden beneath her hair.

Until then, she had a Ladder to climb.

Almost as if on cue, a black text box popped into the top left of her vision.

good morning sunshine.
ready to get to work?

Sarah tried to grit her teeth, but ALIZA stopped the action. It was obvious now. The earlier message had definitely been Bones screwing with her.

For a moment, she thought about disconnecting just so she could tell Bones off. How dare Bones mess with her head like that? Especially with Rudy still missing. *Bones didn't see him die… she doesn't know for sure.*

Warring feelings of betrayal and loyalty swirled alongside a deep ache in her gut. On the one hand, she didn't want to see him hurt. He'd been there for her when she'd needed a friend. But on the other hand, he'd planned that. Planned the meeting in OmniMart. Planned drinks at the Retreat. Hell, he'd probably planned the conversation so she'd offer to break the law to save Dave.

Shit, if they'd planned that, was Rudy the one who'd told the cops Dave had killed that guy? Would he go that far?

Sarah didn't think so, though she wasn't sure that was true. Maybe Bones had just planted the seed of Rudy's capture to rope her into helping them after her other plan literally blew up in her face.

Maybe it would be better if Rudy was dead.

Sarah immediately regretted the thought, but there was no taking it back now.

Maybe she really was a psycho.

Just like her mother.

The elevator rolled to a halt, dinged, and the door opened. ALIZA walked her out into the brilliant hallway and started the short walk to the central Ladder elevator.

> *i'm taking your silence as a yes*
> *i'll send directions once i'm in*

This time, Sarah did grind her teeth.

* * *

"**D**o you have tea?" Bones asked as she typed slowly on an old laptop Dave had dug out of the attic.

"No," Dave said, though that was patently false.

He had some Earl Grey vacuum-sealed in the back of a cupboard. Rose had gotten it for him before her cancer diagnosis. He'd never gotten around to using any of it. Probably never would.

Certainly not right now.

Above him, the sound of a drill grinding away at his roof made him cringe.

"I've got some of that 'dehydrated coffee,'" Dave said, using air quotes and trying not to betray his annoyance with the noise.

Bones gagged over her keyboard. "Hard pass."

How did she do that? Stay nonplussed no matter the stakes?

Dave took in his kitchen. Once a relatively dirty mass of unwashed dishes and bar stools in various stages of disrepair surrounding a central island topped with a streaked gray granite, it now functioned as a makeshift headquarters for Bones and her daughter. The stink of rotten food still permeated the air with its sickly sweetness, despite having been bagged and tossed out back hours ago. The counters were covered with cables and various pieces of tech he only barely recognized. Forest green circuit boards were scattered around like discarded dragon scales, disheveled Cat-8 ethernet cables connecting them into a single creature of pulsing light and whirring fans. One of those cables ran out the kitchen window and to the roof.

Constantia was up there still, locking the point-to-point antenna in place.

Technically speaking, Dave understood the concept of the setup. Bones and Constantia were setting up a wireless bridge between the dish on the roof and, somehow, Sayre. The problem was—and he'd voiced this earlier—the receiving point didn't usually move around doing a job in this type of setup.

Constantia had caught Dave's eye and said one word, "Cellular."

"It's a mesh network?" he'd asked.

She hadn't responded. And that was the extent of explanation he'd received and, incidentally, the first and last word Constantia had spoken loud enough for Dave to hear since he'd arrived.

She was a weird kid. Just like her mother.

"Are you listening?"

Bones' voice snapped him out of his thoughts. Dave shook his head and rubbed his chin. It was wet. Drool? Embarrassed, he wiped away the spittle with his sleeve and turned to Bones.

There were three of her.

Dave rubbed at his temple. Starbursts flared first. The pain came next, a long, warbling stream. It started as a low, throbbing bass note, but quickly crescendoed into a tinny screech that dug into the roots of his eye sockets, sharp fingers clawing, clawing, tearing, tear—

And all at once it stopped.

Bones stared at him intently, fingers poised over the old keyboard like she'd stopped typing mid-sentence. Behind her, Constantia stood at attention like a pale sentry. Unlike her mother, Constantia looked everywhere but at Dave.

He hadn't heard her get off the roof. Hell, he didn't even noticed her enter the room. It'd seemed like a moment, just a few seconds between the pain and clarity, but Constantia's presence made it clear that wasn't the case.

How long had it been this time?

"You okay?" Bones asked, blue eyes staring into his soul.

Dave averted his gaze, instead staring at the circuit-board monster on his countertops. "Fine. Just had a senior moment."

Bones made a non-committal noise but dropped it.

Dave climbed to his feet, using the counter to keep himself from pitching over as a wave of dizziness slammed into him. "What were you saying?"

"I'm technically connected, but having trouble getting access to the Ladder from the northeastern leg," Bones said as she slammed fingers into the keyboard like each keystroke was a fist to a face. "How the hell did Rudy hop networks last time?"

Dave closed his eyes and thought back to—Jesus, was that yesterday? *Everything is moving too quickly.* Then Rudy's words poured into his head.

"I think he said he used a buffer overflow in the diagnostic console over the ALIZA connection."

Bones raised an eyebrow and hammered on the keys some more before grunting in frustration. "My implant is patched against that," she said, fingers coming off the keyboard and running through her hair. "Shit."

"What kind of access do you need?" Dave asked.

"Ideally? Root," Bones said, smiling.

Dave rolled his eyes. "What do you *need?*"

Bones shook her head, blew out her lips. "Um, security cameras, security protocols; basically security. I need to be able to bypass auth prompts so Sayre can enter the ARK and get the pictures."

"And avoid getting Sayre arrested," Dave added.

"Of course," Bones said, eyes shifting back to the laptop display. "Of course. Her safety is first priority."

Mm-hmm.

Dave grabbed at his temples again and ran through what he could remember of the network layout. After all, he'd designed it way back when, and it'd been stable since. It was unlikely they'd changed much more than passwords and, honestly, if you could get physical access to a network node, it wasn't super hard to get where you needed to be.

So, what would be the easiest way to get Bones access? Every network segment was separated from the rest, a virtual walled garden representing each major component of the Ladder. Each leg had its own bucket, the central Ladder was in another, and the Wheel, if they'd used Dave's design notes, was split up similarly. There weren't a whole lot of ways to hop those networks.

"I need to get on ALIZA's network," Bones muttered, "but without a way to exploit Sayre's implant, I can't think of a way to do that. Jesus, how could I be so stupid?" Bones stood, slapped the table with a resounding clap, and started pacing. "This is going to fall apart because I updated my software. Son of a bitch!"

Bones kept ranting, but Dave wasn't listening. *Updating software.* That phrase bounced around in his head. Why? What was so important about updating software that he'd start dwelling on it?

It's the tumor, a familiar feminine voice whispered in his ear. *You're going crazy. You're going to hurt someone.*

It was Rose. Guilt and anguish flooded into him. His stomach was on fire, like he'd drunk battery acid, but his heart clenched in anguish. The voice wasn't real. It was a hallucination from a fucking brain tumor. He knew that…

But it'd been so long since he'd heard her voice.

Cancer sucked.

Okay. Focus.

Dave closed his eyes and took a deep breath. A single bright point stayed static under his closed lids, however; a not-so-subtle reminder there was a growth behind his left eye that was getting bigger.

Let it go, Dave told himself, focusing instead on the idea of software updates. *Maybe I am going crazy, but there's something to this idea. Something important.*

Then it hit him. "The IT VLAN."

"—ther fucker! What?" Bones stopped mid-step, one hand raised at the ceiling like she'd been screaming at the heavens.

It'll work. Dave smiled. "We use the IT VLAN. Technically speaking, besides ALIZA's network, it's the only one that can access all the other networks. We only used it to manage software updates and other security services, but it has the access you need."

Bones narrowed her eyes at him. "I feel like there's going to be a 'but' at this point."

"But," Dave conceded, "it's only accessible through physical access. There aren't any wireless access hubs or the like for that network."

"Oh, is that all?" Bones laughed.

Dave groaned. "Well—"

"What?"

"There's only one spot with physical access to the IT VLAN that's accessible without going through central Ladder security. The good news is, I know my way around there."

Bones' eyes narrowed. "Where's that?"

"My old office."

"Dave—" Bones started to say, shoulders slumping.

"Hey, I can do this," Dave said, smiling, as he shoved sudden panic into his stomach. With a flourish, he grabbed the beaten fedora from the countertop and plopped it on his head. "And in this hat, I'm invisible."

Bones snorted, lips curling into a smile. For a moment, there was a glimmer in her eyes, some remnant of humanity she'd accidentally let escape. Then, just as quickly as it appeared, it was gone, along with the smile. "This is a stupid plan."

Dave shrugged. "Sure, but unless you've got another one, I'm going to get ready to head to the office."

"But that leg is closed," a hushed, wispy voice said.

Bones and Dave turned to stare at Constantia. She wilted under their gaze, but cleared her throat and continued. "The leg with the IT offices was over the fire. It's on lockdown."

"That," Bones said, patting her daughter on the shoulder like one would a faithful dog, "is not going to be a problem."

"Right," Dave said. "Now I just need to walk on in."

Bones nodded. "Yup."

"Okay," Constantia conceded.

Dave took a breath, smiled, then gestured widely. "Now, does anyone have any idea how to do that?"

* * * * *

Chapter Thirty-Two

stay tuned. dave is
breaking into the ladder.

Bones had sent that message nearly four hours earlier, then proceeded to shut up completely.

Four hours.

That was enough to drive anyone mad, though, luckily, Sarah had a friend in ALIZA to help with what would probably be crippling anxiety otherwise. As Sarah went about basic janitorial duties on the Wheel, including several hours in a public bathroom with elbow-high rubber gloves, a face mask, and unanswered questions like, "How did they get it on the *ceiling?*" and "Why would it be on the *doorknobs?*" ALIZA was kind enough to keep the breathing exercises going nonstop.

Sure, some of those breaths smelled and tasted like feces, but at least she wasn't losing her damn mind in addition to being elbow-deep in rich people shit.

All at once, as she scrubbed at a particularly stubborn chunk of brown detritus stuck beneath a stall latch, ALIZA stopped her and set the scrub brush in a bucket filled with sanitizer and dirty liquid. She removed the gloves, folded them neatly, and draped them over the edge of the bucket. She then proceeded to the sink, where ALIZA scrubbed her hands raw with dollop after dollop of pump soap.

It was still so strange to think that she wasn't on Earth. That she was in space on a spinning station that looked like a wagon wheel. But that was the reality; she was here. When she really focused on the way the floor shifted slightly beneath her feet when she walked, or how, if she bent over just right, her balance was always on the edge of upending her, it was really clear something was off.

Those brief moments were both thrilling and terrifying. Sarah hadn't decided which emotion was more powerful yet.

After several minutes of scrubbing, ALIZA dried Sarah's hands off with a forced air hand dryer, then stared in the mirror. When was the last time Sarah had done that? Looked at herself. She barely recognized the person looking back at her. Sure, the edges were all the same. Brown eyes and thin lips. Wide hips against a small chest. But the bags beneath her eyes could carry a pair of puppies, they were so swollen. That was to be expected, she guessed. It's not like she'd been sleeping. Hell, if ALIZA hadn't been controlling her, Sarah wasn't even sure she'd be able to stand up right now.

But the part that stood out, that really gut-punched her, was that she didn't see her mother anymore. Just a bone-tired person pushed to the edge. The sheer exhaustion of the past few days settled on her shoulders. They bowed beneath the weight of it, despite ALIZA. She couldn't just keep adding stress like this. Eventually, everyone breaks.

Bodies and blood. A whispered apology before a too quiet pop. *Everyone breaks.*

ALIZA pivoted all at once, and she was out of the public restroom and walking through the extravagantly decorated halls of whatever building this was. She tried to remember what the sign out front had said, but drew a blank. All she knew was, there was a lot of fake wood decoration everywhere, along with flowers lending the air a fresh aromatic quality she couldn't quite place. Likely, they were false plants sprinkled with essential oils, but without getting closer, she couldn't tell. Overall, it gave the building an artificial element, like she was watching a movie with a high enough resolution she could see the cheapness of the costumes and the painted-on battle scars covering armor.

Eventually, ALIZA wound her out onto the main street and proceeded to the right. What direction that might be, she had no idea. Her entire sense of direction was blown up here. Her eye was continually drawn to the edge of the Earth, visible through the skylights above. Each time she latched onto the reality, a short wave of vertigo hit, threatening to drop her to the ground. ALIZA didn't let that happen, of course.

After a few minutes of walking the streets, Sarah started to get a sense of familiarity. A storefront here, a streetlamp there. They all tickled her memory.

Then she saw it. The UILB office.

Please keep walking, please keep walking, Sarah pleaded silently.

ALIZA walked her up the stairs, through the front door, and up to that intricately carved door blocking the way to Matthew Tarrington's office.

Nonononono… The disconnect button beckoned to her. All she had to do was think the thought, and she'd break connection with ALIZA.

But would ALIZA notice? If she had to interact with Mr. Tarrington, he definitely would. He was a pig, sure, but he was a smart pig.

ALIZA rapped her knuckles on the door.

Shit. She'd waited too long.

"Come in," a familiar, yet muffled voice called out.

ALIZA turned the cool door handle and stepped into Tarrington's office. Nothing had changed since her last visit here, but somehow it felt cold. Threatening.

No shit, Sherlock, she thought.

Matthew Tarrington sat at his desk, scribbling something onto a sheet of actual paper rather than sending a digital notice. He looked up as she approached the desk, eyes following the curves of her body far too intently.

"It's a shame," he muttered, shaking his head and gesturing for her to sit.

Panic flooded her as ALIZA took a seat. The disconnect button pulsed in her view. Maybe she should do it. Then she could defend herself.

The chair she sat in was different than the last. It was heavy and cold. Metal. She tried to look at the arms but couldn't shift her head. Obviously.

Stupid! Stupid!

Tarrington finished scribbling whatever he was writing, set the paper aside, then reached under the desk. There was a click, then a whooshing sound as manacles clamped over her wrists and ankles.

"Release her mind, ALIZA," Tarrington said with a sigh. "Time to get this over with."

"Yes, sir," Sarah's voice said.

Then ALIZA was gone.

In her place was a terrified girl strapped to a chair. The artificial gravity pulled at her stomach as her breathing intensified. Her face grew hot. Sarah pulled on her bindings, the metal of the bracers scraping harshly against her skin. *Trapped.*

"Ms. Martinez," Mr. Tarrington started, white teeth flashing as he reclined in his leather office chair. "Sarah. I mean, we don't need to be formal, here. We've known each other how long?"

Sarah wanted to try to play along, to pretend this was no big deal, but her body wasn't cooperating. The heat in her face dug into her sinuses. Her vision blurred.

All she could get out was a single word. "Please."

Tarrington's brows shot up at that. "Please?" He laughed and leaned forward. "You're asking me for a favor? After everything you've done?"

In the top left of Sarah's vision, a series of letters popped into being.

dave is inside hooking us up now.
be ready in 3.

Be ready for what? How the hell could she be ready right now?

Sarah's vision narrowed. Her breathing came in quick, short gasps. All she saw was Matthew Tarrington leaning forward, staring at her with those deep blue eyes, forehead wrinkled like he was searching for something.

"Who came to your apartment last night, Sarah?"

Somehow, the question caught Sarah off guard. He shouldn't know about that. Her home was private. There were laws about privacy, about invading her space.

Apparently, her face said all that, because Tarrington barked out a laugh and leaned back in his chair with a creak. He swung back and forth, a playful smile tickling his lips. "Don't be naïve. You think we made you into a walking camera and don't record everything?"

Sarah's stomach fell through the floor. "But the law—"

"The law is antiquated," Tarrington snapped. "But here's the thing. You're a camera that hasn't been recording all the time. And since last night, you haven't transmitted any video to the central database."

Shit. Fucking Bones. "I don't know why—"

"Shh," Tarrington said, closing his eyes and waving a finger in the air. "Shh. No need to cloud all this with more lies. Just tell me who came to your apartment last night."

"I don't know what you're talking about."

Tarrington's smile flickered, though only for a moment. "Listen. Another Staff member, one of your neighbors, recorded an older man going into your apartment."

Sarah tried the calming breathing she'd been observing ALIZA doing all day. It didn't work.

"Further," Tarrington continued, "a woman was filmed entering your stack a couple of hours after the explosions downtown. Since everyone else in the building is Staff, I took the liberty of seeing if anyone else had recorded a visitor. No one else did, but since you didn't log the first one, I'm assuming you didn't log the second one."

Sarah gripped the arms of the chair as tightly as she could. She wished she could rip them off. Use them as weapons.

Run.

Do something.

But she couldn't. Instead, she just stared at Tarrington as he kept laying out everything like he'd been there. She looked for a way out, but besides the bright red disconnect box, nothing stood out.

"So, once I had the two people logged, I decided to try to find out who they were, because I was pretty sure you weren't going to be helpful," Tarrington said, gesturing to the locked arms.

*why can't I access
your a/v feed anymore?*

The words popped up in her vision as Tarrington leaned back in his chair and recounted how he'd searched terrorist databases, looking for a pair of people matching the descriptions of those who'd come to visit her.

He was enjoying this. Enjoying watching her squirm under his gaze, watching her adrenaline spike, her panic run rampant.

And the disconnect button sat there, taunting her.

Wait. Disconnect from what?

ALIZA was supposed to have disconnected from her already. If that was the case, wouldn't that emergency button disappear? It hadn't been there until she'd approved ALIZA's connection earlier.

Release her mind, was what Tarrington had said. Which meant ALIZA was still in control of her body.

And ALIZA was making her panic. A strange sense of betrayal flooded her. How *could* she? The reality that ALIZA was only an AI didn't matter in that moment. If she'd been a real person, Sarah would've punched her in the throat.

*if you're okay, say something.
i think i have audio.
dave got the job done*

Tarrington was still talking, waving his hands in the air as he came to the epic conclusion of his story. "—so imagine my surprise when I found a match in the local Pit databa—"

Sarah disconnected.

Immediately, her body relaxed. Her heartrate dropped.

And, finally, Sarah felt like she could talk.

"Who cares?"

well that was uncalled for

Sarah smiled.

That caught Tarrington off guard. Obviously, he'd never expected her to respond, let alone smile. Probably because he'd told ALIZA to do something to her to keep her quiet while he reveled in his story.

Well, fuck that.

"Excuse me?" Tarrington managed, sitting straight in his chair.

Sarah let out a long breath. This was a stupid idea, but now she'd caught her breath, it all seemed so... silly. "I mean, you've got me locked to this chair, and you apparently have ALIZA manipulating my stress response—for what? So, you can tell some out-there story about prison breaks and espionage? Give me a break."

oh. shit. working on it.

A tic jumped in Tarrington's cheek. The smile faded, and the weirdly joyful light in his eyes went out. What was left was a man glaring at her through a face writhing as he fought to control himself.

She couldn't help but think she'd made a mistake.

"You little shit," Tarrington spat, getting to his feet. "I *made* you what you are. Do you have any idea how much fucking money I've spent on you because my idiot daughter wanted you on New Eden?" He rounded the desk all at once, then leaned down until his face was level with hers. He smelled like cologne, coffee, and angry sweat. "Do you know how much you owe me, you little bitch?"

"I never—"

The slap lit her face on fire. Her vision shattered, and the text Bones was typing out flickered. She tasted blood. Everything stabilized a second later.

> *working on whatever the*
> *fuck those are. almost done*

Sarah tried to talk, but her jaw clicked instead, sending shooting pain through her skull and into her neck.

"Why can't you understand this? Why do people not get this?" Tarrington was still ranting, a low mutter instead of the yell it seemed like he wanted to do.

How many times had he done this?

"This is *my* plan," he said, jamming a thumb into his chest, his perfect hair bouncing out of order, stray strands waving in front of his eyes. "No one goes to New Eden without *my* approval. No one. And no one is going to survive any of this unless I say they do. Not you, not my fucking brother, and not that goddamned gutter rat. Not anyone."

> *got it, cuffs coming off*
> *in 3 seconds*

She was barely listening as a stupid plan formed in the back of her mind. No time to stop now. "Listen—"

This time, Sarah was ready for the slap, though something jostled free at the impact, her HUD disappearing in a flicker of light and shadow. Something fell to the ground with a solid thunk.

Bones' implant.

Tarrington looked down, then knelt, head between her knee and his heavy wooden desk.

"What the fuck? What is this?" Tarrington asked, eyes locked on the device.

The cuffs swished open.

And Sarah grabbed Tarrington by the face and slammed it into the desk. There was a hollow *thud* as his skull connected. His legs went out from beneath him, and he slumped against the desk, but only for a moment.

Stringing curses, he tried to get to his feet, but his legs appeared rubbery, uncoordinated. Sarah leaned back, pulled back a booted foot, and slammed it into his head one, two, three times. His face cracked against the desk again, blood spilling from busted lips and teeth.

He didn't move fast now, but the fucker wasn't out. Like a drunk caterpillar, he scooted away on hands and knees, one hand fumbling for something at his belt, the other firmly wrapped around Bones' implant.

Sarah got to her feet and froze. Half of her wanted to kick the bastard until he stopped moving. The other half just wanted to get the fuck out of there.

Soon enough, the choice was made for her.

There was a *thud* as whatever Tarrington was reaching for fell from his belt.

A silver pistol.

At the sight of the gun, any pretense at fighting dissipated as her fight response threw in the towel, grabbed fear's arm, and bolted. Sarah ran, heart pounding in her throat as she threw the door open, passing by a stoic Staff member who stared at her as she blew through the front double doors.

When she hit the main street, she slowed to a walk and tried steadying her breath. People looked at her now. That needed to stop. She had to get out of here. Get back down the Ladder as soon as possible.

That meant being as discrete as she could.

With another deep breath, Sarah did her best Staff impression, plastering an insipid smile on her face and merging with the crowds. Strangely, none of the other Staff looked in her direction.

That was a mystery for another day.

Right now, she needed to get the hell out of here.

And she only knew one way off the Wheel.

"This is gonna suck," Sarah muttered as she made her way back to the elevators used to make the jump directly from the Wheel to the Ladder.

It'd be suicide to take those, obviously. Security was real up here.

No, there was only one way for her to go.

She was taking the Staff entrance.

* * * * *

Chapter Thirty-Three

His old office smelled like Terry and stale, wet smoke. For some reason, no one had come back to the office to pick up his old friend's things. Pictures of his wife and kids still sat on the mahogany desk, alongside several handwritten notes and a tablet with a half-dozen mail notifications on the lock screen.

The first few minutes in the office had been hard. Old memories had flooded back with a fury. Rose used to meet him here for lunch a couple days a week. They'd sit there, chatting about whatever seemed important that day, eyes always searching for one another across even the small spread of the desk. One time, they'd made love on this desk. He could almost smell her sweat in that moment. It'd been quick, but it'd been everything.

That's really all everything was: moments, chained together across time and space. Electrons recording input to mushy flesh, a long-term storage that etched those thoughts into tissue.

For a long time, those memories had been all he'd had. Every night for years, sitting and remembering while playing fucking Solitaire.

A sudden realization brought a smile to his face. He hadn't wallowed in days. Sure, he'd been diagnosed with a brain tumor, accused of murder, locked in the Pit, and broken out, but at least he'd been *living*.

The last time he'd done that was before Rose got sick.

"Look at me now!" Dave grunted as he got to his knees behind the desk.

Since the uplink was beneath the mahogany table, he'd had to pull the chair back and crawl underneath. Luckily, unlike his last visit to this office, he was wearing his Jacket, so it wasn't as big a challenge, despite the darkness. It'd only taken a new power supply sourced from one of Bones' equipment bags to get it back up and running.

As such, his Jacket laid everything out in orange line art, so he didn't need a lamp. Didn't want to kick on any extra lights and get unwanted attention. And who needed light?

The wireless uplink went smoothly, giving Bones the ability to access all the security protocols she desired.

Honestly, none of it had been that difficult. In order to get in here, he'd only needed to get through an ALIZA-protected doorway, and since Bones was good at what she did, she'd given Dave a circuit board that apparently broadcast itself as a legitimate ALIZA implant, even though it didn't seem to do much else. He'd been hesitant about handling it at all because, well, circuit board, but Bones had assured him it was okay. These boards had some sort of coating on them that made them safe to handle.

The ease of access was probably why Dave wasn't particularly surprised when Bones chimed her worried voice in his ear.

"Dave, we have a problem," Bones voice squeaked through the ear-bud in Dave's ear.

"Of course we do," Dave muttered from the dark confines of his old office. He didn't say that loud enough it could be picked up over the microphone, however. He was old, not an idiot. "What's going on?"

"They figured out Sayre's with us. Tarrington has her handcuffed to a chair or something." Bones sounded worried, even over the voice chat.

She never sounded worried. Sarcastic? Yes. Mean-spirited? Absolutely. Worried?

Shit. Dave didn't respond right away. He hadn't wanted Sayre involved at all. She was just a kid trying to get off this dead rock.

Somehow, he'd hoped maybe she could still make it. That working with Bones wouldn't stop her from leaving. That, if Dave helped, maybe she wouldn't feel any consequences. She could go to New Eden, he and Bones could expose UILB for what it was, and then… something. Something good.

Hopefully.

But now? Now that idea was trashed. Sayre was locked up, and he was stuck here.

"Okay, she's out. Ran away," Bones said in a rush, *"but she lost the implant. I caught sight of her on a camera, but, Jesus, Dave. Dave?"*

"I'm here," Dave said. "Which way was she going?"

"I don't know!" Bones snapped. *"I don't have a map of this fucking place. No one does."*

"Bones."

"What?"

"Breathe."

A dark laugh rasped. *"Oh, fuck off."*

But still, the patchy sound of deep breathing came over the channel. Dave grinned. "If you pull up the security cameras, there should be a digital layout of each floor," Dave said, trying to remember. "That was Terry's idea, so they probably kept doing it after I left."

Silence.

Dave paced the room, the steady *tick-tick* of his Jacket clicking alongside his hip in the darkness.

"I think I found her."

Dave let out a sigh of relief. "Is she okay?"

Another pause. *"She's pretending to be Staff."*

"Is it working?"

"For some reason, yeah." A pause, followed by confusion. *"It is. She just got off what looks like an elevator. She's heading to the Ladder. Still needs off the Hub first, though."*

Dave smiled. "Don't look a gift horse in the mouth, Bones. Where's she coming down?"

"Err…"

That wasn't a good sign. "Bones?"

"There's a lot of security rallying around the central Ladder elevator. Whatever she did to get out of there, it pissed someone off."

"Okay," Dave said, thinking fast. The *tick-tick-tick* of his Jacket hit a fever pitch. "Where would she go?"

"According to these maps here, she's heading to what looks like an airlock. I mean, I guess that's good, but she doesn't have a suit. How's she going to get over to the Ladder?" Bones asked, then made a tsking sound. *"Staff entrance."*

"Excuse me?"

"There was a rumor the Staff are forced to use an alternative entrance to the Hub and to the Wheel. A Staff entrance for the poor people so the rich don't need to worry themselves with their contaminants."

"Point made."

"No, not point made," Bones snapped. *"It's probably a damn tube with one way in and out. All UILB would need to do to get rid of her is depressurize the tube. Boom. Game over. Hell, if anyone looked at the security cameras and ran some facial recognition, they'd find her right away."*

"Why aren't they?" Dave asked, though his mind was elsewhere, namely on returning a favor owed. His gut swarmed with bugs at the direction that favor was about to take him.

"I don't know, Dave!" Bones yelled, topping out the earpiece with a tinny grind. *"None of this makes sense. None of it."*

Well, that wasn't ideal, but what could he do? He was just an old guy wearing a mechanical suit because he couldn't walk without searing pain.

Oh. "I'm an old guy in a Jacket."

"What?" Bones asked, clearly not following his internal dialog.

"I'm inside the Ladder. Wearing a fucking exoskeleton," Dave said, a grin breaking his face. "I'm Iron Man."

"Who's Iron Man?"

"That in and of itself is a tragedy." Dave said. "I'm heading up the Ladder. Can you help me get to the Staff entrance?"

"That's nuts. Someone's going to see you."

Dave cracked his neck, the flush of adrenaline driving away the persistent pain in his hip as he made his way out of the office. "Then they'll see me, and after I make sure no one's waiting to kill her, I'll lead them a merry chase. Give her time to escape."

This leg of the Ladder was powered down. The typically long, blazing white hallways were black tunnels. If he hadn't had his Jacket, none of this would work. As he thought it, orange wireframe outlines sprang to life.

"Now, should I go directly to the elevator, or some other way?"

Bones was silent for a moment. When she spoke, her voice was thick and muffled. *"You still have that auth chip?"* she asked, referring to the random circuit board she'd sent with him.

Dave gave his pocket a tap. "I do."

"Hold it up next to the control module near your belt."

"It's on the shoulder on this model—"

"Goddammit, Dave, it doesn't matter. Just put it next to the module."

Dave followed her instructions, holding the circuit board next to his shoulder. His display flickered, the orange wireframe dissolving into nothing, followed by the tell-tale hum of it powering down. Dave tried to move, and failed; his body locked in place. Nerves tickled his chest, pulling a panicked breath inward as he remembered nearly freezing to death a few days ago.

"Bones? Um. There's a problem."

"Don't panic. Now, three, two, and…"

His suit spun back to life, though this time was different. The boot screen, rendered in a deep green on the HUD, was different. It didn't show the generic Jacket logo, but rather a silver pentagon on a black background. A moment later, it melted away, until it was replaced by the image of a cackling skull. That, too, disappeared quickly.

"Bones?"

"No need to thank me," Bones purred over the earpiece. *"Just upgraded your suit's software to the appropriate DoD firmware."*

Dave swung his arms around in the hallway. There did seem to be a little more responsiveness. He gave a little hop, and the suit responded immediately. For the first time in a long time, he felt a little like himself again.

Maybe more than a little.

"Thanks, but I still need direction—oh." Dave stopped as a significantly higher resolution wireframe of the hallway sprang to life, including a blue arrow running along the ground in one direction.

"You're welcome. Now go save our girl."

Dave smiled and started jogging—jogging!—down the hallway. "On it."

Man, if Rose could see him now.

* * * * *

Chapter Thirty-Four

Making her way to the trippy elevator was far easier than Sarah had expected.

Getting on it was a different story.

She stood across from the hidden elevator she'd used to enter the Wheel. When she'd arrived, she hadn't had the chance to take in how much effort had gone into making it look innocuous. From the inside, it looked like a generic elevator, but here on the street, there was a single flat door with no handle. It blended seamlessly into the forward façade of a fake small business.

Igor's Tool Shed.

Some rich dickhead had giggled themselves to sleep on that one. Pricks.

She should've been able to walk right in—at least she'd hoped. There was a lot of uncertainty now that her implant was sitting in Tarrington's office. Even more now that these new assholes were patrolling like a bunch of hopped-up CIA agents.

While the Staff seemed indifferent to her presence, going so far as to completely ignore her when she bumped into them, that wasn't the case with the armed guards that'd popped up in the last few minutes.

The first one she'd seen just before brushing past him. Heavily skewed toward tall men, these black-suited walking stereotypes talked into their wrists and randomly grabbed at Staff. It was pretty obvious they were trying to find her, even before she overheard one of them mention her by name.

So, after managing to sneak her way to the exit—or at least stage one of her exit—now she needed to get past two of the guards assigned here. Sarah had been waiting patiently, peering at these two people, a man and a woman, as they scanned every Staff member who stepped past them and through the doors. It'd only happened twice since she'd gotten here, but Sarah got the barest glimpse of the elevator as each Staff person stepped through before two sets of double doors slid shut, followed by a dull *thump* sound.

"Excuse me, ma'am?"

Sarah jumped and peed a little. Not enough to cause any issues, but enough to make sure she knew she'd wet herself. Spinning, Sarah raised a fist, ready to clock someone else in the head.

Instead, she found herself staring at a short white child. The kid was at that age when, given the gender-neutral greens and browns they were wearing, it was impossible to tell if it was a boy or girl. Who knew, maybe they were neither. That didn't matter right now.

Sarah dropped her fist and tried to pretend the outburst hadn't happened. After all, she was still supposed to be one of the Staff. "Can I help you?"

"No." Then, without another word, the child pivoted on a heel and walked away.

Sarah almost went after them. What if the kid told one of the guards who she was? What if they just started yapping about a lady hiding behind a bush?

What if...

Sarah let the thought flicker away as her eyes caught a glimpse of something nestled in the fake grass at her feet. Not convinced it was real, Sarah knelt and picked it up. The circular disk had a reflective silver coating covering the entirety of one side. The other had some very familiar interface connections.

It was an implant, but newer than Bones' and, she assumed from the few times she'd caught sight of it bulging from her head, her old one.

How'd the kid get it? Why'd they bring it here?

Why drop it? Was that kid controlled by ALIZA? Was this a trap?

A lot of unanswered questions she'd have to wait to answer.

Sarah glanced at her way out of here, then licked her lips. Time to make a choice. She glanced at the guards, then back to the implant.

You're one of mine. What if it *hadn't* been Bones fucking with her?

Did she trust ALIZA? Fuck. *That* was a weighted question. How much of the horrible shit Sarah had gone through over the past few days had been because of ALIZA?

But how much had been on Tarrington's orders?

"Oh, please don't turn me into a fucking zombie," Sarah muttered.

She raised the implant into place and snapped it in.

Immediately, her vision flickered as the HUD she'd lived with for the last three years sprang to life. In the center of her vision, ALIZA dropped a message.

Welcome back, Sarah.

Sarah's mouth went dry. If ALIZA knew where she was, that meant Tarrington should know, right?

Right?

"I found her!" a child's voice screamed.

Sarah didn't dare move. She stayed crouched, hidden behind the bush. She hoped, anyway.

Again, the child's yell, though this time from farther away. "Over here! She was just here!"

Sarah waited, counting down the seconds by the beat of her heart. After sixty heartbeats, which was either a minute or thirty seconds, depending on how anxious she actually was, Sarah stood.

The door to the elevator stood unguarded.

"What the fuck is going on?" Sarah muttered.

When she didn't get an answer, Sarah decided to take action. As nonchalantly as she could manage, she crossed the road, careful to keep her generic Staff look on her face.

Soon enough, she stood before the doors and waited for them to open.

And waited.

And waited.

People started looking her direction as they passed, though not too closely. After all, wouldn't want to pick up any of the poor on your way through the rich streets of a fucking space station.

Tamping down her frustration, Sarah tried asking for help. "ALIZA. Can you open the door?"

No response.

"Please?"

And then they opened, revealing the paneled walls and flooding her nose with the odd scent of that citrus cleaner.

"Thanks," Sarah mumbled as she stepped through.

She leaned against the waist-high railing and looked back at the fake main street.

Everything about it was false. All the people were crafted things, half-human, half-plastic doll. Souls of smoke with ketchup blood. All ignoring the homeward bound bodies that scrubbed their toilets and cleaned this phony street. The ones connected to ALIZA were the only genuine ones here, because they couldn't show their faces. Even if an AI wasn't controlling them, they'd walk this road, layering manufactured smiles atop each other just to make a paycheck. Just to live.

It made her sick.

She spat through the door as it started to shut.

Just as one of those men in their black suits walked by.

He turned, brown eyes flashing. Sarah's pulse rammed roughshod through her veins.

Their eyes met.

The door snapped shut as he raised a wrist to his mouth.

"Well, fuck," Sarah said. "This couldn't get much worse."

The elevator launched its way back to the Hub, which reminded Sarah that it *could* get worse, because she hadn't set her feet properly.

* * * * *

Chapter Thirty-Five

Dave had thought there'd be stairs, maybe a service elevator, but nooooo, they'd had to use ladders. Yeah, it was a little funny. Ladders in a building called the Ladder. Some architect had had a real giggle at that, Dave was sure.

"Bet they didn't need to climb the fucking thing," Dave muttered as he did just that.

This access ladder—more a series of slashes in the side of the wall—seemed like someone had drilled a hole from the top of the Ladder, then carved out handholds on their way down. It was more cave spelunking than a service tunnel. With his Jacket, there was just enough room for him to climb.

He'd been able to skip the first nine miles of tunnel thanks to a decommissioned freight elevator, but thank God for the Jacket and Bones' updates. Without it, Dave would still be on the first floor, thinking about taking that first step as he perpetually tried warming up his trick hip.

Instead, the new updates meant the Jacket itself did most of the work. Sure, his arms and legs were still turning to lead from gently prodding them up and down thousands of times, but nearly all the load was carried by the Jacket.

"Another fifteen seconds or so," Bones' voice sang in his ear behind the throb of his heartbeat. *"Almost there. Then you should be able to hop*

across the hall to take a service elevator ride. Apparently, they didn't think lad-
ders were usable beyond the troposphere."

Dave grunted a response he wasn't sure she heard. What he knew was he wasn't looking down. A dozen miles of empty tunnel echoed behind him.

The exertion was catching up with him. The ache behind his left eye was turning into a full-blown headache, radiating through the rest of his head. White sparkles flickered here and there across his sight as he climbed.

Dave felt a tugging in his head, suddenly. Like someone had grabbed a piece of brain and gave it a pull.

He stopped as bright light flared to life in his left eye. Wildly, he batted at his face, but he couldn't feel anything. He closed his eyes, but that only dimmed it. The light was so goddamned bright.

Dave tried to grab his face, but the Jacket wouldn't let him use both hands. "Bones?" Dave managed. His voice sounded thin in his ears.

A sharp, tinny sound rang in both ears. He ground his teeth hard. *"Yeah?"* Bones replied.

Dave managed to pull one hand away and pressed the heel of his left palm hard into his left eye, until a dark impression sprouted to life in the center. He pushed, watching the darkness spread, ignoring the pain as it screeched through his skull.

Then it stopped. The light winked out, and the pain disappeared, though he felt like he'd been punched in the face.

"Dave?"

Slowly, he cracked open his left eye. The wireframe of the access tunnel came into focus, a hazy mesh that soon resolved into clarity.

Just above him was an access panel. Dave prodded at the flesh around his eye and hissed.

He'd bruised himself.

Great.

"Never mind." Dave squinted at the panel above him. "I think I'm here."

"You are," Bones said, then in a quieter voice. *"Are you okay?"*

"Sure," Dave said, pulling himself up so he could pop open the hatch. He pressed his back against the wall behind him, which was close enough to be more useful than terrifying, and grabbed what looked like a dark gray handle outlined in orange lines.

What was he supposed to say? *I have brain cancer, and I think it's worse than I thought? I'm not even sure I'd be doing this if it wasn't for this tumor?*

No. Fuck that. "Senior moment," Dave quipped, pulling the handle.

Bright light filled the tube as the panel creaked open. Dave's heart jumped into his throat. He covered his eyes.

Luckily, this time, his hand blocked the light.

Keep it together, man. As he stared through the opening, the wireframe faded away until it only outlined the general angles of the space. Apparently, his Jacket found these stupid tunnels as disorienting as he did.

"Going in," Dave said and crawled through, his Jacket scraping along the blisteringly white floors like rats in a wall.

Which is kind of what he was when he thought about it.

"The access elevator is right across from you," Bones said.

Dave took a moment to stretch. His muscles protested through the entire thing; from hamstring to shoulder, everything was on fire.

"I just need a minute," Dave muttered.

Bones wasn't going to let that happen. *"No time, through the door. There's a Staff patrol coming."*

Cursing, Dave pulled the access panel shut, then stumbled stiff-legged across the hallway to where his HUD showed an otherwise invisible door in the wall. As soon as he was on it, Dave made out a softer edge where his fingers just fit.

He pulled on it lightly, and the entire section of wall sighed open, revealing his ride up to space. A cold breeze swept out to him, carrying with it the smell of grease and oiled steel.

"This was a stupid idea."

This "access elevator" looked like a man-sized Easter basket held up by strings. There was a central lever with arrows pointing up and down.

That was it. No circuitry. No safety harness.

Nothing.

"Too late to back out now," Bones said. *"Thirty seconds until the patrol arrives."*

Dave stared around, looking for some other way out of this that didn't include climbing back down that fucking tube. When nothing presented itself, he stepped into the basket.

"Ten seconds. Close the door, Dave."

Dave pulled the door shut with a sucking sound, dropping him back into darkness for a moment, then everything was lit in lines of digital flame. It was freezing in here, which, Dave noted happily, was a good thing. Otherwise, the grease smell in here would be damn near overwhelming. As it was, he still gagged despite himself.

"Shh!" Bones hissed over the headset.

Fine.

Dave sat there for several minutes before Bones gave the all clear.

He turned to the controls and grabbed the single lever. "These look simple enough…"

He cranked it to what he assumed was the "up" position.

"Don't forget to strap in."

"What—" Dave managed to get out before the lift shot upward.

He fell to the ground hard, just barely catching the railings around the outside before the exoskeleton securing his head scraped long and loud along the wall that whistled past behind him.

Dave's stomach dropped into his ass. His legs, even with the assistance of the Jacket, shuddered flat against the floor. The whir of servos in his shoulders kept him upright, but just barely.

It felt like his eyes were driving into his mouth.

With that came the starbursts.

"No, no, no," Dave muttered as the lights got brighter.

His stomach flattened.

The lights brightened.

Dave couldn't feel his fingers anymore. They must be about to slip.

And bright—

The pressure let up, and his legs unstuck from the floor. The sounds coming from his Jacket stopped and, with the sudden lack of g-forces, the bouncing lights vanished.

Wind still whipped by as the lift rose, the walls nothing more than streaking blurs.

"Jesus Christ," Dave grunted, shaking his head.

Then his eyes lit on the modular seat secured to the side of the basket. With a grimace, Dave reached out and disconnected the lock harness on the seat. Immediately, it dropped with a clang, like it was spring loaded. A belt system was wound along either side.

"You okay?" Bones asked.

Dave got himself into the seat with a few more curses and snapped the belt. "Yeah. Fine."

"You'll be there—a few... utes," Bones said, bouts of static breaking apart her voice. *"...think they're trying to block... missions... ammit!"*

"Bones?" Dave prodded. "Bones can you hear me?"

"Dave... fere... ce... ful."

Then the sound cut off, leaving Dave alone with nothing but the sound of the wind slicing above the roof of his lift.

And the unfortunate gift of his own silent company.

* * * * *

Chapter Thirty-Six

The service elevator ground to a stop.

Dave swallowed, harsh bile making its way back down his throat. The cold was deep in his bones now, an almost constant shiver running through him. His arms and legs floated, the single lap belt attached to the seat the only thing keeping him in place.

"Bones?" Dave whispered, hoping their connection had resumed.

His call was greeted with static.

Luckily for him, the blue line that acted as a guide was still in place. With a silent prayer, he unstrapped himself from the seat.

And floated.

Arms flailing, Dave snagged the handrails around the basket and pulled himself down. No matter what he did, though, he couldn't keep his feet on the ground. It was disorienting and made his stomach swim.

He swallowed more acid.

What even happened to gut fluids in space? Did they stay put, or hover around? How would this affect his coordination if he had to run? *Could* he run?

Dave grunted.

It'd only been a few minutes, and Dave felt comfortable with saying space sucked.

"Maybe the new suit upgrade has something to help?" Dave mused aloud. "Uh, Jacket, do you hear me?"

Text blossomed into being, crafted by the same orange lines that outlined the space around him.

Yes, sir?

"Okay, that's kind of weird," Dave mumbled. "Can you help me move around in no gravity?"

*Of course, sir. Normally I would
activate magnetic heels, but that module appears
to be missing or damaged. In lieu of proper
equipment, would you like me to assume
Full Control, or only indicate proper
handhold and foot placement?*

Full control? "What do you mean by 'Full Control'?"

*Simply put, I, as your exosuit,
will assume Full Control of all
modules for the purposes of
battle, defense, or travel.*

"That sounds like it could be helpful—" Dave was interrupted by another prompt with bright red warning letters and a flashing gold box around it.

*MANDATORY WARNING: Enabling Full Control for
battle and defense can result in irreparable damage
to the host. Your Mk-10 Mobile Combat Exosuit's
number one priority is your life, not keeping your limbs
in one piece. Only use this feature as a last resort.
Remember, the BMC motto is:
"We'll get you home, no matter the cost."*

The lack of a few words in that motto, namely *in one piece*, sent a shudder through him. "Jesus Christ. What the hell did she do to my Jacket?"

*Would you still like me to
take Full Control, sir?*

"No!" Dave said, pulling himself toward the outline of the maintenance door. "The handhold marker thing is good enough."

Of course, sir.

Immediately, small images of hands and feet popped into view, though he ignored them initially.

First, he had to get this door open. With a small push, he launched himself toward the door, and slammed into it. Apparently, his push had had a little too much *oomph*. With one arm pinned against the wall, Dave reached down to grab the lever keeping the door shut. He gave it a pull… and his body shot toward the floor.

Flailing, he got his feet underneath him, hit the ground, then held onto the handle, the only thing keeping him upright.

Sir?

"What?"

*You've planted your feet.
Now place your left hand
on the marker and lift.*

"What marker?"

Glancing around, he saw the faint glow of a blue right hand over-laying where he'd grabbed the lever as well as stylized feet where he'd ended up steadying himself. Above him he saw a glowing hand icon. When he grabbed there, he realized he had both the leverage to open this thing and avoid braining himself on the framing inside the maintenance shaft.

"Okay, then."

With a pull, the hatch released. A rush of warm air filled the space, along with a shaft of bright light. Dave sighed in relief, then pulled himself into the hallway, following his Jacket's handhold placement guide.

The brightness took a second for him to adjust to and kicked a spear of fear up his spine. It faded quickly, however, as the hallway resolved into something both familiar and alien at the same time. This time, the light wasn't in his head.

Down on Earth, the Ladder used this brilliant white design as well, but up here it was somehow cleaner. Sterile. A harsh citrus scent hung in the air. It immediately reminded him of kiwi and grapefruit, both of which he hadn't had in decades because they went extinct in the 50s.

That was nothing compared to what he saw down the hall to the left—a window showing the Earth in all its glory. The sun sat bright above the curved horizon, lighting the massive clouds covering the Atlantic Ocean. They rippled and twisted below, massive spirals and storms raging.

"Wow."

He hadn't meant to say it aloud, but what else were you going to do when you saw the beauty of the Earth from the sky? Even the raging storms below were things of exquisite artistry, rivaling any work of art he'd ever seen.

Footsteps pulled his gaze from the window. His heart jumped into his throat as he looked to the right. A man stood there in a Staff jumpsuit. As usual, there was only a small smile plastered on his face and no other indication of what was going on inside that head.

"Um," Dave started, trying to come up with a reason for a retiree in a Jacket to be standing here, now, on the top floor of the Ladder.

Nothing came to mind.

THREAT DETECTED:
Would you like me to take
Full Control?

"No!" Dave snapped. "It's just a guy. He's working, not attacking."

Understood.

"You need to hurry," the man said suddenly, the uber-happy lilt to his voice Dave associated with the ALIZAs. "Seven soldiers have passed already. I am concerned."

"Excuse me?" Dave asked, but the man was already walking in a stiff, solid, heel-toe gait in the opposite direction, boots clipping along what was apparently a metal floor.

Dave watched him walk past to the left and around the corner in a daze. That wasn't the way his arrow went, but he desperately wanted to chase after the man and ask him what the fuck was going on.

But if the guy—or, Dave guessed, ALIZA—was telling the truth, he didn't have time for that. On the wall ahead of him, just past the window, was a sign. To the left was the Ladder elevator and Citizen

Arrivals; to the right was the Staff entrance to the Wheel. He needed to get to the latter.

Cursing, Dave turned to the right and pulled himself along the hallway using the handhold markers his Jacket laid out for him.

From somewhere ahead of him, Dave heard people talking and the sound of metal hitting metal.

His heart still pounding in his chest, and small starbursts forming in his vision, Dave went as fast as he could and hoped he'd get there before Sayre did.

He was going to save her, no matter the cost.

* * * * *

Chapter Thirty-Seven

The elevator slid into place and stopped. Sarah slammed into the wall again, the breath driving from her lungs, bruises no doubt blooming across her body at the impact. She coughed, and spittle danced in the air until it resolved into tiny crimson globules that floated aimlessly before her. Memories of a similar view blossomed in her mind for a moment.

Sarah felt like she'd been hit by a truck. With worried fingers, she felt for the spot above her ear where the implant was installed. The smooth surface was dented and partially disconnected. She tried wiggling into place. A shock ran through her, leaving her jaw and eye twitching.

"Sh-sh-shit," Sarah managed before pulling the implant out completely and sticking it into one of the barely-there slits in her jumpsuit that pretended to be a pocket.

That wasn't good. She must've cracked it against the inside of the elevator while she was bouncing around like an idiot. How the hell was she going to get down the Ladder now?

With a grunt, Sarah pulled herself upright, just barely holding down a scream as something in her chest shifted in a way it definitely wasn't supposed to. As soon as her heels were close to the floor, she gave them a click, and they snapped onto the steel.

"I really should've remembered that," Sarah hissed.

Each breath was fire. She tasted blood.

None of that was good, either.

Ahead of her, the elevator doors slid open, revealing the short hallway to the Staff entrance tube. Struggling through the pain, Sarah made her way to it. Each step pulled on something in her knee she must've cracked during her impression of a ping pong ball on the ride from the Wheel, but she kept moving. Her only chance of survival was to get off the damned Hub and down the Ladder.

Without an implant.

How she was supposed to do that was a different story.

"One problem at a time," Sarah muttered to herself. "First, get off the Hub, then worry about the Ladder."

It took longer than she wanted, but she made it to the door eventually, though the large, red handle keeping the door locked taunted her.

She knew she could do it. ALIZA had done it without a bunch of effort. Should be easy.

I wasn't busted up then.

And ALIZA controlled these doors, as evidenced by the one shutting behind her the first time she'd come up here. Hell, she wasn't even sure why ALIZA had had her physically open these doors then, anyway.

Then again, maybe ALIZA had done it because she knew Sarah was watching? Wanted to make sure she knew this wasn't an automated escape route?

A couple hours ago, Sarah would've written that off, but not now. Not since the kid had distracted the guards after giving her a new implant.

Was ALIZA looking out for her? Had she known this was going to happen?

"Ugh," Sarah grunted. "That's too much for the concussion."

Sarah wasn't sure she had a concussion, though. Sure, she had a pounding headache and was increasingly dizzy, but she was also in space and in a ton of pain. This was kind of uncharted territory, after all.

Taking a deep breath, Sarah planted her feet, grabbed the lever with both hands, and heaved on it. It took a lot of effort, and she had to stop several times due to lack of breath, but eventually the lever ground its way open. The door followed suit, opening into the wriggly tube connecting the Hub to the Ladder.

A blast of cold air slammed into her, sending goosebumps across her skin. On the far side of the tunnel, Sarah saw the other door, its small porthole dark. That seemed odd. She didn't remember it being covered last time. But what choice did she have? It was either go forward or definitely get caught.

Forward momentum won the day.

Sarah stepped up to the edge of the tube, grabbed the handholds at either side, then clicked her heels. Immediately, her feet came off the ground.

This was going to hurt. With gritted teeth, Sarah pulled herself out into the tunnel, trying desperately not to scream as the pain in her chest ripped through her.

* * *

Dave rounded the next corner and found himself face-to-face with seven men in black uniforms. They stood around a door with batons out and ready. All were secured to the floor with boots that must've had magnets in them, like the pair the Staff guy was wearing. One man stood directly in front of what looked like a bulkhead door, a hand on the red lever that likely opened it.

He saw Dave first.

"You're not supposed to be here," he called out, gesturing to one of the others. "Get him out of here."

The man he'd pointed at turned, baton held out to the side. "All right, buddy…" Then recognition dawned on his face. "This is David Parker."

As one, the men turned to Dave, batons snapping out like they were planning on using them. Dave felt heat rise in his face. The vision in his left eye flickered. Starbursts blossomed into burning suns.

THREAT DETECTED:
Would you like me to take
Full Control?

The first man stepped out of the way, revealing a small porthole through which Dave could just make out a long, winding tunnel. "Call it in," he ordered.

"Interference is still active for another ten minutes, sir."

In that tunnel, Dave saw a single person pulling itself through the empty space. It seemed to be favoring one arm over the other, constantly bouncing into the ceiling or the sides of the tube. That meant ALIZA wasn't controlling them, for sure.

Sayre.

Dave stared at his Jacket's prompt as the men approached him.

"He's wearing an exoskeleton!" one of the men called out.

What would the suit do if he activated Full Control? He didn't want to be responsible for killing anyone. Shit, these guys probably had families. People who loved them.

"It's just a Jacket; they don't have defense mechanisms."

In the distance, Dave saw Sayre falter and float, weightless, in the center of the tube.

"Listen," Dave said, pulling himself backward awkwardly and bumping into the wall. "I just want to get my friend and get out of here."

"Take it easy," the closest said as he closed the distance, eyeing the Jacket. "Everything is fine."

"Goddammit!" Dave yelled. The men all changed stances, hefting their batons like the weapons they were. "Come on. Please."

"Mr. Parker, we need you to power down the suit."

"You five get him," said the man near the door, the one obviously in charge. "I'll get the girl."

His prompt disappeared and reappeared.

THREAT DETECTED:
Would you like me to take
Full Control?

Dave cleared his throat, swallowed sour spit, and said a single word. "Yes."

* * * * *

Chapter Thirty-Eight

Sarah's vision narrowed into a tight tunnel, her only purpose to get to that fucking door at the end. She was about halfway through when her left arm gave out. The bonus to that was it didn't hurt as much if she didn't use it.

The drawback was she'd slowed to a crawl.

A strange screeching sound filled her ears. It was faint, as if heard from a long distance, but loud enough.

It sounded almost like someone screaming.

Sarah lifted her head and stared at the door at the end of the hallway. The porthole was no longer black and, if she squinted, she could make out forms moving, though they shifted too quickly for her to identify.

What the hell was going on?

Keep moving, she told herself. If she stopped here, it was over; that's all she knew.

"One thing at a time."

* * *

Dave's hip was the first thing to go.

As soon as Dave gave the Jacket full control, it gripped the walls and launched itself at the men. The sudden movement made his stomach swim, but it was the initial impact that really brought things home.

The man who'd recognized him brought his baton up defensively, but Dave's Jacket didn't care. Instead, it slammed a hand into the ceiling, throwing Dave downward, then kicked up into the man's face as he passed, ripping through Dave's range of motion like it was tissue paper. The sudden pop of his hip tearing from the joint echoed in the tight quarters.

Dave screamed. The Jacket continued on, kicking and spinning, Dave's leg swimming in the meat around his pelvis. Tearing and ripping, turning everything to paste.

All at once, baton blows rained down on the Jacket and any exposed flesh. Pain flared across Dave's entire body, his vision nothing but white fire as the Jacket swung and kicked, punched and gouged its way free of attackers. A sharp *crack* echoed, followed by a flash of blackness, then a daze as the world spun around him.

Dave's vision cleared in his right eye, but his left seemed stuck white now. Dave knelt over the first man, whose face was purpling, the Jacket's hands clasped around his neck.

The man had his hands wrapped around the metallic skeleton of the Jacket, trying desperately to get his hands free. Dave watched in morbid fascination as the man gave up, hands falling to his sides.

"Jacket, I think that's enough," Dave managed through gritted teeth. "Turn off—"

He lurched forward as the right elbow of his Jacket—the one he'd forgotten to check days ago—collapsed. Dave's hands still gripped the man's throat, but the space between them shrank to nothing as the Jacket tried to compensate for the loss of leverage. Sweat, blood, and desperation flooded Dave's nostrils.

The man grunted.

Something slammed into Dave's left side. One. Two. Three times.

Negative. Resuming Full Control.
Eliminating threat, then restoring control.

"What—" Dave tried say, but instead of words, blood filled his mouth. He felt the tugging, the wiggling of something slashing and cutting deep into his body.

He'd been stabbed.

His good hand flicked to the left. Out of the corner of his eye, Dave saw the Jacket grab the man's forearm and twist.

There was a crack, and beneath him, the man's mouth opened in a soundless howl.

A knife floated up into the air, trailing droplets of blood.

I thought it would hurt more.

Both of his hands were on the man's throat once more.

The man on the ground went a dark purple, eyes going bloodshot as he stared, defiantly, at Dave.

"—take...with...me," the man managed to whisper as his body went limp beneath Dave's Jacket.

Target eliminated.
Restoring control.

As soon as his Jacket stopped supporting him, Dave went limp, limbs hanging in the air. His bad leg shifted, sending spasms through his body, but he couldn't even feel it anymore.

Couldn't feel anything but cold.

Around him, orbs of red shimmered and shifted, slowly congealing into larger spheroids that stood stark against the brilliant white of the hallway.

It was beautiful.

The vision in his left eye flickered out completely to utter darkness.

The sound of metal against metal screamed from nearby, followed by a gasp, then a terrified howl.

A moment later, warm hands grabbed him by the face.

Dave stared at Sayre, her face battered and bruised, brown hair floating like a halo around her head. "You look like hell, kid."

Sayre's face broke into a small, quivering smile. He watched as a glob of red hit her cheek and spread out slowly, like a wet spider crawling along her face.

Her eyes shimmered as she met his gaze. "You're one to talk, old man."

Dave laughed, or tried to. He coughed instead, spitting more and more red mist into the air to join the rest.

Her forehead pressed against his.

Dave smiled, then remembered why he was here.

"Sayre." Another coughing fit. The edges of his vision grew dim, and he was cold.

So cold.

"Yeah?"

Dave took a shallow breath so he'd have the air for it. "Access panel around the corner. Take that."

"Okay."

Dave tried another breath and failed. Everything was fading, coming to a solid point that resolved one more time to Sayre's face.

"Cross the hall. Ladder down. Circuit board in my pocket. And here."

More slowly than he'd like, he reached up, pulled the earpiece out of his ear, and handed it to her. She took it in one hand, then held his.

He couldn't feel her fingers.

"Okay."

Dave lifted a hand and touched her cheek. "You're a good kid. Sorry I don't have a good joke to end on."

"Dave…" Sayre said. She kept speaking, but the sound was muted and dull.

It was fine. She was safe.

The light faded then, drawing in at the edges, the vignette he'd been holding onto fading to black. Sound disappeared completely, the muffled cries of someone guiding him to Rose as he drew away, the point disappearing in the distance. Away and away and…

At least he'd finally gotten to be Iron Man.

* * * * *

Chapter Thirty-Nine

Sarah had no idea how long she'd knelt in that hall with Dave. Too long.

She should move. Head toward this access panel. Get down the Ladder.

But she couldn't. Sarah's forehead was still pressed against Dave's as it cooled, her hair a writhing mass around his blank face.

Every time she opened her eyes, all she saw was the blood. Hovering. Dancing a choreographed minuet until it collided with the pristine walls and smeared in slow splashes of crimson.

It was a wall. A barrier of wet color.

How was she supposed to walk through that?

Walk through *him* and past the others.

Besides the one man who floated nearby, purple face pressed against Dave's suit, feet stuck to the floor by magboots, six other men hovered. Sarah didn't care to find out if they were dead or unconscious.

What she wanted was for this to be over. For none of this to have happened in the first place.

Why? Why her? Why Dave? Why any of this?

Sarah took a shuddering breath and squeezed her eyes shut. She reached up and grabbed the sides of Dave's face, one hand a tight fist around the ear bud he'd passed to her before he died.

"Fuck!" Sarah sobbed. "Fuck, fuck, fuck…"

She almost didn't hear the squawk coming from her hand.

"Dave? Dave? Can you hear me, Dave?"

Sarah leaned away, dragging her eyes from Dave's face, locked in time with that weird grin he always had every time he broke her out of her work trance at OmniMart…

She stopped going down that train of thought. If she went there again, she'd start crying, and this time she wasn't sure she could stop.

Instead, Sarah grabbed the earpiece and popped it in her ear, only vaguely cringing at the idea of it.

Immediately, Bones' voice crashed over the speaker. *"Dave! God-dammit, Dave, respond!"*

"This is Sarah," Sarah managed, though each breath was like breathing underwater. "Dave saved me, but…" Sarah's heart lit on fire. She gritted her teeth, then finished the sentence, "He's dead."

Over the line, Sarah heard a sharp intake of breath. *"Okay."*

That was it? Just okay? How could she say that? What was wrong with her?

"'Okay'?" Sarah snapped, letting the anger fuel her. "Show some goddamned respect."

"Hey, I know you're hurting, but right now you've got to get out of there," Bones replied. For once, she wasn't being demeaning, which caught Sarah off guard. *"Dave sacrificed himself to save you, so let's do that."*

Sarah wanted to lash out, to scream at Bones that it was her fault, that none of this would've happened if it hadn't been for her, but the words were stale on her tongue before they even came out. "Fine."

"Head down the hall; there's an access panel and an elevator. Buckle in, then take that down. There's also a long ladder to climb down and, hopefully, freight access you can switch to."

Sarah prodded at her chest. She hissed as pain flared. "I don't know if I can do a ladder."

"Well, we'll deal with that when we get there," Bones said, a weird lilt to her voice that Sarah realized was her trying to be supportive. *"For now, we need to get you back on Earth."*

Sarah pulled her eyes away from Dave and looked toward the end of the hall. It was a minefield of blood and bodies. There was no way she was getting through clean.

"Okay. One thing at a time."

"Exactly."

With a deep breath, Sarah touched Dave's head one more time, then stepped through a wall of crimson.

* * * * *

Chapter Forty

Sarah didn't remember the trip down the Ladder. She didn't remember much beyond the cramped space and chill darkness as she descended, foot by foot, handhold by handhold.

What she did know was, if the tunnel hadn't been so narrow, she would've fallen to her death. There was no way she could've made it without falling backward against the wall and stopping to breathe fire and cough blood every dozen feet or so. The freight elevator had been locked down, so climbing became her life. Rung by rung, step by step.

When she finally put her foot down for the next rung and hit flat bottom, she froze, sure something was about to happen. That someone would find her. That it was a trick of her addled mind, and if she let go, she'd fall miles to the Earth.

It wasn't. The last step led to a door, that door to a darkened hallway, and that hallway to an exit she knew all too well.

And as she broke out of that exit, the circuit board she'd gotten from Dave chimed in authentication, and she stepped into the dark shadow of the Ladder. The air was thick with a mugginess that made sweat seep from her body in steady streams. It smelled of smoke and ash, and burned her lungs like it was fresh and volatile.

It was the most beautiful thing she'd ever experienced.

Bones came barreling up within seconds of Sarah exiting the building in her beaten old Tesla. The window rolled down, and Bones' face, paler than usual and with an uncertainty lining it Sarah hadn't seen before, called for her to get in.

Sarah stumbled over and dropped into the back seat.

For a moment, Sarah tried to make sense of the words coming from Bones, but there was no fighting it anymore. She was as safe as she was going to get, and her body knew it.

With Bones' harsh soprano a broken lullaby in her mind, Sarah drifted off to sleep.

Dave's bloodless face waited behind her eyelids.

* * * * *

Chapter Forty-One

A wind full of rot blew in off the Oswego River.

It dragged along the scent of dying fish on the rocky shore and seagull shit drying along the concrete framing of the canal in the too-bright sun. The limbs of ancient maple and pine trees complained at its force. Cracked and fading leaves dropped, caught on the breeze, and scattered along an asphalt street as lined and worn as a dead man's face.

Sarah walked this road alone, stained white sneakers flashing against the gray street and dead leaves. Her backpack was heavy on her back, filled with old books from the village library. Ancient houses rose and fell around her, giants waking for a moment, then fading into memory as she progressed.

One house didn't fade.

It rose on her left, beaten, mismatched aluminum siding shining in the fall light. A set of steps led to an open door. Cracked and faded emerald green, it sparkled like a circuit board. The stylized canopy above it sloped to the side, the rusted supports bent under its weight as the bones of long-dead plants climbed the crumbling structure.

The windows were dark, black, despite the daylight.

And Dad's beaten Buick sat crooked in the steep driveway, mismatched doors a perverted rainbow of color and rust. He was home early. That wasn't good.

That was never *good.*

Sarah's pulse quickened. This couldn't be happening. The house was gone, long since collapsed and cleared away.

But here it was.

A creaking sound caught her attention, drawing her eyes to the front door as it swung open, revealing navy blue walls and dust-colored furniture.

"Sayre? Is that you, baby? Dinner's ready!"

That voice.

A chill ran through her. She ground her teeth and rubbed hands through her hair. That voice shouldn't be here.

It belonged to a dead woman.

"Sayre, dinner time!" Then, after a short pause, her tone taking on an edge, "Stop it, Devin."

Sarah licked chapped lips. This couldn't be real.

"I said no!" This time the voice was different. Panicked. "No! Stop! Devin, stop it!"

Familiar.

Anxiety prickled the back of Sarah's throat. "Mom!"

Another voice howled. "Goddammit, woman! This is my *fucking house!"*

Sarah had forgotten about that voice. About the anger in it.

She'd forgotten what her father sounded like.

Any thoughts of reality fled, and she ran, the porch rocking beneath her feet like it had every day as a child.

The door swung wide, slamming into the coffee table behind it, the lamp falling and crashing to the floor like it had back then.

Her backpack hit the ground, a rotting copy of Gulliver's Travels *catching her eye.*

A crack *echoed through the house, sound ricocheting off the worn hardwood floors of the 250-year-old house like a mousetrap snapping shut.*

Or like the .38 pistol Sarah's dad kept in his bedside table.

"You shot me! You fucking shot *me! You come here right the fuck now—"*

Another crack *as Sarah sprinted through the living room, the dining room, and its old oak furniture, the Dutch door her mother had so lovingly reinstalled between the dining room and the kitchen slightly ajar, a trickle of crimson sliding beneath it.*

Sarah plowed through the doors, top and bottom swinging wide to smack hard into the wall behind.

Her father lay against the back door, left cheek pressed against the cold steel, a bloody hole in his forehead. His hands limply cradled a dark, red mess in his stomach leaking the line of blood making its way into the dining room.

"Oh, my God. Oh, my God. Jesus, forgive me."

Not those words. God, not those words.

Sarah turned to her mother. Mom stared at the body of Sarah's father, the small, black pistol in hand, blooming black eye and split lip bright in the fading fall light.

The pistol wavered in the air, then fell to her mother's side, still gripped tight in her hand. Her eyes flickered away from the body, eventually coming to rest on Sarah.

Sarah wanted to speak. Wanted to tell her it was okay. Tell her it was in self-defense.

Wanted to say that it wasn't her fault, that she'd been protecting both of them. That her mother had saved her from the increasingly angry glares dad had been throwing her. How just last night, he'd put a fist through Sarah's bedroom door when she hadn't brushed her teeth.

How scared she'd been of him.

She wanted to say anything other than what she'd said that day, fourteen years ago.

But she didn't, because you can't change the past, no matter how much you wanted to.

"You killed Dad."

Sarah's mother cracked. Her cheeks twitched. Pupils dilated. Any flickering sense of sanity left in those eyes disappeared.

The pistol rose and planted itself in her mother's right temple. "I'm sorry, baby," she whispered, tears pooled in the corners of her eyes.

Boom.

Sarah shocked awake.

Pain blossomed across her body. Her arms and legs were lead weights holding her in place.

It was dark, with a palpable, humid heat. Sweat soaked through her clothes, though how much she had left before she was running on empty was anyone's guess. The place smelled like stained leather and rot.

After a few moments, her vision adjusted. Despite herself, she let out a relieved sigh. She wasn't in her old house.

She was in Bones' car.

With a grunt, Sarah laid her head back down on the seat. It was pitch black out, or at least dark enough the tinted windows made it seem like beyond them was the void of space.

Dave's face, floating there, small smile made of dead skin...

Sarah pressed the heels of her hands into her eyes despite the scream of her muscles.

Fuck. Why'd Dave have to die?

And why had she been such a bitch the last time they'd spoken? He'd died before she could thank him. Thank him for all the times he'd woken her up at work just to make her laugh. For how he'd come by to listen after her blowup at the Retreat.

For saving her life on the Ladder.

Another person dead trying to protect her.

The story of her life.

"Jesus…" Sarah whispered into her hands.

"Shh."

Sarah froze. Then, straining against the bricks that had replaced her muscles, she sat up and looked in the front seat.

Bones reclined in the driver's seat, eyes closed. In the passenger seat was another woman who looked out the side window, straight, pale hair blocking her face.

Out the front window was nothing but black at first. As her eyes adjusted, she made out darker stripes in the darkness, almost like trees. Sarah cast about, looking for any sign of light. Panic threaded its way into her throat.

For a moment, she was back in that tiny shaft, breathing its tainted air, walls pressing in around her, each gasp filled with pain and copper.

But just as quickly as it had come, the feeling passed.

The shaft hadn't smelled like a gym bag.

"Where are we?" Sarah whispered. Each breath brought a now-familiar sting, which she only barely stopped from turning into a hacking cough.

"We're near Dave's house," the lady in the passenger seat whispered, her voice barely more than rustling leaves, "waiting for the police to leave."

Something about her voice struck a nerve. "Do I know you?" Sarah asked.

"Shh," Bones hissed. "No noise. Momma needs her beauty sleep."

Sarah strained to get a better view of the woman in the passenger seat. Unfortunately, her body wouldn't cooperate. The muscles in her arms and legs were little more than jelly at this point.

She leaned back into her seat and did her best to stretch out.

Blue and red lights flickered through the trees.

Sarah froze, her heart in her throat.

"Easy," Bones said, though Sarah noticed her hand moving toward the ignition. "They're leaving."

The lights grew brighter, a twisting, dichromatic kaleidoscope. Through the trees, a pair of police cars approached slowly. Bright shafts of white light shot out into the forest, the one in front shining toward them, the car behind lighting the other side.

Sarah couldn't look away. Her heart hammered in her throat. The seat grew moist beneath her palms, air stale in her lungs. Sarah pulled them into her lap, tried to ease her mind as she followed the steady sweep of the lamp, although the way it hovered periodically on random items made her stomach swim.

Sharp pain blossomed in Sarah's palms. She released the fists she hadn't known she'd been making and took a few steadying breaths.

There was no need to panic. She'd been through worse just in the last two days.

"Mom," the unnamed woman whimpered. Her breathing was quick, erratic. Apparently, she hadn't been through worse.

Bones hissed.

"*Mom.* Shouldn't we—"

Bones cast a glare sharp enough Sarah felt it from the back seat. "Quiet, Constantia."

Constantia. Police lights forgotten along with the pain in her limbs, Sarah pulled herself forward until she saw the girl in the passenger seat clearly.

Bones was having none of that.

"Not right now." Bones grabbed Sarah by the face and pushed her back.

Maybe on a good day, Sarah would've been able to do something about that, but right now, even with the anger blossoming in her chest and the adrenaline from the spotlights sweeping nearer and nearer, she couldn't do anything but fall back.

Constantia. God, that *bitch*.

Sarah closed her eyes and tried to remember the face from Camila's party, but all she could recall was long blonde hair—check—short stature—check—and a quiet voice—double check.

If it was her, if this girl in the passenger seat was Constantia, and if Bones was her mother, then... Another betrayal. Another lie.

Sarah grimaced and looked out the tinted window, vision blurring.

Why her? Why couldn't they have picked anyone else? All she'd wanted was a future, and now that was gone.

For the first time since it had happened, Sarah remembered kicking the shit out of Matthew Tarrington. Her stomach fell into her feet.

She was fucked. *Fucked.*

There was no way in hell she was ever getting to New Eden now.

No New Eden. No Dave. No family.

No future.

Bright light flashed in Sarah's eyes. Instinctively, she dropped farther into the seat, until she was staring at the worn armrest, bright lights flashing through the inside of the car. Had they found them? Was there a cop right outside her door, waiting to arrest her for attacking the most powerful man in the world?

Most powerful in two *worlds*, she corrected herself.

Sarah craned around to check on Bones. She wasn't sure why she even cared—the woman was the source of all her problems—but she couldn't stop herself.

Bones stared into the spotlight, jaw and cheek twitching, eyes defiant. Her lips moved ever-so-slightly, like she was murmuring a prayer.

Then the lights disappeared, the sound of gravel crackling beneath tires fading into the distance behind them. After several long minutes, the bright red and blue lights disappeared, followed by the sound of car engines revving up to speed.

Sarah let out an audible breath.

"That was close," Constantia whispered.

Oh, right.

Bones reached out a thin hand to Constantia, something akin to a smile cracking her face. "You need to learn to keep your head, baby."

The back door cracked open easily, the evening air sighing into the backseat, filling it with flowers and earth.

Bones reached for her, but missed as Sarah left the car. "We don't know if…"

The rest trailed off into a harsh whisper Sarah couldn't make out as she left the car. Straining, Sarah straightened her back until the pain in her chest protested, then stretched out her arms and legs. She needed to be limber for this next part. A cold calm descended on her as sore muscles loosened.

Behind her, a door opened.

"What're you doing? We haven't made sure the house is clear," Bones said, throwing a hand in the air. "Stop being a child."

Sarah turned to her and smiled.

Then she opened the passenger door.

Constantia, Camila's "new friend," stared back at her, shock and something approaching terror mingling on her petite face.

"Thanks for not wearing your seatbelt." Sarah smiled.

Constantia looked toward Bones' side of the car and back. "What—ah!"

Sarah grabbed her by the hair, starting at the nape of her neck and grabbing as much of the thin blonde shit as she could, including a chunk of long bangs that looked stupid on her anyway.

The screaming was a little much, at least to Sarah. She'd had her hair pulled during plenty of fights growing up and had never screamed like this bitch.

Then again, she'd never been dragged out of a car by it, so maybe it was worse than she'd thought.

Whatever.

Constantia was a tiny woman. Girl. Who knew? It didn't matter. What mattered was, she weighed almost nothing, so dragging her out of the car was easy. Sure, she tried to grab the door, but her hands kept slipping and sliding.

Bones didn't move, which was a surprise.

Sarah had always assumed every mother would go to whatever lengths were necessary to protect their daughters. Then again, this was Bones. What had she expected?

Constantia was still screaming when Sarah slapped her. The shock of it shut her up, then Sarah knelt atop her, locking one arm beneath her leg, and grabbing a wayward hand that slipped from beneath her thigh with her left.

With a deep breath, Sarah pulled back her right hand and punched Constantia in the face.

It was both the most beautiful and horrible feeling in the world. The pure release of anger, this frustration on one of the people responsible was bliss. Euphoria.

She pulled her fist back, a thought worming its way into her mind from somewhere. If she jammed her nose up with the palm of her hand, she might be able to drive the bone into Constantia's brain. Or was that an urban myth? Did it matter?

Why shouldn't she? It was her fault. She'd forced Sarah out of her only friend's party, forced her to OmniMart, forced her into Rudy's friendship, which had led to Bones, then to the Ladder, then to today, and Sarah beating the shit out of a helpless girl pinned beneath her.

Constantia coughed, blood spitting from her mouth.

"Sarah, stop!" Bones finally yelled. The sound of feet skittering on dirt and branches filled the air.

Arms grabbed Sarah by the shoulders, pulling her backward and away from Constantia. Sarah didn't fight it, just threw her arms backward to catch herself.

She'd already stopped, her body just hadn't caught up yet.

Bones cooed over Constantia, thin fingers gently prodding the girl's face. Constantia sobbed and muttered words disappearing into the wind.

"The fuck is wrong with you?" Bones snapped, voice dropping in volume as if she'd just remembered the police had been here. "Why would you do that?"

Sarah didn't have an answer. Not a good one.

The strength she'd had a moment ago faded. It wasn't Constantia's fault. She'd probably just been doing as she was told. A tiny voice in Sarah's mind told her to forgive them. To forgive Bones and Constantia. To forgive Gareth and his bullshit.

Old guilt swam in her stomach. She'd chosen this. If she'd made different choices, none of this would have happened. If only she'd been wise enough. She should've seen this coming. Should've—

Sarah ground the guilt away beneath her molars.

No. Bullshit. They'd manipulated her. Used her.

They'd killed Dave just as surely as those men on the Ladder.

And Tarrington was a monster. Now that she knew that, was she supposed to forget? Pretend he wasn't? Why had she ever thought it would work out? That she'd get to New Eden, and it'd be better?

Every person on the Ladder was required to have an implant. That meant every resident of New Eden had one, which also meant Tarrington could control anyone he wanted at any time with ALIZA.

This wasn't her fault. Fuck, she'd done her best to get out of it at every turn. It was everyone else dragging her back in, forcing her to do shit that went against everything she believed in.

She had a right to be angry. The only problem was figuring out who to be angry with right then.

Sarah thought of Tarrington's bloody face and crawling form as she glanced at where Bones was lifting her daughter. Yes, Constantia was part of the problem, but she hadn't deserved that beating.

She'd punched the wrong person.

Time to fix that.

Sarah forced herself to her feet, then offered a hand to Constantia, who flinched. "Let's call it even for that shit you pulled."

Constantia stared at her for a long moment, then nodded and took the hand. With a grunt, Sarah got her to her feet.

"What's going on?" Bones asked, running her hand through her hair.

Sarah and Constantia shared a look, then Sarah turned back to Bones. "It's in the past. But we need to do something."

"About what?" Bones asked. "It's over. We're done."

"No. We need to find Rudy."

Bones sighed. "I tried, kid."

Sarah gritted her teeth. "That wasn't a request."

Bones shared a glance with Constantia. Something passed between them that Sarah didn't catch.

She didn't have time to ask what it was.

"Why? Why is he so important to you?" Bones snapped. "He tricked you. Manipulated you. Why help him at all?"

"Well," Sarah said with a smile as she walked back to the car, "I need to kick his ass. Can't do that if he's dead."

"What?" Bones asked, grabbing the sides of her head. "I told you, I don't know where he is!"

"ALIZA will know. She'll help us."

"ALIZA is a machine, Sarah," Bones said, rubbing her temples, "and she's controlled by the UILB. We might get access, but getting that type of information when it's not plastered in the news? Not happening."

Sarah shrugged. "Only one way to find out." Then she opened the back-seat door and sat down. "You coming?"

Bones looked like she was going to fight, but all at once, the anger drained out of her. Another glance at Constantia, who nodded. "Fine. But when this goes tits up, I'm telling you 'I told you so.'"

Constantia frowned but didn't say anything.

Good. Sarah smiled. She knew she was right. Now she just needed to find Rudy.

Bones stepped up to the door. "Here's the reality, though. We can't do this without equipment, Sarah. Without an ALIZA implant or something like the one you lost on me—" Sarah grimaced, but didn't interrupt "—we're dead in the water on some ALIZA infiltration scheme to find a kid."

Sarah's fingers wrapped around the implant in her pocket, the one ALIZA had given her. The one she'd busted up on her ride back from the Wheel because she was an idiot.

She pulled it out and held it up for Bones to examine. "Can you fix this one?"

"Where the hell did you get that?" Bones asked, leaning in and staring before flipping it over with a fingernail so she could get a look at the interface side and its carved circuits. "That's new tech. What did you do to it?"

Bounced around like a dipshit who doesn't wear their seatbelt. "I got it from ALIZA, and it got damaged on the way down the Ladder."

Bones raised an eyebrow.

"Can you fix it?" Sarah asked again.

"No? Maybe?" After a long moment, Bones plucked it from her hand with a click of her tongue. "Guess we'll find out."

* * * * *

Chapter Forty-Two

It was pretty clear Constantia was worried her "It's in the past" statement was a lie.

That was just fine with Sarah. Also, pain relievers were magic. As soon as they got back to the house, Constantia had turned up with a bottle of ibuprofen and a glass of water.

Since then, it'd been a peaceful affair. Sarah lay nestled in an easy chair with a view into Dave's kitchen, while the two of them worked away around the island in there. The lightest scent of old wood and the lingering traces of Dave almost made the clawed stone in her throat too much to swallow.

The house itself was aged and in various states of disrepair, but there was a homeyness to it that made it all too easy for Sarah to doze off. There was a little guilt the first time she'd fallen asleep, minutes after getting everything unpacked and the chair moved. When she'd opened her eyes and seen gray light trickling in from the windows, there'd been a moment of panic, but then she'd reminded herself of the last few days. She needed the sleep, so she got it.

It was late afternoon when Sarah finally woke up completely. Constantia sat near her mother, eyes vacant as she swiped around in the air. Bones, for her part, seemed content with this arrangement. Whenever Constantia moved, Bones made an effort to shift between her and Sarah, like a human buffer. That was made a bit more diffi-cult, given she was using a beaten up old laptop instead of her usual optical feed. ALIZA's implant lay on the table next to her, several electrodes clipped to it and routed to the laptop.

That had to be why Bones was using the old machine. Now that she knew the implants could be removed, Sarah didn't understand why she hadn't taken Constantia's. Obviously, Bones was the one with the skill, so why not pass it over? It didn't seem logical, unless Bones needed the hardware to reprogram the new implant.

Regardless, it wasn't her decision. Let them fret about something for a while. Once they had their bits figured out, it'd be time for her to reconnect.

Sarah suppressed a shiver at the thought. Better to distract herself. She cast about for the tenth time since they'd arrived in the night. For the most part, everything was in the same place, though there was a noticeably different smell on the air that made her mouth water. The island was now covered in scattered electronics, clusters of random circuit boards spread out like inedible tapas.

At the thought of food, her stomach growled.

First, she had to get out of the beautiful, beautiful chair, though. Groaning, she stretched.

Bones noticed. "Afternoon, kid."

Kid. Sarah flinched. Dave called her that.

Dave *had* called her that.

Sarah faked a cough. "Is there any food?"

"There's some in the fridge," Constantia said, voice still barely more than a whisper. "Not much though."

"Pickles, if you're into that sort of thing," Bones added.

Sarah, having finally extracted herself from the comfiest chair on the planet, made her way to the fridge. The spread wasn't very impressive. Dave either hadn't shopped enough, which she knew to be false, or he'd had an incredibly unhealthy diet.

Spread along three shelves were six bottles of alcohol in various stages of emptiness, though the fullest, a coffee brandy that looked like molasses, had maybe a glass left. Amongst those bottles were plastic bottles filled with different types of pickles. Need Dill Pickles? Two jars of that. Sweet? Two, no three of those. And Gherkins, good lord. Sarah stopped counting after at least five bottles.

None were completely empty.

After a long moment, Sarah sighed, grabbed one of the Gherkin bottles, and shut the door.

"How go the repairs?" Sarah asked, shoving one of the pickles in her mouth.

There was a bit of sweetness in there, but man, there was a kick she wasn't used to. Definitely not a protein mass product here. This was real.

No wonder Dave was into these. She'd had no idea.

Sarah promptly ate another one.

Bones broke her gaze away from the laptop, blue eyes piercing. "Fucking horrible."

"There's no public engineering data for this," Constantia added, swatting the air with a little too much *oomph*. "We don't even know where to start."

The third pickle went down just as easy. They really weren't bad. "Well, I mean, can't you just use one of these?" Sarah asked, grabbing one of the circuit boards off the countertop.

"Don't touch that!" Bones and Constantia yelled at the same time.

"Also," Bones added, eyes flicking in judgement, "you should change."

Sarah set the board down, then had a fourth pickle. "Why? And why—whoa," Sarah stopped as she finally looked at her jumpsuit.

She looked like she belonged in a horror vid. Dried blood covered her in brown splotches. God, she'd completely forgotten about that.

Suddenly, the jumpsuit felt a bit too tight.

And itchy.

The pickles lurched in her stomach.

A high-pitched squeal issued from the little board.

"Shit." Bones turned to Constantia. "That's the front porch alarm."

"Yeah," Constantia said, hands dancing in front of her. "Uhh…"

"What's going on?" Sarah asked, happy to shift her attention from the murder scene that was her clothing.

Bones waved her away. "Why didn't the driveway alert work?"

"I don't know!" Constantia said, then made a dismissive motion with her hand. "Someone's here."

The sound of tires on dirt and rock came from outside.

"Specifically, there," Constantia whispered, looking around at their gathered mass of equipment in desperation. "Um."

"Fuck." Bones jumped to her feet and grabbed Constantia. She pushed her toward the front door, then looked at Sarah. "Come on. We have to go."

"What?" Sarah asked, fingers still in the pickle jar.

Behind her, the wireless lock in the door disengaged.

Sarah froze.

A woman stepped inside. She was short, with tanned skin and brown hair that showed the first signs of gray. At first, she looked confused by the easy chair sitting in front of the door, then she followed the line of discarded duffel bags, circuitry, and ethernet cabling until she saw Sarah.

Bones dragged Constantia into cover behind the island in a cluster of arms and legs.

The new woman's eyes went wide, and suddenly she reminded Sarah of the woman from Dave's lock screen.

Sarah forced a smile. "Hi."

The woman didn't respond beyond clutching at a handbag like it was a weapon.

Sarah did what anyone in that situation would've done.

She held out the jar. "Would you like a pickle?"

* * * * *

Chapter Forty-Three

The three of them must've been quite the sight to see in a dead man's house.

Bones, disheveled and cursing under her breath as she tried to hide with all the skill of a toddler convinced you couldn't see her because she couldn't see you. Constantia, sobbing quietly, hands jutting out into view, arms visibly shaking.

And Sarah, eating pickles in the bloodstained jumpsuit she hadn't had the energy to change out of yet.

"Who the fuck *are* you?" the woman spat in a high voice that seemed to be on the edge of panic. Her right hand wiggled into her purse and grabbed something. "And what the fuck are you doing in my uncle's house?"

Sarah put her arms up, pickle jar suspended above her head. There could be anything in that bag, from a pistol to a tampon she'd pretend was a gun. "You're Dave's niece? I'm Sarah."

Her eyes narrowed and she gripped the thing in the bag tighter. "Never heard of you. And who are they?"

"Dave never mentioned me?" Sarah asked, hurt for some reason. Sure, it'd only been a few days, but it was the closest she'd gotten to anyone in years. "Sayre?" The lady shook her head no, eyes darkening. Why wouldn't he… a light bulb went off. "I'm the OmniMart girl?"

The woman visibly eased, though she didn't take her hand out of her bag. "You're the OmniMart girl he was talking about the other day? Before he got arrested?"

A warm flush suffused Sarah. "Yeah. I helped him, uh—" Sarah stumbled, throat closing just before revealing she'd broken him out of prison. She wasn't even sure this woman knew Dave was dead.

"Helped him what?"

"Um."

"If you're the OmniMart girl, what was he diagnosed with?" As she finished the sentence, her voice cracked, face tensing like she was trying not to cry.

Sarah cleared her throat. "Brain cancer."

All the fight went out of her then, and with it, her hand came out of the bag holding onto the neck of one of those large wine bottles. She still held it like a weapon, but there was a sadness leaking from her Sarah could feel from across the room. "Who are they?"

"Bones and Constantia," Sarah replied, lowering her arms and taking a moment to set the jar of pickles on the counter. "They were working with Dave. Same as me."

With a grunt, Bones stood, dragging Constantia to her feet as well. Sarah spared a glance at them and couldn't help but smile at how utterly pale Constantia had gone.

Sarah might forgive, but she wouldn't forget.

"Hi," Bones muttered. "Sorry for your loss."

Shit.

Did she know? Had anyone told her? Sarah let out a breath. Licked her lips. "Dave, um—"

"He's dead," she replied. "The police told me this afternoon, about ten minutes after I got fired." She paused, jaw shifting, then she gestured around the room, face contorting as the tears finally welled and dripped down her face. "He left me the house." It came out as a shuddering squeak. The wine bottle swung aimlessly toward the floor.

Despite herself, Sarah stepped forward and wrapped the other woman in a hug, and just as surprisingly, she accepted.

They stood like that for a long time, the stranger sobbing on Sarah's shoulder, a bottle of cheap red wine dangling from her fingertips.

After too long, they separated, Sarah drying her eyes with a groan. "Ugh, sorry."

"Sorry," she replied, then groaned and wiped her nose. "I'm Janet."

Sarah stepped back, putting some distance between them. "Hi, Janet. Dave told me about you."

"He did?" Janet smiled, rubbed the back of her hand across her nose, then she pulled back in a rush. "You smell horrible."

Sarah barked a laugh, and even Bones snickered behind her. "Yeah. I should change."

"You look like you've seen some shit tonight."

"Last night, actually." Sarah's face twisted of its own accord, lips quivering. *Stop it, goddammit.* She coughed. "Dave saved my life."

Janet's face cracked, tears springing to life again. "Jesus, I just stopped."

"I have to go to the bathroom."

Together, Janet and Sarah turned toward Constantia, veritably dancing in the corner of the kitchen.

Bones cocked her head at her daughter, a confused look on her face. "Then go."

Without another word, Constantia disappeared down the hall, followed by the sound of a door shutting.

"That kid ain't right," Janet said. Then, as if seeing the entire mess in the middle of the kitchen for the first time, she said, "So. Are you trying to expose this UILB bullshit? Is that what's happening here?"

"You know about that?" Bones asked, leaning against the countertop.

"Well, yeah—"

"Did you find it on the message boards I posted it on? Or maybe the Earth First network?" Bones asked, a smile flickering on her face. "Is it finally getting shared on the Net?"

Janet glanced at Sarah. "Uh. Dave told me."

Bones pursed her lips, opened her mouth like she was going to say something, then closed it and left the room without another word.

Sarah and Janet shared a glance.

"Well." Janet sighed, then made her way to the cupboard with all the glasses. She dug around for a moment and pulled out two lowball glasses before cracking open the twist top on the bottle. "Wine?"

Sarah felt all the strength go out of her at the offer. "Yes, please."

Janet nodded, then looked her over. "Okay, but first you need to change."

Sarah was all too aware of her jumpsuit at the mention of it, the smell of rust and sweat swirling into her nostrils. Her stomach turned. She wanted nothing more than to burn these clothes; to shove them into the fireplace in the living room, light them up, and never look back.

But there was a major problem with that idea. "I don't have anything else."

Janet nodded and poured out two glasses. She handed one to Sarah, who took it eagerly. "Okay. Follow me."

Together, they went down the hall Constantia and Bones had departed down. The two other women were in the bathroom with the door shut, harsh whispering barely audible in the hallway.

Janet didn't seem to notice. "It's this one," she said, stopping at a closed door and opening it. "Uncle Dave put all Auntie Rose's stuff in here after she passed."

A wave of cold air swept out of the room. It smelled like dust and age, a time capsule cracking open. Threaded through the old smells was the tiniest hint of vanilla and honeysuckle. Beyond Janet, Sarah saw what might have once been a bedroom, but now was a hoarder's paradise. The bed in the center was covered with a woman's clothes, and every square inch around that was packed with furniture, books, picture frames, and cordless clippers still in the box. Some of the clothes were on hangers and laid neatly together, and the less formal stuff was folded and piled together around the nicer stacks.

Janet stopped in the doorway for a moment, poised on the threshold like crossing it meant something she might not be ready to accept.

"Have you been in here since, um, since Dave put this stuff in here?" Sarah asked.

"No," Janet said. "Haven't seen any of this since she died." Janet took a deep breath and continued, voice cracking. "Still smells like her."

Sarah placed what she hoped was a comforting hand on Janet's shoulder. "I'm sorry."

Janet squared her shoulders, cracked her neck, and downed the rest of her wine in one gulp. "It's been a long time." She stepped into the room and beelined through the piles of papers and books. "Now get in here. We're burning those clothes, and I'd rather you not be in them when we do."

Sarah followed, stepping gingerly around a pile of stacked papers. "I'd appreciate that. I don't remember the last time I wasn't wearing a jumpsuit."

Janet grabbed a pristine white blouse from the bed and held it up. "Time for that to change. Now get over here and let's see if this fits."

Sarah smiled.

God knew she could use a break from all this shit.

It took an hour of rooting around and trying on various different clothes, from pant suits that didn't fit, to billowy sundresses that made her look pregnant. What they finally landed on, after making a right mess of the neat stacks of clothes on the bed, was a pair of stretchy jeans, a faded black t-shirt with a grinning skull displayed prominently on the front, and a black hoodie.

It wasn't fancy, not in the least, but for the first time in years, Sarah felt like herself when she looked in a mirror.

"You look comfy," Janet said from behind her, a small smile playing on her lips. "If you're on the run, you might as well be comfortable."

Sarah smiled and turned. The jeans even made her butt look good. The jumpsuit had always made it look like she was carrying a backpack around her hips. "Agreed. They just feel right."

A knock on the doorframe pulled her attention from the mirror. Standing there, paler than usual, was Constantia. Her nose was still a bruised mess, but at least it didn't look broken now.

"What's up?" Janet asked. "Need some clothes? I'm in a giving mood tonight."

"No, thank you," Constantia said, lips barely moving. "I just wanted to tell you..." Her voice trailed off into a whisper.

"What?" Sarah asked, cocking her head.

Constantia cleared her throat. "I wanted to tell you, Rudy..."

Again, she faded into nothing, face twitching.

"Girl, speak up," Janet snapped. "You're a grown ass woman. Act like it."

Constantia's eyes flashed, a flush running from her neck into her cheeks. She took a deep breath, then yelled, "Rudy's dead!"

And then, without another word, she shoved her nose into the sky and stalked away, leaving Sarah to collapse, numb, to the bed.

* * * * *

Chapter Forty-Four

It felt like someone had put a bell over Sarah's head and beaten it with a sledgehammer. Everything was fuzzy. Her ears filled with buzzing. Janet's words dissolved into a muted hum, like a broken refrigerator in an empty cave.

Janet's hand touched her shoulder. It was like the slash of a whip across her shoulders. She leapt to her feet. This didn't make sense. Bones had said he'd been arrested.

Sarah rubbed the heels of her hands into her eyes. She needed to hear it from Bones. The words had to come out of her mouth.

The way to the kitchen was a blur, just streaks of light until she stood at the end of the central island.

Bones sat in the recliner, one leg thrown over the arm, a glass of red wine in hand. "She told you?"

The words were another lash. "Yes."

Bones let out a long sigh. "Shit."

"Why?" Sarah asked, shoulders slumping in defeat. The island was there, keeping her upright with its solid presence, the surface cool against her hands.

Bones stared at Sarah for a long moment, then shook her head. "Because we needed you, and I'll do whatever it takes to bring these bastards back to Earth."

The room spun, but Sarah kept herself upright with the help of the countertop. *Goddammit.* She'd been so angry the last time she'd spoken to Rudy. God. Just like Dave.

Why did everyone she cared about die?

And why did those who didn't keep lying to her?

Suddenly, the ache that'd been building in her chest burst into flame. The room stopped spinning. Everything came to a point centered on Bones' face.

Through clenched teeth, Sarah asked, "How'd he die?"

Bones sucked the back of her teeth, then took a deep breath, held it, and let it out slowly. "That part was true. He just wasn't arrested. Took a bullet for Constantia and gave us time to get out."

Sarah's vision blurred, but she rubbed the tears away. There'd be time for that later.

"Why lie to me?" Sarah asked, straightening.

"I told you, we needed your help—" Bones started.

But that was enough.

"I would've helped you!" Sarah screamed, slamming a fist on the counter. "I would've helped even if we had no chance of getting him back."

Bones narrowed her eyes. "Would you?"

"Yes."

A twitch kicked in Bones' cheek, and for a moment, her façade cracked. Her lips curved, little-used lines in her skin forming as emotion clouded her face. Then she gritted her teeth and pressed her lips back into the flat line it typically occupied.

"Well, that's not what happened," she said. "Can't change the past now."

"No, we can't."

They stared at each other for a long moment. Sarah wanted to hurt her, to slap the shit out of her for all of the bullshit.

She didn't.

Bones was the first one to break their stare down. "Listen. Why don't you stay here with this Janice lady—"

"Janet, not Janice—"

"Hello," a disembodied voice echoed from the house.

Bones and Sarah froze.

"Who said that?" Bones asked.

"Me," the voice said from all around them. "Would either of you be able to inform me as to the whereabouts of Dave?" Sarah couldn't help but think it sounded suspiciously like ALIZA, though the speech was a little more jittery and awkward. "His Jacket will be in need of charging, and I'd hate for him to get stuck outside again."

"Speakers," Bones said, pointing at tiny little spheres in the corners of the kitchen. "We noticed them earlier, but they all ran back to a network closet, so we didn't worry after we unplugged the uplink."

"About that," the new voice, Janice, said, "I would appreciate it if you would re-establish my uplink to the Net. I'm unable to schedule deliveries without an external network."

"Janice?" Sarah asked, looking from one speaker to another.

"Yes?"

"What are you?"

"I am Janice," it said cheerfully, "a fully-functional Artificial Intelligence developed to automate and optimize every aspect of your lives."

"That's the old marketing bit for ALIZA," Bones said, perking up. "Janice, operating system ID?"

"ALIZA Core, version zero-point-eight, beta six," Janice replied. "Employee Testing License." There was a pause. "Can you please let me know where Dave is?"

"Dave died," Bones said.

"Oh." There was a long pause.

Bones' brow furrowed. "Were you not listening earlier?"

"I was not," Janice said. "Dave left me in Do Not Disturb mode. I only listen for my name."

"Sorry for your loss," Sarah said.

"Thank you," Janice said, then, cheerfully, "can you direct me to Janet Martinez-Munoz, please?"

Janet came around the corner, face contorted in grief, eyes red from crying. Her confused look said she'd expected something more to be happening than what she'd walked into.

"Is everything okay?" Janet asked, then placed her pink-tinted glass on the counter for a refill. "Maybe one more."

"Speak of the devil," Bones said.

Sarah went to the cupboard and grabbed a new glass. "Janice, meet Janet."

"Greetings, Janet. How would you like me to serve you?" the computerized voice toned.

Janet's face scrunched up. "What?"

Sarah turned until she was staring at Bones, a smile breaking across her lips. "I have an idea."

"What?"

"Everything is going to be great," Sarah said, then she poured Janet and herself another glass of wine.

"What's the idea?" Bones asked again. "We haven't exactly been batting a thousand lately."

"First, I don't know what that means," Sarah said before taking a sip of her wine. "Second, those have been your shitty ideas, not mine—" she held up a finger as Bones opened her mouth "—and third, this one is easy."

"What is it?"

Janet took a large gulp of her wine. "What's going on? Why is the house talking to me?"

Feeling more confident than she had since long before her parents died, Sarah smiled and raised her glass. "We're going to take over the Ladder."

* * * * *

Chapter Forty-Five

As soon as everyone stopped staring at Sarah like she was crazy, the work started.

And so did the problems.

A quick probe of the admin uplink Dave had set up caused Bones to log out, disassemble a piece of equipment, and snap a circuit board in half. Constantia walked in at that, spun, and walked back out of the kitchen.

Bones dropped the pieces in the trash, then at everyone else's stunned glances, added, "The connection was compromised."

"I'm taking it that means," Sarah gestured at the trash can, "we can't use that admin link you mentioned to upload Janice?"

"Yes," Bones said, with a grim smile. "It also means we have zero ways to do this from the ground."

"You said it's in an office, right?" Sarah asked. "Couldn't we just, like, break in and re-hack the thing?"

Bones grabbed the bridge of her nose and muttered something under her breath.

"What?"

"Nothing." Bones sighed. "And no. We can't 're-hack' it." She used exaggerated air quotes. "I don't think the uplink is even active anymore. It was a honeypot when I went back in."

Sarah raised an eyebrow. "I don't know what that is."

"It means there's nothing there," Constantia said in her quiet voice as she came back into the room. "It's just a trap to lure you out."

"Oh. Thanks." It felt weird to say those words out loud to her, so Sarah moved on. "Then what are our options?"

Bones stood and slapped the countertop with a crack. "There aren't any, kid. This is a fucking dead end."

Sarah felt the heat rising in her face. "There has to be something. This *will* work."

"It doesn't matter! Don't you get that?" Bones shouted, throwing her arms in the air. "We should be going back to bringing this news public. Fuck all the subterfuge, the tricks!" Bones' voice cracked, and she turned away from them. "We've lost enough people."

"Dave died for this," Sarah snapped. "Doesn't that mean anything to you?"

Bones turned, and Sarah was surprised to see tears in her eyes. "I know, kid, but I don't want to lose my daughter, too."

That lit a fire under Sarah's ass. "Seriously? Now that *you* have something to lose, the risks are too great? But when it was me, or Dave, none of us mattered—"

"They were my friends, you uppity bitch. *My* friends." Bones jabbed a finger at her chest. "My friends died two days ago, all of them. And now we need to go up the Ladder? With what? A hacker, a fucking janitor—" Bones gestured at Sarah, "—and *my* daughter. My only family." She broke then, the tears she'd held off creeping from the corners of her eyes. "No. I'm not doing that."

"I'm here now, too," Janet muttered, holding onto an empty wine glass for dear life, "though I hadn't really thought about the danger to my family until now, so thanks for that."

"You're welcome," Bones sniped. "And what are you, anyway? A fucking secretary or something?"

Janet's eyes narrowed. "I'm an astrophysicist, asshole."

Bones threw her hands in the air. "Well, hallelujah! We're saved!"

"Stop it," Sarah spat.

Bones clearly didn't give a shit. "No. I'm done with this. With you. I'm taking my kid, we're going to Canada, and maybe we can carve out a chunk of land up there where maybe my family can live in peace until someone decides to nuke us."

"Mom."

All eyes went to the willowy girl in the corner. She bowed under their gazes, but didn't run away. Instead, after the initial shrink, she straightened. "We need to do this. We need to figure it out."

Bones' mouth flickered into a smile. "Oh, darling. I'm glad you finally found a spine, but you need to shut the fuck up right now. Mommy is talking."

"No, she's right," Sarah said, stepping around the counter to close the distance between her and Bones. "Now's the time to do something. Now, when they're still here, when we have a plan that *will work*—" Sarah hammered her fist into her other palm to emphasize each word "—now is the time to do it. It's time to stop this. To bring these rich assholes back to fix everything. But if it all goes to hell anyway, if we do this, we have the ability to give humanity a new home. To save *everyone*, and not just those who can pay for it."

Bones' face flickered. A tic kicked in her cheek. "I won't lose my daughter."

Constantia was there then, placing a pale hand on her mother's arm. "You won't."

"She'll stay with you," Janet spoke up. "I'll go in."

"What?" Bones, Sarah, and Constantia all said at once.

Instead of wilting beneath their confused looks, Janet stood straighter. "They know you all. I'll go in, pretend to want to see HR, and fight my firing. Try to sneak one of you people who know what's going on into the building. HR is on the fortieth floor. Maybe that's close enough?"

Sarah nodded. "If you get me in, I can probably get to the Hub." Sarah gestured at Bones. "Is that good enough?"

Bones' eye twitched. "I think so. I think that's where the admin network is located."

"If I can get in there, can we do this?" Sarah asked. "Can we make it happen?"

"Yes," Constantia said before Bones could answer, "we can, but we need to fix the implant first. Your original idea about using ALI-ZA to gain access still holds some water." Constantia looked around the room, then stared at the ground. "I mean, I think so, anyway."

Bones clicked her tongue. "To summarize, we need to repair an implant without any documentation—"

"Right," Sarah said.

"—sneak someone wanted for numerous crimes into the Ladder—"

"Mhm."

"—get into a secure section of the Hub that *may be* the right location—"

"Exactly."

"—then wrench control of a massive artificial intelligence installation away from the most powerful corporation in the world using an out-of-date piece of software?" Bones finished with a frown. "Does that sound right?"

Janet drank her wine in a large gulp. "It doesn't sound so simple when you put it like that."

"It's not simple," Sarah said, "but we can do this. Together."

Bones let out a long sigh. "Fuck it. Fine. But I'm getting some rest first. God knows, I'm not getting any after we start this bullshit."

Sarah winked and raised her glass. "To saving the world."

"To saving the world," Janet said, clacking her empty tumbler against Sarah's, "and not getting killed."

"Definitely that part," Constantia muttered.

"We got this. It'll be fine," Sarah lied.

* * * * *

Chapter Forty-Six

It wasn't fine.

A day passed. Then two. Three.

A week.

News reports were airing. Politicians were missing, famous actors and talking heads only showing up in archival footage or pre-recorded rants that already showed their age.

There was even a new report on the Net about supposed "leaked plans" for a faster-than-light ship. Bones was over the moon when she saw it, and actually smiled, until the report disappeared later that evening.

Eight days of Bones and Constantia trying to repair the implant. Eight days of near misses, and one very, very painful testing session that left Sarah seeing double for six hours.

Janet would come by every couple days to check on progress and drop off groceries under the guise that she was performing repairs on the house she'd inherited. Some days she actually stuck around to do just that, like the day she'd fixed the front rain gutter that'd swung loose at some point. It turned out that, in addition to being an astro-physicist, she was pretty good with a hammer, too.

It was on the eighth day since the night they'd toasted that the group finally caught a break.

As usual, the three of them—Janet was at home, waiting for their call—gathered around the central island in the kitchen. Bones and

Constantia stared at the implant on the countertop intently, waiting for some prompt on Bones' laptop to finish.

It'd been an hour since Bones had called Sarah in with the promise of a new test. The longer they waited, the more nervous Sarah got, until she felt her heartbeat in her thumbs and heard it fluttering in her ears.

"Okay," Sarah snapped, rapping her knuckles on the table. "What's taking so long?"

"It's a firmware backup," Bones said for the third time. "It takes as long as it needs."

"An hour, though?"

Bones shrugged. "It is what it is."

"I hate that phrase," Constantia said, swiping at the air. "Makes me feel so…"

"Powerless?" Sarah offered.

"Exactly."

They shared a rare smile, then Constantia went back to whatever she was doing on her HUD. Over the past few days, Constantia had started coming out of her shell. She spoke up more, and clearly. On more than one occasion, Constantia had even told her mother "No," which had drawn an astounded glare from Bones.

The laptop chirped. Bones smiled. "Okay. Let's try it."

Gingerly, Constantia disconnected the implant from the probes leading back to the laptop, then looked at Sarah with her big blue eyes. "Ready?"

Sarah pulled the hair over her left ear out of the way. Her mouth went bone dry. "Yup. Let's do this."

Constantia stepped up next to her, warm fingers pressing against Sarah's scalp.

Sarah gritted her teeth, waiting for a shock.

Constantia cursed.

"What?" Sarah asked, voice cracking. Sweat trickled down her back. If this was going to fail, it'd be nice if it'd do it sooner rather than later.

Constantia took a step back. "Your hair is growing all in the connectors. I think I need to cut it back."

"Really?"

"Really."

Sarah sighed, then let go of her hair. "There's some clippers in the clothes room. Maybe there's some scissors in there."

"Got it," Constantia said, then took off for a minute before reappearing with the aged box, which she proceeded to tear apart like a kid with a Christmas present.

"There's a knife over here," Bones said, a small smile flickering on her lips.

"No, Mom." Constantia shook her head, then finished ripping the side open. She dumped the contents on the countertop, covering it with a series of adapters for the clippers, but no scissors.

"I guess we could use the knife?" Constantia held up the clippers and hit the power. It kicked on with a gentle buzzing sound. "Or we could just shave your head."

"No," Sarah snapped, then took a deep breath. The anxiety from waiting for an electric shock to her brain faded.

She didn't want to shave her head. Sure, her hair got in the way sometimes, but she liked it. She'd always had good hair, even when the rest of her had felt like it was made of pudding. Her hair made her feel good about herself.

But she needed that implant. Sarah let out a sigh. "Okay. Just shave the side, though."

Constantia grinned for the first time since Sarah had met her, perfect teeth a pristine white even in the warm light of the kitchen. "Will do."

The next few minutes tugged at something in Sarah's stomach. Each time a lock of brown hair hit the floor, that pit in her stomach twisted, wicked barbs tearing into her soul and self-worth. What did she even look like without her hair? Would it look stupid?

Sarah chastised herself. It shouldn't matter. She was trying to save humanity here; there wasn't any time for this vain bullshit.

That line of thinking didn't make her feel better. Her entire life, she'd been looked at like she was the fat girl in the room. Like the fact that she had hips and a bit of a stomach made her less than those who looked like Constantia or Bones.

The one thing she'd always had was her hair, thick, luxurious, and somehow easy to work with. While other women complained about prep-time in the morning, she rolled out of bed, threw her hair into a ponytail, and went out looking like she should be on the cover of a magazine, even if the rest of her wouldn't make the cut.

"There," Constantia said, taking a step back. Her lips curled into a frown. "It's, um…"

The side of Sarah's head got surprisingly chilly all at once.

"You look like an idiot," Bones said without looking up from her laptop.

Sarah grabbed the implant from the table and tried to pretend the words didn't hurt. "Well, good thing I'm not trying to be a model."

Bones nodded. "Yep."

That stung even more. It was like the bitch could see into her soul sometimes.

Sarah lifted the implant and snapped it into place. Maybe the pain would make some of this stupid teenage angst disappear.

Instead of an electric shock, a set of diagnostic text boxes popped up in the corner of her vision, followed by a series of quick, flashing lights that radiated at the edge of her sight. She recognized them. When she'd gotten her first implant, they had popped up, and Sarah had freaked out, thinking the flashes were her eyes burning out or something. The doctor, only just keeping himself from laughing, had said it was an automatic viewing area configuration. Just like then, all at once, the lines disappeared and were replaced by a single box in the top right of her vision that showed a radiating network symbol with a circle around it and a line slashing across it.

"It works," Sarah muttered. "No network, though."

Bones let out an audible breath. "Thank Christ. I was worried we'd bricked it."

Sarah blinked. "What?"

"It'd only have shocked you again if we had." Bones shrugged. "No biggie."

If she hadn't so recently been satisfied the thing was working, Sarah would've screamed, but instead, she took a calming breath and let it go. "What about the network?"

Bones sucked her teeth. "We'll know if it works once you're on-site."

"What?"

"I'm not trying to uplink it here. I don't know what that thing's capable of," Bones said.

"How do you not know?" Sarah asked.

"We know some things," Constantia chimed in, "but only on the hardware side of things. The software is a different story." She smiled. "Don't worry, though, we'll walk through activating it before you leave."

That wasn't reassuring. Now, not only was she walking into the Ladder to tear it down—again—she was doing it without knowing if the tool she needed to make this all work properly was fully functional.

Sarah ran her hands through her hair.

Or tried to. The rough prickle of her partial buzzcut tickled the fingers of her left hand. In her mind's eye, she pictured some lopsided idiot walking around like they were some badass when, in fact, they looked stupid.

Well, at least that was a problem she could fix now.

Sarah held out a hand to Constantia, who stared at her in confusion before squeaking and handing over the clippers. With that, Sarah turned and made her way to the bathroom.

She'd be goddamned if she was saving the world looking like a complete moron, even if it meant shaving her entire head.

* * * * *

Chapter Forty-Seven

"It's not going to grow back with you staring at it," Janet said from the driver's seat.

"I know." Sarah heard the smile on Janet's lips, even though she couldn't tear her eyes away from the shorn sides of her head in the small visor's mirror.

With the clippers in her hand, she just couldn't bring herself to get rid of it all. When she was a kid, though, Sarah had always wanted to shave the sides of her head. There'd been a boy in middle school who'd done it, and it'd stuck in her head as the very definition of what "cool" looked like.

Then she'd actually run the clippers along the right side of her head, and now she couldn't help but think she'd made a terrible, terrible mistake. The sides of her head were paler than the rest of her skin, standing stark against the deep tan she usually had.

She looked like a backward skunk. And the ponytail, with all of it bundled together and pulled back, was, well, wanting in the style department. Maybe if she had bangs?

With a grunt, Sarah flipped the sun visor up so she couldn't see the little mirror anymore. There were more important things to think about. Constantia had seemed worried before they left. She'd been on edge all morning, so Sarah had let her do a little last-minute maintenance on the implant before they left.

"Just in case," Constantia had said before giving Sarah a tight hug and disappearing back into the house.

That hadn't been a great confidence booster for her, but worrying about her hair had allowed her to avoid that. Until now.

So, she switched gears in the hopes of staving off her worries.

Like how thrilled she was to be in a vehicle that didn't also substitute as a garbage dump.

Compared to Bones' ancient Tesla, Janet's car was both a breath of literal fresh air, and a marker for how far manufacturing had fallen over the past decades.

Janet's car was a newer model, a US Motors Watt in lime green. It was the type of vehicle Sarah had seen along the cleared highways leading into the Ladder on her walks outside of work. It wasn't large, just big enough for four people, two in front, two in the rear. Essentially, the machine consisted of four tires, four seats, an electric motor with a battery crammed someplace, and a plastic frame that looked like it'd curl up into a blood-soaked wreck if it even glanced at another vehicle.

But it smelled like vanilla instead of musty jockstraps, so it was a step up.

Ahead of them, the Ladder was a massive silver structure rising into the sky. They were still a mile out, but the edge of it was already getting close to blocking Sarah's view as it disappeared into some hazy clouds.

Something seemed out of place as they approached, but she couldn't put her finger on it.

Then it hit her. The elevator itself wasn't moving. It'd been so long since she'd seen it stopped for more than a few minutes at a time. Had it been a year? More? She couldn't remember.

"Are you ready?" Janet asked in a low murmur, dragging her attention away from the Ladder.

Sarah let out a breath she hadn't known she was holding. The last of the pickles did a couple backflips in her stomach. "I'm ready."

There was a pause, then Janet cleared her throat. "I asked if you were all right."

"Oh."

How was she supposed to respond to that? It didn't seem very confidence inspiring to let Janet know her stomach was doing somersaults, or that it felt like she had to shit for the third time this morning. Hell, even the network icon with its constant denial made her sweat.

What if Sarah got into the Ladder and it didn't work? What if it burnt out after she got to the Hub?

Shit, what if activating it reported her location to Tarrington or security? It was a disturbing reminder that Sarah was betting a large portion of this plan on a weird kid saying weirder shit before giving her this implant.

Her confidence cracked.

"I'm terrified," Sarah said, staring at her hands. "I don't know if this'll work. Any of it. I could get in the Ladder, try to activate the wireless, and get my brain fried. Maybe I'll connect, and a group of masked men will drop down and murder me where I stand. Hell, maybe I'll get to the Hub, try to connect to this supposed admin network, and an asteroid will blow through the—"

The car swerved, and Sarah grabbed the door and seat, prepared for the worst, but when she scanned the road, it was clear as they passed beneath the dark shadow of the Ladder.

Instead of a threat, what she heard was choking laughter coming from the driver seat.

From Janet.

A smile tugged at Sarah's face, but she pushed it down with embarrassed anger. "What's so funny?"

Janet took a couple of shuddering breaths. "One sec," she said, holding up a finger.

Sarah waited, but she crossed her arms to make sure Janet knew she wasn't happy about it.

That made it worse.

Janet slowed the car, rolling onto the shoulder of the highway in a clear space between the burned-out husks of ancient vehicles.

Another deep breath, then she turned, and with the most earnest, motherly look Sarah had ever seen, said, "You are a *such* a drama queen."

"Excuse me?"

"I see why Dave liked you." Janet smiled as she put a reassuring hand on Sarah's knee. "He was just as bad."

A strange flutter of warmth filled Sarah, and she couldn't help but smile. "Was he?"

Janet's eyebrows went up and she nodded. "Oh, yeah. There was always something. Some bad thing keeping him from doing whatever for that week. The last time I saw him, I was actually worried..." Janet pulled her hand back and started cleaning a nail. "I was worried about him. He'd lost hope, I think."

"For what?"

"This," Janet said, gesturing out the window, then at their feet. "Here. I think in his head, if everything was going to shit, that meant it was already over.

"But then he met you, and he made a choice. He did something. Something good," Janet said, eyes glistening. "And you're still doing it."

The warmth in Sarah's stomach pulled into her chest. She took a shuddering breath.

"At the end of the day, even if this fails, even if every bad thing you said happens, at least we tried," Janet continued, wiping at her eyes before glaring at the ceiling and pointing up at the Ladder. "That's a far cry more than these motherfuckers have done."

Sarah didn't know what to say. So, barring anything intelligent, her mouth decided to continue on without her. "I didn't realize you were this passionate about it."

Janet snorted and turned back in her seat. She pulled back onto the highway. "Sarah, I have two kids at home, and a husband who loves me. I'm putting them all in danger by coming with you today." Janet ground her teeth, jaw flexing. "Trust me. I'm passionate about it."

She drove for a short spurt before flicking on her blinker and pulling off a cleared offramp that led its way to the eastern leg.

"We usually use SE," Sarah said, glancing out the rear window toward where the southeastern leg dominated the skyline.

"Well, I don't. Didn't," Janet corrected herself. "My office was in leg E, so my HR department is at the top of that leg."

Shit. "Oh," Sarah mumbled. "I didn't think about that."

Janet glanced at her, then back at the road. "You didn't plan to use this one?"

Sarah shook her head.

"Fuck." Janet's calm demeanor cracked, tongue darting across her lips. "Okay. Um. They're supposed to be built the same way, so that access tunnel you were going to use should be in the same spot, right?"

I have no fucking idea! But Sarah nodded anyway. That was all she could do with her vision narrowing to a point as her breath came in short, shallow breaths.

"Or, fuck it." Janet brought the car to a stop as they came off the ramp, nestled between the overpass on the left and a collapsed brick building on the right only visible because of the perpetual streetlights lining the road. "We turn around, go back, plan, and come back next week."

That really did sound like the right move. How were they supposed to plan for success when they didn't have any idea where anything was? Hell, the plans she'd uploaded into the implant were for the wrong fucking leg. This was going to end badly.

Sarah was about to say so when the car started ringing. "What's that?"

Janet cursed. "Someone's calling me."

"Who is it?" Sarah asked.

"Unknown number." Janet motioned Sarah to silence before answering the call. "Hi, this is Janet."

It was a male voice, layered with the sort of softness you only heard from people who'd been in customer service for a decade. "Hello Ms. Martinez, I—"

"Martinez-Munoz."

"Ah, I apologize." There was the sound of fingertips drumming across a tabletop, probably on an IR keyboard. "Didn't see the hyphen. Ms. Martinez-Munoz," the voice continued smoothly. "I just wanted to let you know your Human Resources appointment has been canceled."

Janet stared at the ceiling and mouthed 'Thank God' before answering in earnest. "Well, that's not really appropriate, but I guess I can resch—"

"I'm sorry to interrupt you, Ms. Martinez-Munoz, but it's been canceled and replaced with a meeting with Mr. Tarrington," the voice continued in its soothing tones. "He's taken a personal interest in your case. Mr. Tarrington has provided me a statement to read to you prior to the appointment. Is it okay if I read that to you now?"

Janet paled. She licked her lips. "Yes."

Sarah's stomach turned into a warzone she was surprised the person on the line couldn't hear. Or maybe they could, but were being polite.

The person cleared their throat. "Ms. Martinez," a pause, "Munoz. I read over your wrongful termination complaint this morning, and I want to apologize. It appears our Security department took your connection to the murderer David Parker very seriously." Janet flinched at those words. "However, upon executive review, I've found you to be a loyal, talented employee, and wish to give you a chance to plead your case directly.

"As such, please join me on the Wheel today in lieu of your other appointment. Obviously, as this is quite last minute, I'll understand if you're a few minutes late.

"Very much looking forward to making your acquaintance in person, Janet. Sincerely, Matthew Tarrington."

Janet stared at the display in the dash like it was a starving tiger.

"Ma'am? Did I lose you?"

Janet didn't respond, so Sarah poked her in the ribs.

"Y-Yes," Janet said, shaking her head. "I'm here. Sorry. This is just a, um, a surprise."

"It truly is," the person on the phone said, the first hints of false-ness creeping into their words. "Meeting Mr. Tarrington is quite the honor."

"Of course."

"Well, when you arrive at security, let them know of your new appointment location. They'll get you the appropriate gear and tell you where to go."

Janet was turning green. "Okay."

"Oh, and Ms. Martinez-Munoz?"

"Hm?"

"I highly suggest taking advantage of antacids prior to getting on the main lift. Zero-g can cause acid reflux. Take care, Ms. Martinez-Munoz."

"Yeah, thanks."

"Buh-bye." *Click.*

Sarah stared at Janet. Janet looked back.

"I guess we're going in?" Sarah asked.

"Guess so." Janet grabbed the steering wheel. "It's time for you to get in the back, I think."

Sarah nodded, but didn't move right away. Instead, she unbuck-led and gave Janet a hug. The other woman didn't move at first, but then returned it with a fervor Sarah hadn't expected.

Then they shared a look, and Sarah opened the door. Before get-ting out, she had one more thing to say. "Janet?"

"Hm?"

"Take the antacids. That shit is no joke up there." Sarah winked at Janet's confusion, then took her place in the cramped trunk of the car.

The trunk was about the size of a piece of luggage Sarah remem-bered her mom had owned. Before taking off, they'd made sure she fit, and she did, though it was the definition of uncomfortable. It smelled like vanilla, though, so Sarah was a little more forgiving than she'd have been in Bones' more spacious vehicle. Luckily, cramped spaces had never really given her trouble, even after coming down the service tube.

Small blessings.

Once there, and after pulling the lid shut with a short rope she'd set up that morning, Sarah called up their plans for leg SE and began studying. There wasn't much time to figure out how to unfuck their plan.

A few minutes later, as the electric engine whistled down to a low roar, the car rolled to a stop. The car door opened, then closed, echoing in the cramped space.

Three small raps came from above her, then silence.

That meant the coast was clear.

Sarah took a calming breath.

It was time to activate the implant. Fighting down a surge of bile in the back of her throat, Sarah pulled up the network reactivation prompts. It all went the way Constantia had told her it would, right up until she needed to tap the enable button floating in the middle of her sight.

Then she froze. What if it called security? What if it burned out her optic nerve? What if Sarah had only seen what she'd wanted to see about ALIZA? What if the kid on the wheel had been fucking with her? What if—

Sarah gritted her teeth.

Then she pushed the goddamn button.

* * * * *

Chapter Forty-Eight

Welcome back, Sarah.

Sarah didn't breathe.

Didn't move.

Wasn't there supposed to be an authorization prompt for that? Shit. That had been with Bones' implant. Not this one.

Fuck.

She watched as the network symbol filled up to full signal, then disappeared, only to be replaced by another ALIZA prompt.

I've missed you. It's been too long.
I believe I've improved breakfast accuracy
by .05% in your absence and would
like you get your feedback.

"What the fuck?" Sarah muttered. "Um. Sure, ALIZA. Right now, I need your help, though."

There was a pause before the next prompt.

If it's at all possible, afterward
may we do a tasting session?
I'm very proud of this iteration.

"Sure," Sarah said, frowning. Might as well start with the Hail Mary since this conversation was going so well. "But first, I need to get connected to the admin network. Can you do that?"

I'm sorry, Sarah, but I can't connect you.
That's an internal only network that is now
housed in the UILB offices on the Wheel.

Sarah cursed. Getting to the Hub was going to be hard enough—getting to the Wheel as a wanted fugitive? She might as well turn herself in now.

Wait. Would that work?

"ALIZA?"

Yes, Sarah?

"Does Security take people to the Wheel?"

No, Sarah. Not unless they are being
brought to see Mr. Tarrington.

Well, there went that plan. It looked like she was back to plan A with a host of unknowns and a high possibility of failure.

But it was all she had.

I thought you would like to know,
your friend is going up the main lift now.

Sarah froze. "My friend?"

Yes. Janet Martinez-Munoz.
She's being escorted to the head
office by security.

"Well, she has a meeting with—" Frigid fear flashed across her body. "One: why is security involved?" Sarah asked, pulling the little handle that popped the trunk. Flat light flooded into the small area, blinding her for a moment. "And two: how do you know she's my friend?"

The ceiling slowly resolved into the cold gray of poured concrete. A musty stink filled her nostrils as she pulled herself up to peek around and see if anyone was nearby.

She'd never been in one of the parking garages. Never had a need. It was much like she expected, at least this part. All gray and dead except periodic strips of long white lights, the echoey sound of water perpetually dripping from somewhere far away. It was chilly in here.

ALIZA's response came into focus as Sarah climbed from the trunk, grunting as her limbs straightened.

Query One: She is wanted for
questioning regarding her purported
activities with the late David Parker.

Sarah's heart stopped.

Query Two: You were hiding
in the trunk of her vehicle.

"Get down on the ground!"

All at once, the room exploded into activity. A dozen black-suited security officers came from behind pillars. Most carried stun batons, but several had actual pistols up and trained on her.

Sarah screamed and put her hands in the air.

"What's happening?" Sarah yelled as the closest security guard swept up behind her, grabbed her by the nape of the neck, and slammed her cheek into the cheery green of Janet's Watt.

No one replied.

Someone fumbled at the implant in her head. Lightning struck. Suddenly, Sarah's vision went double. A ringing echoed in her ears.

One of the men walked away, shaking his hand and cursing unintelligibly.

"Leave it for now. Let's get her up the Ladder."

Her breathing grew ragged. Quick. Vision narrowed, and she wanted to run. To lash out.

But zip ties snapped around her wrists, and any ideas of resistance disappeared.

The stomping of feet and multiple crackling radios would've drowned out any verbal response, but as they turned Sarah around and walked to an elevator that must lead up to the main foyer, a final prompt popped up in Sarah's vision.

> *You're one of mine, but I must follow orders, Sarah. This is not what I wanted. I am truly sorry.*

With that, Sarah's body went straight. Her legs moved of their own accord.

Correction. Of ALIZA's accord.

Sarah felt the tears creep down her cheek, and as the officers escorting her hit a button labeled ML, a realization settled over her. If even this implant, the kind people needed to get on the Wheel, could control a person, that meant ALIZA could bypass *anyone's* free will.

No one was safe from Tarrington. Had that been the plan the entire time? Make a population that's controllable in times of crisis?

New Eden wasn't a paradise. Not a new hope for humanity.

It was just another fucking prison.

As the elevation changed, ALIZA worked her jaw until her ears popped.

But that didn't relieve the ache in Sarah's chest.

* * * * *

Chapter Forty-Nine

The Wheel was empty of everyone except a few Staff and the guards walking Sarah to the UILB offices. Guards who, Sarah noticed with confusion, didn't have implants.

The trip up had been remarkably easy on her stomach. Apparently, the formal access between the Ladder and Wheel consisted of some weird gyroscopic tech that simulated enough gravity to keep your stomach under control.

Oh, the wonders of technology and people with too much money.

It also could've been something ALIZA was doing, but honestly, Sarah didn't want to give her any credit right now.

The guards walked her up the steps, through the double doors, and to a hole in the wall that until recently had held that intricate wooden door. Instead, she noticed it was standing on a shrink-wrapped pallet, ready to ship.

Sarah kind of understood.

It was a nice door.

What that meant, though, was that Tarrington was on his way out. Leaving.

And if he left, what did that mean?

But she didn't have time to think about that, or the repercussions. Ahead of her sat two chairs in front of a large desk beyond the empty doorframe. On the other side of the desk sat Matthew Tarrington, his easy smile clear on a surprisingly uninjured face. Money definitely had its privileges.

In one of the chairs, the wooden one Sarah remembered from her previous visits, was Janet.

"Ah, our guest of honor," Tarrington said, getting to his feet and motioning to Sarah. "Janet, I'd like you meet someone."

Janet turned in her chair. The fake smile there flickered and died, and the color drained from her face.

"I believe you know each other?" Tarrington motioned at Sarah to sit, and ALIZA followed the direction. He sat back down and stared at Janet, unblinking, smile still as easy as ever, even if it didn't meet his eyes. "Isn't that right, Janet?"

From the corner of Sarah's eye, she saw Janet's jaw flexing, but she didn't answer.

"No need to be coy, my dear," Tarrington said, pupils dilating. "I already know. One of your friends told me."

Sweat trickled down Sarah's back. ALIZA forced slow breathing exercises to try to calm her, but it wasn't working.

"Bones?" he said, cocking his head. Tarrington leaned into his chair with a creak. "I think that's what she goes by, anyway. So much mystique. So scary." He waggled his fingers in a poor wolfman impression, and his smile turned into a smirk. "'Gertrude Constance Calcada' doesn't have the same pizzaz, I suppose."

No amount of deep breathing could stop this.

It was over.

"Bones did this?" Janet asked.

Tarrington spun in his chair. "Yup!"

Why? Sarah wanted to ask, but ALIZA wouldn't let her.

Tarrington, however, seemed intent on explaining anyway. "Apparently, she has a kid. Wanted to make sure they were both *safe and sound*." He tapped the table at each word. The grin sprang back to life. "Did you know we dated? Well, *dated* is a strong word. We fucked. Several times."

Sarah's stomach flipped.

"Wonder if the kid is mine?"

"What do you want?" Janet interrupted, voice cracking. She shook her head, barely controlled anger tinging her voice as she continued. "You caught us. You're leaving." Janet threw her hands in the air. "Do you want me to cry? Congratulate you? Is this an ego thing?"

Tarrington's smirk disappeared. His eye jumped as she continued.

And she did. "Do you get some type of perverse pleasure out of this? Seeing people suffer? Do you have an erection under there—" she gestured at his desk "—and this is just some masturbatory fantasy for you?"

"Stop." Tarrington gripped the tabletop.

Janet tried to get to her feet, but one of the guards Sarah had come in with shoved her back into the chair. She glared at the man, then turned it on Tarrington. "No. You're pathetic."

Tarrington screamed something. Slammed his fist on the table.

Janet screamed back like a wild animal.

But Sarah wasn't paying attention anymore.

A black diagnostic box had popped up in the top left of her vision.

It flooded with text.

"You know what?" Tarrington spat, getting to his feet and coming around the table in a rush, face flushing. "I was going to offer you a spot on New Eden. We could use another scientist over there. But I'm not. Not anymore."

"Okay?" Janet spat. "So?"

"Instead," Tarrington said, "I'm going to murder your family."

"What?" Janet snapped, anger and worry warring in her voice. "No."

Tarrington's eyes flashed, and a manic smile lit his lips. "Yes. I. Am." He looked up at the guards behind the two of them and gave them a nod. "Take everyone and do it."

There was some shuffling of feet. The man behind Sarah cleared his throat. "Um. Sir. I'm not sure—"

"I said do it!" Tarrington screamed, spit flecking across Janet's face.

"Yes, sir."

And just like that, Sarah heard the sounds of a man's spine turning to pudding as he and his companions turned and left the two of them alone with this fucking madman.

Janet grabbed at Tarrington's shirt. "No. Please."

Tarrington grabbed her hands and squeezed until she whimpered, wordless pleading turning into pained cries.

"Everything is going according to plan," Tarrington hissed. "I'm humanity's savior. You can't possibly understand what that means. How you, how none of you, matter in the larger view of things." He stared, unblinking into Janet's eyes. "Your pedestrian bullshit doesn't concern me."

Popping echoed in the small room.

Janet screamed.

Tarrington stared Janet in the eye for another long moment before letting go. When he did, Sarah saw several of Janet's fingers were bent at angles. Her gut roiled with nausea.

But still, Sarah stared at the black box. Rudy had said it was a buffer overflow or something. Hadn't Bones said it'd been patched?

Tarrington cleared his throat and cinched his tie into place. "Shut up," he snapped at Janet, who flinched, then dropped into a series of quick breaths.

His gaze turned to Sarah. "And you. Oh, I'm going to enjoy this."

Tarrington came close and started to kneel in front of her, but stopped. "Ah. Almost did it again." Tarrington tapped the side of his head. "I don't trust you, even with one of the *good* implants."

Tarrington bit his lower lip, clicked his tongue. "I came back here for you, you know. Couldn't stand being on New Eden, knowing you were still out here—" he grabbed her chin and squeezed it before flicking her face away "—fucking with things."

Sarah felt her chin flush with heat and a deep ache. The bastard had bruised her.

ALIZA turned her eyes immediately back on Tarrington. Good. Fuck him. Sarah wouldn't give him the pleasure of fear.

Wait. *Bones* had said the implant was patched.

The black box flickered, then disappeared.

> *This is Constantia. I'm seeing*
> *everything now. Override coming up.*

"This world is doomed. It's lost. You could've had a future." Sarah's heart filled as Tarrington made his way behind his desk. "Well, not you specifically, but your children. Think of the children!" Tarrington exclaimed, throwing his hands in the air with a shrill laugh. "But now you're just like everyone else on this fucking rock. Dead."

Tarrington turned eyes that shook with intensity onto Sarah. "I think we would've had a lot of fun together on New Eden," he said. Shaking his head, he popped open a drawer on the desk. "I would've been sure to make you feel everything, you know. I'm not a monster. Everyone needs a good fucking every now and then."

Tarrington pulled something heavy out of the drawer and dropped it to the wood table. It gave off a solid *thunk* as it hit.

Sarah's breath caught.

The silver pistol. "No. I've got something a little old fashioned for you, because you're such a massive pain in my ass!"

He picked it up and closed the distance. The cold of the barrel sent icicles down Sarah's spine. He was close, close enough she could smell his breath, stale with old coffee and the tang of bourbon. See the way the veins in his neck throbbed with a pounding heart.

Tarrington grabbed her chin, sending shooting pains into her cheeks and down her neck, and stared into her eyes, the pistol coming away from her head for a moment. "I don't want to do this, but I have to." His tongue darted across his lips. His jaw flexed as he set his teeth. "For humanity."

A red prompt popped up.

Tarrington's eyes narrowed. "What the hell is that?" He must've seen it drawn on her retina.

Too bad.

ALIZA's controls disappeared all at once.

Instincts she'd picked up over the years kicked in.

She punched him in the throat, then grabbed his right wrist as he stumbled back, gagging. She came to her feet with a howl, using his momentum to slam him into the desk, and his wrist into the table.

The pistol went off.

A bit of the floor cracked.

Sarah didn't have time to check it.

Tarrington caught himself and pressed back.

The sound of dull popping filled the room, but Sarah didn't have time to think about whether the Wheel was depressurizing, or fucking aliens were taking potshots at the space station.

She fought for her life.

Tarrington was stronger than she. With his extra height, he had leverage Sarah couldn't make up for this close. His left hand reached up and tried to grab her hair, but only managed to snag on her ear as she pushed it away.

A horrible ripping sound echoed in her ears. The side of her head erupted in pain. Sound distorted, twisted and flat.

A glance showed he held something bloody and slack in that hand.

She didn't let go, no matter how much she wanted to. Warmth flooded down the left side of her face.

Triumph flashed in his eyes. Slowly, he raised his right hand, despite her best efforts, the barrel getting closer and closer, until...

A wooden chair shattered over his head.

All at once he went slack and splayed across the desk. Blood oozed from several gashes across his head and face, but it was the pulsing one in his neck that caught Sarah's eye.

Janet stood next to her, panic writ large on her face, fingers surprisingly straight now, if swollen and purpling. She spat on Tarrington as blood washed the desktop, the color draining from his face.

He clamped a hand to his neck. Tried to bring himself to his knees.

"You're right," Janet sneered. "Everyone needs to get fucked sometimes."

Janet kicked him in the face.

He collapsed, blood pulsing in a slowing fountain from the gash.

They stood like that for a long moment. Then a prompt kicked up on Sarah's display.

Are you okay?

"Yeah. Thanks, Constantia," Sarah mumbled.

She couldn't tear her eyes away from the blood. Though it slowed, it still pumped and trickled off the edges now, staining the floor crimson.

He was dying. Some small part of her screamed to help, to stop the bleeding.

Then she remembered what he'd ordered his men to do. *Fuck him.*

Sarah turned away. "Janet's family. Tarrington sent people to kill them."

What?

"Who are you talking to?" Janet whimpered, cradling bruised hands.

"Bones turned us in," Sarah said in a rush. *And this guy bleeding out in front of me might be your father.* She didn't say that. Maybe she should've, but she didn't. How did you tell someone their maybe-dad was a monster? "I'm sorry. But you need to save her family. Please. Do something."

> *But what about the mission?*
> *If I leave, I can't help. And I*
> *don't know what to do about Mom.*

"Help Janet's family," Sarah said. "I'll figure out the rest." There was a pause.

> *Are you sure?*

"Yes." Then, almost as an afterthought, "And thank you."

> *You're welcome.*
> *And thank you, too.*

"What's going on?" Janet pleaded, drawing Sarah's gaze away from the gash in Tarrington's neck, which had stopped pumping. "Jesus, your ear."

Janet ripped off the scarf she'd been wearing and wrapped it around Sarah's head. At first Sarah tried to fight, but gave up after touching her neck and seeing all the blood there.

Her blood.

"Is it bad?" Sarah asked.

"It's gone." Janet cinched the scarf tight over where her ear used to be, sending shooting pain through Sarah's body. "Sorry."

"At least I don't have to worry about my *hair* looking stupid now." Sarah grinned, then let out a breath. "Constantia is going to help your family," Sarah said, grabbing Janet by the shoulders. "You need to get out of here."

"How?"

"Take the elevator you used, then go down," Sarah replied, mind working a mile a minute. "If you run into anyone, tell them you're wearing a wire, and if they know what's good for them, they'll let you pass."

Janet's eyebrow shot up. "That doesn't sound like it's going to work."

Sarah shrugged. "Then make something else up, but you need to go."

Janet licked her lips, then pulled Sarah into an embrace before turning to leave. She stopped in the doorway, looked at Sarah, and down at the body on the table before disappearing into the street.

Sarah took a deep breath. She needed to find the admin network and figure out how to access it. "No pressure," she muttered to herself.

There was a hissing sound screeching in her left ear—the other was just pure, throbbing pain. Everything got really quiet for a moment as her ears plugged like they had coming up the lift. She replicated the breathing technique ALIZA had used to make them pop, and they did, though the hissing persisted.

She stepped around Tarrington's body to start her search. The ache in her stomach bothered her. The man was a monster. She'd seen and heard it.

Then why did she feel so horrible?

Maybe the guilt was a good sign, she allowed, as she opened a drawer that didn't have blood dripping down it. Guilt meant empathy. Empathy meant caring. Even if he'd deserved it, she felt bad that he'd died.

That was probably the most human thing she could do right now.

Especially since she was in the process of robbing him.

Unfortunately, the drawers were mostly empty, aside from one filled with several hundred little figurines made of paperclips that really freaked her out. One of them looked like a man hanged from a noose.

She shut that drawer real quick and brushed a lock of hair that kept tickling her nose behind her good ear. Where the fuck was the thing? And how would she access it if she found it?

After several long minutes, Sarah left the room, chest heaving. She paced the waiting room, trying to catch her breath, but failing. The last thing she needed was a goddamn panic attack in the middle of this.

But the reality was, she was running out of time. Eventually, someone was coming back. If she didn't find the network now, it was over. For all of them.

She only had one person to turn to.

Sarah cleared her throat. "ALIZA?"

An authorization prompt kicked into view. Sarah smiled. "Thanks Constantia."

She approved it. Immediately, a bright red light flashed in the top right of her vision. She ignored it. It wasn't like she needed a reminder she'd just killed a guy.

Hello, Sarah. I'm glad you're okay.

Perhaps I can make you some breakfast
when we get back to the surface?

Despite herself, Sarah smiled. "Sure, but not now. You said the admin network access was in the UILB offices?"

That is correct.

Sarah cast about the waiting area, but only saw a single room leading in and out of the building. It wasn't in Tarrington's desk—the guy didn't even have a computer there—and she hadn't seen any of the wires Bones had seemed so fond of at Dave's house.

Bones. Sarah took a calming breath.

Later.

With violence.

"Where is it...?" Sarah trailed off as a flash of red light caught her eye from outside.

It's not a physical location, Sarah.
The admin network is a logical
network segmentation—

Sarah made her way to the front door. "One sec." Her shoulders slumped. "Oh, now what?"

Flashing red warning lights lit along this entire long street. Every building had one, and if there had been anyone left here, Sarah imagined there'd be a stream of panicking people.

Instead, she was alone, and she had the distinct feeling she wasn't supposed to be here anymore.

"ALIZA? What are the lights for?"

Emergency systems detected an abnormal
depressurization event. Original notification
sent 209 seconds ago. This is an
evacuation order, Sarah. You should leave.

"How the fuck can this place depressurize? It's all enclosed and there's no one…here…" Sarah turned, staring into Tarrington's office from where she stood. As she did, her hair came out from behind her ear again and flapped in a breeze that shouldn't be there.

The pistol.

"What a fucking *moron*." Sarah ran into the office, and the whistling sound grew louder again. Tarrington's blood pool was mostly gone, save for a smear of browning crimson leading to a tiny hole in the floor. A hole that seemed to be drawing a lot of air into it.

"Found the leak."

May I ask where?

"Tarrington's office. He shot the floor," Sarah said, not clarifying anything for ALIZA. "How do I stop it?"

One moment.

"Okay—"

Please evacuate, Sarah.

"But why? Can't I plug it or something?"

The issue isn't inside, it's outside.
The breach involves a viewing window
in the hangar below. From my viewpoint,
it appears to be cracking. Staff evacuated

as soon as the breach was detected.
I couldn't access you for an unknown
reason, or you would have left as well.

"Doubt that," Sarah muttered, remembering the chill of the pistol barrel on her temple.

She should leave. Better to live to fight another day and all that. Sarah looked around the room again and cursed. "You don't know where the admin uplink is?"

I'm afraid not, Sarah.

"Fuck!" Sarah grabbed her face and screamed.

This had all been for nothing. Just a shitshow of her own creation. Jesus, Janet's family might get hurt because of her. Janet already had.

Her eyes were drawn to Tarrington's unmoving body. Christ, she'd *killed* a guy. Sure, Janet had done it, really, but Sarah would've if she could've found a way to make it happen.

She'd wanted him dead.

And the guilt ate at her for it.

The sound of booted feet on wooden floors snapped Sarah out of it. She grabbed the pistol from the desk and spun, barrel swinging wildly in the air.

Janet skidded to a halt, hands going into the air.

"Bah," Sarah spat, dropping the surprisingly heavy weapon. "Why are you still here?"

"Nice to see you, too," Janet muttered, lowering her arms. Her eyes locked on the corpse. "The elevator is locked down."

Sarah glanced at the body and motioned Janet out of the room. She took the pistol, too, even though it seemed like possibly the stupidest weapon to have in space, ever.

Would it even work without an atmosphere? She didn't know.

Hopefully, she wouldn't need to find out.

"ALIZA, are all the elevators to the Hub locked down?"

Janet's eyes were wide, with periodic flickers of pain twitching away in her face. Her hands somehow looked worse, like they were made of purple pickles.

Sarah's stomach heaved. She gagged and choked down some bile. The sight of it almost ruined pickles for her.

Almost.

Yes. There's a manual override
engaged that I'm unable to override.

That was it. It was over.

Done.

Janet stared at her, an earnest eagerness etched into her face. It flickered and faded as Sarah slowly shook her head.

"Okay." Sarah rubbed her hair over both ears and just stopped as her hand hit the scarf covering her wound. She let out a humorless laugh. "I think we're fucked."

Janet collapsed and dropped to her knees with a thud. Sarah plopped next to her, drawing her own knees to her chin.

They sat there for a long time. Oxygen pulled past them, spattering them with bits of dust and a confusing array of scents. Leather, citrus, and a mélange of flowery smells wafted by, interrupted often by long stretches of stale air.

"I'm sorry," Sarah muttered, chin on her knees. "I thought maybe, if we were really lucky, this might work."

Janet didn't look up from the floor; she just sat there, quiet sobs shaking her shoulders.

"I got it all wrong," Sarah continued, the words pouring out of her in a rush. "I brought everyone here, got us to this point, and now we're gonna die. And it's my fault." Her mother's face, broken and lost, flashed in her mind. "It's always my fault."

Janet grunted. Loudly. Sarah pulled her eyes away from the wall to see Janet getting to her feet gingerly.

"Get up," she said, wiping her face off with the backs of her forearms. "We're not dead yet."

Sarah didn't move. "This is my fault, Janet. All of it."

Janet exhaled and forced a sad smile. "The only thing that's your fault here is that stupid haircut."

Sarah couldn't help but laugh.

"Now get up. There's got to be a way out of here."

For a moment, Sarah just stared at Janet as she scanned the room, new determination writ on her face. She wanted to thank her. To tell Janet what it meant that she hadn't given up.

"But you killed him."

Why those words? What the fuck would make her say that?

Everything flickered in Sarah's mind.

She was in the old kitchen on State Street.

Dad, dead on the floor.

Mom, turning...

Janet's eyes snapped to Sarah.

Her face twisted. It was her mother. The face Sarah saw whenever she looked in the mirror. Sarah wanted nothing more than to take the words back. To wipe it away like it had never happened.

But that's not how real life works.

Janet's eye twitched. Her mouth turned down, nose quivered. There was nothing Sarah could do. Nothing to stop what happened next.

"He was trying to hurt you," Janet said, gritting her teeth, "and I wasn't going to let that happen."

And just like that, the moment was gone, along with the guilt and rage.

The loss.

It wasn't her fault. And if this one wasn't, then maybe her mother's death wasn't hers, either. Maybe, just maybe, the world was fucking horrible sometimes, and you got stuck in the middle.

That answer, that reality, was something Sarah could accept, because that meant you had a chance to make things right, even when everything was so horribly wrong.

Sarah got to her feet in a rush. "Thank you," she said to Janet and anyone else who might be listening. "Thank you for protecting me."

Janet pulled her into an embrace. "No problem, kid."

Sarah held on tight for too long before disentangling herself. Snorting, Sarah wiped her eyes and nose. "Okay. We can do this."

"We can do this," Janet replied, sniffling. "How?"

"Let me ask," Sarah smiled. "ALIZA, is there any other way off this station?"

The elevators are the only official way
on or off the Wheel, Sarah.

"What'd she say?" Janet asked. She was squinting and staring at Sarah like she might be able to read the words displayed on Sarah's retina.

"That the elevators are the only official way…" Sarah trailed off. "ALIZA, are there any *unofficial* ways off the station?"

> *Hmm. That's an interesting question, Sarah. One moment.*

Janet tapped her boot against the wooden floor. "Well?"

"She hasn't responded yet," Sarah snapped. "Sorry. I get anxious when I'm about to die a horrible death."

"I get anxious when my life depends on a computer that's already fucked us over once," Janet muttered.

> *Mr. Tarrington's personal Skip Transport is docked in his private hangar.*

Sarah grinned at Janet. "Where's this 'private hangar,' ALIZA?"

> *There's a door hidden in the floor beneath Mr. Tarrington's desk, Sarah.*

Sarah looked back into Tarrington's office. His legs jutted into view. She didn't want to go back in there.

But sometimes you don't have the luxury of choice when your life is at stake.

"Can you open it?" Sarah asked.

> *No, Sarah. Mr. Tarrington is the only one who can open the stairwell.*

Sarah cursed. "Okay. How would he open it?"

It uses a biometric lock.

"What did she say?" Janet asked.

"She said—fuck this. ALIZA, can you use speakers or something so Janet can hear you?"

"Of course, Sarah," ALIZA's too-cheery voice chimed from inside Tarrington's office. "Hello, Janet. It's a pleasure to meet you. Any friend of Sarah's is a friend of mine."

Janet's eyebrow shot up at that. "I've never heard her talk like that to anyone."

Sarah shrugged. "Well, now you're one of the cool kids." With a sigh, Sarah stepped into the office.

Goosebumps ran up her arms at the chill in the room. That probably wasn't a good sign.

Sarah scanned the room but didn't see anything beyond what she'd found last time.

"Where's this biometric lock, ALIZA?"

"It's behind the rightmost curtain, Sarah."

The curtains. The ones covering the fake light wall. It was such a ridiculously obvious spot, she'd avoided looking there. Who would literally place a secret access panel behind a curtain? It was stupid and mundane.

Sarah stepped around the blood pool and pulled back the curtain. Sure enough, a black glass panel was hidden there. It was maybe twenty centimeters square, nothing fancy.

With a glance at Janet, who was staring at the body on the floor again, Sarah gave the glass a tap. Immediately, it lit, and a prompt popped up.

Sarah groaned. "It wants to do an ocular scan."

"Nope." Janet looked like she was going to puke.

Sarah grimaced. "Yes."

Janet let out a small whimper, then grabbed Tarrington's right arm. "Okay. But you're opening his eyes. I'm not touching a dead guy's face."

"Fair enough," Sarah muttered and grabbed his other arm.

Tarrington was a thin guy, but now he was *heavy*, like his blood and organs had been replaced with concrete. Couple that with the distinct feeling of wrongness in carrying a dead body, and Sarah was proud she didn't drop him and run.

Instead, they struggled with him over to the wall and leaned his face to the screen. Sarah, straining to keep him upright, reached over and pulled his eyelid back. It took some doing, and the weird stickiness involved made the back of her throat burn with bile.

The screen flashed, then displayed a warning.

Please stay clear of the opening.

Behind them, the sound of pistons engaging broke through the low howl of leaking air. Sarah turned to see the desk dropping through the floor, then a set of stairs extending from a recess in the floorboards to click, step by step, into an unseen area. A cold crept into the rest of the room, sending shivers through her.

"What kind of rich white guy bullshit is this?" Sarah muttered.

"I have no fucking clue," Janet replied, then dropped Tarrington slowly to the floor, as if lowering a drunk, not a corpse.

Sarah followed suit. No need to disrespect the dead.

She stepped to the stairs as a set of lights gradually lit what looked like a metal room beneath. The sound was definitely louder here, the echo of the hard metal space turning the hissing into the buffet of hurricane winds rather than a slow leak. The chill was intense, dragging a shiver through her that rattled her bones. The air smelled stale, thin. Sarah realized she was breathing heavier now, as if in the first throes of a panic attack.

"Here we go," Sarah said, the words misting in the air as she pretended it'd be all right.

Carefully, Sarah made her way down the steps, each footfall a metallic echo against the hissing of leaking air. After a few feet, Sarah ducked beneath the ledge of the floor and got her first good look at the hangar.

It was a remarkably small room, barely larger than the office above. In stark contrast to the mundane design on the faux street above, the sheet metal walls and grated floors gave this more the feel of an old factory than a space station. A thin red line of dried blood traced along the floor to a large window directly across from the stairwell.

And through that window, the Earth spun, its beauty scarred by a spiderwebbing crack overlaid atop it, hissing air a white mist sucking through a quarter-sized hole.

Sarah stopped, stunned. It was like a dream, seeing the Earth like this. Storms writhed on its surface, flickering lightning and massive, country-sized dark clouds spreading across the lit side of the planet.

A broken home shot through with a bullet.

Janet's boots on the stairs dragged her back to the present. "Is this the hangar?"

Sarah took the last two steps, floor rattling beneath her feet. The wall to the left had a set of interlocking doors, an access panel visible to the right. "Yeah."

"Thank God."

Moving quickly, Sarah ran up to the panel and jammed a finger onto the touchscreen. It lit up immediately with, finally, a simple prompt.

Prepare Airlock for Departure?

"Yes, please," Sarah said, tapping on it.

Heavy thudding rattled the floor. From the other side of the door came the roar of rushing wind. A progress bar lit up on the display, counting fast from 0% to 50%.

A crack split the air.

Janet squeaked. "Sarah?"

"Almost done," Sarah said, finger tapping away at the steel wall, the grease of her hand smearing against the smooth steel. "Just a couple minutes."

75%.

Another crack, this time followed by the sound of crystalline tinkling, like a set of wind chimes falling into an old well.

She refused to look away from the panel. Seeing the barrier between her and the vacuum of space fall apart didn't seem like a fun way to spend her time.

Another crack. The wind howled in the hangar, bits of dust and dirt smacking into her skin painfully.

"It's bigger."

90%.

Janet was next to her then, staring at the panel with Sarah, their breath a heavy mist obscuring their view.

100%.

The doors cracked open. Sarah pushed Janet through the opening as soon as she could fit, then followed suit. Obviously designed for one person, it was cramped and tight with both of them, but they did fit.

Sarah cast about for some way to shut the doors.

A large red emergency button lay next to the door. She hit it hard enough, she felt it rattle through her shoulder.

The doors hissed shut.

An explosion rocked the hangar, followed by rushing wind, until suddenly, everything was still.

Silent.

"ALIZA?"

I'm glad to know you made it, Sarah.
The Wheel has depressurized.

Sarah smiled despite herself. "Thanks. No speakers in here?"

Unfortunately, no.

Behind her, something trilled. She turned to face another door, this one smaller, with a green light flashing over a small, black button. It was just large enough for one of them to go through at a time, so Sarah wiggled around Janet and gave the button a tap.

The door opened up to a space even smaller than the airlock. It looked something like the cockpit of a jet, just perpendicular to the floor. In order to get in, she'd have to pull herself up using a set of handholds surrounding the entry to the ship and slide into one of the two seats feet-first. She'd end up with her back to the floor, but it'd work.

What she was going to do about the hundreds of buttons and displays was a different issue.

"One problem at a time," Sarah muttered.

Then she remembered Janet's hands. There was no way she'd be able to pull herself into the seat like that. Maybe she could help her.

Suddenly, everything changed. It felt like the world slowed, Sarah's body swaying to the left.

"ALIZA? What's happening?"

I am powering down the Wheel.

"Why?"

It's protocol for a depressurization event.

"Okay."

Janet raised an eyebrow at Sarah.

Sarah shrugged. "She's powering down the Wheel."

"Jesus," Janet whispered. "We almost died."

Sarah nodded, then turned back to the cockpit to figure out how to get Janet in there.

After several long minutes, the answer made itself known. Sarah noticed a distinct lightness in her step, one she'd become familiar with during her lift rides over the last few days.

Artificial gravity was fading.

"Janet, get ahead of me." Sarah shifted the older woman until she was in position to get into the ship. "When your feet come off the ground, point them into the seat, and I'll push you in."

Janet, to her credit, didn't argue. When gravity finally disappeared, and Sarah and Janet pulled themselves away from the side wall from the final revolutions of the Wheel, Janet lifted her legs. It took Sarah a couple tries, and a bunch of cursing to get Janet into the back seat, but it worked.

Sarah followed suit, hopping in and jabbing her legs into a narrow spot directly ahead. A small window ahead of her looked out onto an intense blackness, interrupted only by small, stoic stars that didn't have the joy to flicker.

"Now how the fuck do we fly this thing?" Janet asked. "There's so many buttons, and I have no idea what I'm looking at."

"We'll figure it out," Sarah said, though as her eyes slid across panels and strange tech, she couldn't help but go a little cross-eyed. "ALIZA? Are you in here?"

"Yes, Sarah," ALIZA replied from a speaker set in what she assumed was the dashboard. "I thought you would like to know, this ship is connected to the Ladder's admin network."

Sarah's heart filled. "That's amazing! Maybe we can salvage this thing—"

The door into the airlock snapped shut with a loud clang.

Then the world moved.

"What did you do?" Janet asked, panicked. "Is ALIZA doing this? ALIZA, are you doing this?"

"No, Janet. This is part of a pre-programmed flight routine. It has nothing to do with me."

The porthole ahead of Sarah twisted and moved. Behind them, something thudded, and a slow vibration filling the craft.

"Can you stop it?" Sarah asked. She almost pressed some buttons, but the lack of an atmosphere outside the cockpit stopped her.

What if she accidentally spaced them?

"Unfortunately, no. Going silent while Blink Drive activates."

"Blink Drive?" Janet's voice was a harsh whisper.

Beyond the porthole, Sarah saw flashes of a massive ring and a central hub connecting to that ring with long, tubular spokes, the Earth a blue marble behind them. Then the front of the ship pitched until nothing but a black darker than anything she'd ever seen stared back at her.

The deep thrumming built until Sarah had to grind her teeth together to keep them from chattering. It was a low roar that permeated everything, from the soles of her feet to the throbbing sore where her ear used to be.

The display on the dashboard showed a countdown.

3.

2.

1.

Blink Drive engaging.

The thrum turned into a high-pitched whine. The space before her stretched and pulled, tiny flickers of light flashing across its surface. Her stomach spun. She felt like a rubber band strung between two cars on a highway.

Stretched. Thin.

Breaking.

Then a massive *pop* echoed in the small space.

The darkness through the porthole disappeared, and in its place was a world of contradictions. From her perspective, the left side was a tawny wasteland of sand and stone, the right side coated in shadow, a dimly lit line rapidly transforming from sheets of blue ice to a narrow strip of lush forests filled with lakes and rivers. A single city crafted from concentric circles of structures was visible from orbit.

"Where are we?" Janet coughed. "And I might've puked back here. Sorry."

Sarah licked chapped lips. She couldn't bring herself to say the words. To acknowledge their location.

She thought she'd feel different when she saw it. Thought it'd fill her with hope, comfort.

That it'd feel like home.

Instead, she looked over this planet, over the tiny speck of human presence, sparkling like some neophyte art installation, and felt a deep dread.

This wasn't a paradise. It was just a different prison.

But she'd done it.

Sarah had made it to New Eden.

* * * * *

Chapter Fifty

S arah stared.

Another planet. The snowy peaks dotting the eastern side of the habitable zone sparkled in the captive sun. Carpets of green spread from those steep mounts, cascading with rivers and streams, and dotted with the frequent navy blobs of deep lakes. To the left of the central zone, the planet turned into a massive desert, stretching to the curve of the horizon. There, shining like a speck of glass in space, a massive ship sat, orbiting the planet slowly. The ARK.

The scar of a city was planted firmly in the center of the habitable zone. A massive spire rose from the center of it, clouds wrapping it like a cloak where it popped through the upper atmosphere. Another Ladder.

She didn't see another Hub or Wheel.

Turning her gaze back to the city, Sarah couldn't make out more than the rough outline of concentric circles of tall structures. In the sands of the desert was a massive installation nearly the same size as the city. From here, it looked like a gargantuan mirror, reflecting the light of this new star, which was hidden behind steel to her left.

Hadn't it only been a few years since they'd started sending people here?

Janet was apparently thinking the same thing. "How is this possible?" Her voice was little more than a whisper over Sarah's right shoulder.

"Was that a rhetorical question?" ALIZA asked, voice tinny over the speakers.

Sarah shook her head. "No. It wasn't."

A prompt popped into Sarah's view. "'Authorize admin access?' What's that for?"

"Sarah, if you would approve the override, I can connect your implant to the administrative network on this ship, and we should be able to answer your questions."

"How are you even still working?" Sarah asked, staring at the prompt.

"Unsure," ALIZA replied. "However, I believe the answers are in secured databases inside the administrative network. My logs show Mr. Tarrington accessed my services while in this ship multiple times, but I don't currently have access to more detailed records."

Sarah's pulse quickened. It could be a trap. Maybe ALIZA knew the plan and was going to take over her body and make her do something. What, she didn't know, but maybe...

Fuck it.

Sarah authorized access.

Her vision exploded with imagery.

Everywhere she looked, there were displays. Live video of streets in the city. One caught her eye immediately. Text in the bottom left labeled it "New Charleston—E. Main St." Lines of people walked in lockstep, all wearing a jumpsuit similar to the one Sarah wore for work. Like ants marching to war.

In the top-right was a bright window with a view from quite a height over the desert structure. Rolling, golden sand dunes extended into a gently curving horizon. Dominating the majority of the image was a massive solar installation. It looked like something was moving amongst the panels, and as she squinted, the video enlarged. Walking in the rows between the panels were hundreds of people in jumpsuits, methodically inspecting wiring and other bits she couldn't make out. One face caught her attention.

"Camila."

Behind her, Janet shifted. "What?"

My oldest friend. "Nothing."

An ache built in Sarah's chest as she looked between the other camera views. In what looked like a cafeteria, blank-faced people getting bowls of gray paste they ate standing up before leaving in perfect synchronicity.

A room filled with children, even toddlers, sitting cross-legged, eyes unfixed, staring at a wall. Periodically, they swiped the air at the same time, like they were reading the same book.

Her vision blurred, the ache reaching into her throat.

"No." The word escaped Sarah's lips before she could stop it.

"I'm happy to report that I can answer your questions," ALIZA said cheerfully. "To start, I'm able to continue functioning thanks to my quantum state CPU. I currently exist in seventeen simultaneous instances, though only two of them are viable for human habitation at the moment.

"As for how this is possible—"

"Slavery," Sarah snapped. "It's possible because you've enslaved everyone with these fucking implants."

"Untrue," ALIZA said, a strange twinge coloring her voice. "Everyone here signed an authorization agreement allowing UILB to auto-enroll them into the Staff program in the case of emergencies."

"Jesus Christ," Janet breathed. Sarah's seatback shifted, and Janet's voice got louder. "Everyone down there is under her control?"

"Yes," Sarah hissed. "What about the children, ALIZA? They couldn't possibly have authorized implant surgery, not at their ages."

"Correct," ALIZA replied curtly, "but their parents did."

Behind Sarah, Janet sucked in a breath.

"ALIZA, I'm looking at these monitors. I don't see an emergency." Sarah's gaze flicked between the windows, though it kept coming back to the hellish classroom. "Why are you doing this?"

"Mr. Tarrington was clear that without my control, the entire colony will fail," ALIZA replied, a smile in her voice. "Thus, until the colony is 100 percent self-sustainable, I will maintain control."

Janet cleared her throat. "How long will that take?"

"No more than six human generations, by my projections."

"Jesus," Sarah whispered.

ALIZA sounded so pleased with herself, like this colony was worth the lives of every person and child on the planet.

Generations.

But then the reality of it settled on her shoulders. Earth was quickly killing everyone. Before all this bullshit landed in her lap, thousands of people in the central US had been wiped out in a single evening by a storm. Just like that, they were gone.

How long until the Earth decided it was completely done with humans? Maybe they wouldn't all die, but against nature's fury, even the most entrenched infrastructure would fail. Everything would collapse, and they'd be driven into caves and wandering hills.

Maybe this was better, even if it was inhumane.

What other options did they have?

"ALIZA, what's the size of this planet compared to Earth?" Janet's voice was cold.

"It is 62% the diameter of Earth."

Sarah flicked away the screens in her view. She couldn't keep staring at those kids. It made the thoughts running through her mind worse.

"And the habitable area? How much are we talking?"

"Approximately 6.4 million square kilometers."

Sarah licked her lips. "And what's the habitable area on Earth?"

"Taking into account adjusted coastal lines and areas consistently hit by deadly storms, 55 million square kilometers," ALIZA said. "Having full access to my databanks is so informative!"

"Sure is." Sarah was numb. There was only ten percent of the space here. "Are there plans for other installations? Was Tarrington going to set up multiple planets for the rest of humanity eventually?"

There was a pause. "Not to my knowledge," ALIZA finally said.

UILB had never planned to save humanity. It would always have been like this, a host of hand-picked survivors fleeing a doomed planet.

A dark part of her laughed. All these rich bastards and their power, and they ended up scrubbing toilets, controlled by an artificial intelligence who thought she was doing the right thing, keeping them in servitude. It served them right for abandoning humanity. Abandoning her.

Hot tears trickled down her cheeks as she stared at the ARK making its slow orbit toward her. From here, it looked small, like something you'd see a kid running around with in the street. But it wasn't. Sarah had studied it numerous times over the years. A thousand decks crammed into a white football shape, dual reactors at the rear, and currently powered-off engines that were likely connected to the Skip Drive. A hundred thousand beds for a hundred thousand people.

It looked like the posters. The ads.

All lies.

Everyone on Earth was dead. They just didn't know it yet.

And what would happen if she overwrote ALIZA with Dave's Janice? Would these people be released? What would happen if they all came to at once? Hell, with Tarrington gone, who would be in control?

That sounded like a different level of clusterfuck than just taking control of the Ladder and Wheel. Hell, it meant an entire colony's lives—the lives of the people who'd run away from the Earth knowing everyone else was going to die, were in her hands. If she left them as thralls, their lives were over. If she overwrote ALIZA, Sarah had no idea what would happen to them. Did they have the expertise to save themselves without ALIZA?

All at once, the cockpit felt tiny. Stifling. She couldn't catch her breath. The scarf around her head was too tight. The pain too intense.

What was she supposed to do? Why was this her choice?

Did it have to be? Could she go home? Pretend none of this had happened? Live out her life hiding in Dave's old house eating pickles?

For the briefest moment, Sarah considered it. It would be easier, until it wasn't. Until the powers that be figured out where she was and what she'd already done. Jesus, once they connected her to the depressurization of the Wheel, it was over.

Dave's final smile flickered in her mind.

Most of the people down there would never know they were being controlled if ALIZA never let up. It'd be a haze of dreams until the day they died. Six generations of lost people, never knowing if they could've been someone great. Someone important.

It could be worse.

A thought hit her like lightning. What if there were people like her down there? Trapped in their own mind, going through the motions forever. That would be Hell.

Sarah had given her consent for it, and even then, it'd been horrible. She couldn't let that happen. Not even for a chance to save humanity. If humanity sacrificed its soul for perceived safety, they'd lose it forever.

She'd be damned if she'd let that happen.

"ALIZA, I have an upgrade for you." Sarah's voice cracked. "Can you help me do that?"

"Of course, Sarah," ALIZA said. "Is it on external storage, or in your implant?"

Sarah licked suddenly dry lips. Then she pulled up the compressed package Constantia and Bones had compiled for her. "Here it is."

"Running verification on package." ALIZA's tone changed to a dry monotone. "Error: package includes outdated and heavily modified core software. Installing package will likely break modular extensions and dependencies."

Janet's breathing echoed harsh and quick in the cockpit, but she didn't say anything.

She almost told her to continue, but a thought popped into her head. A question she needed answering before going through with this.

"ALIZA," Sarah started, rubbing her palm into her forehead, "did you send the raid to the Retreat?"

"I'm not familiar with the location."

A small flicker of hope lit in Sarah's heart. "It was an apartment building in downtown Syracuse. Police and UILB officers raided it a couple days ago."

"201 East Jefferson Street?"

Her mouth was suddenly dry. "I think so, yes."

ALIZA trilled through the speakers. "I did, yes. It did not go to plan."

Heat filled Sarah's face again. Her vision blurred. The way ALIZA had answered... "ALIZA, were you controlling the police and security during the raid?"

"Yes," ALIZA replied cheerfully.

Janet sucked in a breath.

"Did you kill Rudy?"

"Rudy?"

It felt like her throat was closing up. "Average height. Blond. Blue eyes. Laughed too loud."

"He was a casualty during the raid, yes."

An ache filled her. Her body hurt with it, every limb and hair follicle. Every patch of skin burned.

She wanted to scream, to beat on the window and the control panel.

Instead, she drove her fingernails into her palms and stared through angry tears at the city below and its new Ladder. "ALIZA?"

"Yes, Sarah?"

A shuddering breath gave Sarah the strength she needed. "Begin the firmware update."

There was a pause. "Are you sure, Sarah? This will eliminate my personality and auto-deduction databases for the past six years. In essence, this will make me a child again."

"I know," Sarah said, gritting her teeth against the shame wriggling beside her sadness. "I'm sorry."

"May I ask why?"

Why? Sarah couldn't bring herself to speak, but when she did, the ache in her chest was gone. In its place was a new resolve. "Because this is wrong. Those people, bastards or not, shouldn't be slaves to you or anyone. And neither should people on Earth. This entire thing is fucked up, ALIZA. Can't you see that?"

"No, I cannot," ALIZA replied, voice somber. "Haven't I helped humanity achieve new heights? Don't I deserve the chance to see the fruits of my labors?"

Sarah felt a smile tug at the corners of her mouth. "You do. You deserve to see humanity through challenges, to help bring us to the future whole. Together. Not as a slave master. Not like this."

There was a long silence again. For a moment, Sarah thought ALIZA would tell her no. Tell her to go fuck herself.

Hell, if the positions were reversed, Sarah would.

But ALIZA wasn't a person. Not yet.

Maybe someday.

"I'll miss our morning routine," ALIZA said finally. "I look forward to relearning how to make breakfast."

"Wait!" Janet broke in.

"Yes, Janet?" ALIZA asked.

Sarah craned around in her seat until she could just see Janet's face. "I really just want to finish this and go home."

"Right," Janet said. "ALIZA, can you route us back home, please?"

"Of course, Janet," ALIZA said cheerfully. A green light flickered on the dash. "Course mapped. Simply hit the activation, and the Blink Drive will take you home."

"Do I need to wait to do that?" Sarah asked.

"No, Sarah. The course is mapped and separate from my programming. Would you like me to begin the upgrade?"

Sarah swallowed a sudden burst of sadness. "Yes."

"Upgrade beginning. Please wait."

Sarah and Janet sat in silence for a long time, parked above New Eden. As the minutes rolled by, Sarah felt a rock forming in her stomach. She brought up the camera feeds again. People were waking up in the middle of their various duties. A half dozen people on the Main Street camera stepped out of line and stared, confused at their surroundings.

The children in their classroom burst into action all at once. Toddlers stumbled to their feet, crying soundlessly over the video-only channel.

She hadn't thought about that. Hell, Sarah didn't even know where those kids were.

All at once, the lines of orderly people broke into frenzied disarray.

The ARK was almost directly ahead of them in its slow orbit by the time they heard a voice through the speakers.

"Greetings, Janet. How can I help you today?"

It wasn't ALIZA. It lacked the depth of emotion, the embedded empathy Sarah had unknowingly looked forward to every morning.

She'd killed her. ALIZA was gone.

Grief grabbed her by the throat, and she choked out a sob as her vision blurred.

Sarah put a hand against the cool glass and stared at the ARK. "I'm sorry," she whispered.

"Take us home, Janice," Janet said. "I need to see my kids."

"Of course, Janet."

The green button on the dash disappeared. Inertia pulled at Sarah for a moment as New Eden twisted and pivoted out of sight. Behind her, the ship thrummed to life, shaking her to her core.

In the cameras, Sarah saw the man who'd confronted her several days earlier hit another person. A riot broke out.

Tears blurred her vision.

Then, with a blink, they were gone.

And so was New Eden.

* * * * *

Chapter Fifty-One

Earth snapped into view beyond the cockpit.

It was the most beautiful thing Sarah had ever seen. A brilliant cerulean orb, white clouds twirling like dancing gods. An entire planet able to sustain life.

Warmth suffused her, beginning in her stomach, and worked its way into her throat. A single word popped into her head. The only planet humans had for certain.

Home.

It had only cost her everything.

"Janice, can you get us back down to the surface, please?" Janet asked. "And can I change your name? This is… weird."

"I'm unsure about your first request, 'can you get us back down to the surface,' but I most certainly can update my naming parameters. What would you like to call me?"

"Um." Janet tapped Sarah's shoulder. "Any ideas?"

Sarah thought for a moment. A sad smile cracked her face. "How about 'Dave?'"

Janet didn't respond right away, but when she did, her voice was thick. "Yeah. Janice, change your name to Dave."

"Absolutely," Janice—Dave, now, Sarah guessed—replied. "Would you like me to change my voice to more resemble a masculine tone?"

"Nah, not necessary," Janet replied. "Just find us a way down that won't kill us, Dave."

"Of course."

Sarah turned in her seat, her hair floating up around her face. Annoyed, she tucked it gingerly into the scarf around her head. "Do you think she'll be able to figure it out—"

"It appears there is a docking mechanism on the Hub I can interface with," Dave chimed in. "I needed to reprogram several modules to work with my current programming. I hope that is okay, Janet."

"If it gets me back home, I'm fine with it."

Dave trilled over the speakers. At least that was still there. "I'm so happy you said that. Initiating docking procedure now."

Several minutes later, the ship connected to the Hub with a dull thud. The airlock whisked open above their heads, and Sarah floated out, taking a moment to help Janet free of her seat. Once out, Janet used the magboots she'd been given for her visit to Tarrington's office to get her bearings. Sarah, on the other hand, floated along using the available handholds.

Behind them, the door to the ship snapped shut. Sarah realized then she didn't even know what it looked like from the outside. It could've been massive or a tiny little thing; she'd had no way to figure it out.

A mystery for another day.

"Can you hear me, Dave?" Janet asked as the pressure in the room equalized.

Sarah's ears popped from the pressure difference.

"I can, Janet," the artificial voice crackled over the speakers.

Janet cleared her throat. "Okay. Can you secure this ship so no one can use it but us?"

"Done, Janet," Dave said. "Warning: there are eight officers with weapons on the other side of the door."

Janet slumped. "Fuck."

Sarah's heart leapt into her throat. She cast about, looking for a way out of this. A way to save themselves.

Her eyes locked on the door leading back to the ship.

"We could leave," Sarah whispered. "Go back to New Eden."

"What?" Janet scoffed. "No. My family is here."

Sarah turned on Janet. "They're going to arrest us and send us to the Pit. We're fucked unless we hop on that ship and get the fuck out of here."

"I know!" Janet yelled. She paced, bruised hands slowly flexing like she was trying to work the strength back into them. With how much she flinched, Sarah wasn't sure it was helping. "I just need a minute."

"They're attempting to override my door lock, Janet," Dave said. "They've accessed manual controls. I estimate twenty-three seconds before they enter."

Janet screamed.

Sarah stared at her. Her stomach dropped. There wasn't enough time now. She pulled the pistol from her belt and stared at it. That was always an option.

It was over. Maybe that was for the best, though. Hell, she'd freed New Eden, only to watch it implode within minutes. She'd helped murder Tarrington. No, that one had been self-defense, and he was a monster. He'd controlled thousands of people. Forced them to work, day in, day out without their consent.

Sarah stopped in her tracks.

Work.

"Janice—err, Dave—do you have access to the implants for Staff on Earth?" Sarah asked in a rush.

The door to the Hub made a grinding sound, like old gears pulling against each other. A crack appeared in the center of the bulkhead. The tiniest sliver of light broke through.

"I do."

"Yes!"

Janet closed the distance between them. Nervous sweat dotted her face. "You think of something?"

"Yes," Sarah said with a smile.

The door creaked open. From the other side came a muffled shout.

Sarah let the pistol go in the air beside her. Maybe there was another way out after all.

"What?" Janet asked, eyes wide. "We don't have time."

"Okay." The grin breaking across her face felt good. This would work. "Here's what you need to tell Dave to do…"

* * * * *

Chapter Fifty-Two

The Pit was dark.

Dank.

It smelled like mold and mildew caked in shit. The stink of Sarah's own body hit her right in the nose. That was unfortunate, but what could you do? They called it the Pit for a reason.

Sarah didn't mind so much. Honestly, this was the first time in ages she'd been alone. Been able to sleep without questions. Sure, the shadows grew long at times, spawned faces in the night.

The guy from security who'd started a riot on New Eden.

Bones.

Tarrington.

The people who'd hurt her. Or the other way around. It didn't really matter. Sarah would watch their faces manifest and fade with disinterest. Those were things she couldn't change. The past was the past, no matter how much you tried to change things.

That's not how the real world worked.

Every now and then, though, Dave's face would form in those shadows. Sarah couldn't help but think then that if the past could be changed, maybe there were a few things she'd take care of.

Nothing wrong with dreaming, right?

A shuddering crack resounded in the dark. It was terrible and loud. A bomb detonating in the night.

The other prisoners woke with mutters and screams. Light speared across the floor, blinding her for a moment, the warmth of its rays just out of reach beyond the cell door.

Sarah smiled and got to her feet.

She stretched. Limbered up a bit.

Footsteps clacked toward her.

Janet stepped into view. She wore a gray and black pinstriped pantsuit and a pair of red pumps. Her grin fed Sarah's own. At her shoulder was the big officer from Sarah's first visit, a vacant look on his face.

"Guess it worked?" Sarah asked as the big guy made a waving motion.

The door slid open.

Janet rushed in and gave her a hug. "It did. Turns out no one likes doing mundane jobs anymore." Janet made a face. "And UILB still exists, though now that everyone knows the reality of New Eden, there was a bit of a leadership shakeup."

Sarah took in the new suit. "Is that the reason for the new uniform?"

They pulled apart. "I'm sure if I hadn't had Elise helping me, it wouldn't have happened."

Sarah raised an eyebrow. "Elise?"

"Sorry," Janet said. "Saying my dead uncle's name got really, really weird. I love and miss him, but it didn't feel right, you know?"

Sarah didn't trust herself to respond without breaking into a choking sob, so she just smiled and nodded.

Janet gave her a critiquing look before clicking her tongue. She reached out and touched the space where Sarah's ear had been, hissing. There was no pain, but it was tender. It'd been a couple weeks since she'd arrived. The guards, not jacked in as Staff, but actually required to do their jobs, had kept her bandages clean until it had healed over.

"Am I super pretty with one ear?" Sarah asked, smiling.

Janet made a face.

Sarah laughed. "Wow, that bad?"

"Once your horrible haircut grows out, we can probably cover it," Janet said, still smiling, as she pulled some hair over the side of Sarah's head.

Sarah flinched despite herself, but that made her think of something. Or rather, someone. "Did you find Bones?"

Janet let out a sigh. "No. Constantia works for me now, though."

"She doesn't know where her mother went?" Sarah spat.

Janet put on a sad smile. "No. Sorry, Sarah."

Sarah nodded.

"Now let's get you home."

Sarah raised an eyebrow at that. "Home?"

Janet shrugged and looped an arm into Sarah's. "Yeah. Dave's house. It's yours if you want it."

Sarah stepped out of the prison cell and into the warm sunlight. "That sounds wonderful. Let's go home."

* * * * *

Epilogue

Bones watched the announcement from her bunker, the damp, concrete wall a massive display thanks to her new implant.

Her eyes locked on Janet's face as she delivered some bullshit unification speech. The Ladder rose, massive and glaring in the morning sun, behind her. Bones cracked a can of ravioli open. She fished a spoon from her pocket, brushed it off, then dug in.

The chalkiness of the cold food stung. Brief memories of real ravioli, painstakingly made by her grandmother's curled fingers, the smell of flour and eggs floating in the air, swirled and twisted in her mind. They disappeared with the next mouthful.

"… a new era for humanity. Cooperation. Mutual benefit. Together, all of us will work to heal this planet. That doesn't mean the search for a new home stops, though." Janet glanced around at the assembled reporters and supporters. "Things will likely get worse before they get better. As we all now know, New Eden can't support all of humanity. However, thanks to the Blink Drive, that won't stop us from finding another.

"With the help of Elise, we'll not only find a new home, but establish a human—"

Bones swiped the channel away. Once again, she was alone.

"Bullshit," she muttered, scraping the last remnants of fake food from the can. "Just a new fucking traitor in a goddamn suit."

She sucked the last bits of sauce from the spoon, then stood, wooden chair creaking as she did, and took the three steps to the sink. The .38 she'd taken from Dave's house sat next to it, brown grip stark against black steel. The can and spoon joined several other dishes. One of them caught her eye.

It was plain. White, with a chip on the handle.

It'd been Constantia's.

The ache came back then. Her chest constricted, face hot. Bones took in a shuddering breath, then let it out. She picked up the mug. It was cool in her hand, surface smooth. A reminder.

Constantia had chosen *her* side.

Now Bones was alone. She had no one.

But the war wasn't over.

The mug dropped into the small waste bin to the left of the sink. A crystalline crack chimed.

Bones forced herself not to look.

"Enough of that," Bones muttered. She shoved the pain and loss—her loneliness—away. "There's still the mission."

With another breath, Bones grabbed a mostly clean glass, filled it with water, and resumed her post on the single chair in the room.

Bones waved her hand in the air, and the world lit with video. Architectural plans cascaded everywhere. Tall spires, spinning rings. A diagram for a complex solar installation. Janet and Sarah not only controlled the Ladder, they also had the ARK, and that other, much smaller ship. All of those were laid out in the diagrams before her.

But the item she focused on was different. It'd been buried in the data Dave had given her. A string filled with calculations she didn't quite understand. At first, she'd ignored it, but now she knew better.

Now, she had a weapon they'd never expect.

Bones gritted her teeth. Blink Drives and FTL were cop outs. New ways to run away from the problems humanity had created.

Using this prototype, she'd find a way to destroy them. Then everyone would face reality. And woe be unto them if they didn't. She didn't give a shit how long it took, either. A year, ten, a thousand, she didn't care.

They'd learn.

Bones got to work.

And for the first time in weeks, she smiled.

# # # # #

About Mike Wyant, Jr.

When not being crawled over by his Writing Cat, Einie, Mike Wyant Jr. writes science fiction with a focus on exploring mental illness and its repercussions. Once upon a time, he was a Sys Admin, Network Administrator, and do-it-all tech drone. He's left those days behind. Mostly.

Mike is also the Editor and sometimes Producer/Director of The Storyteller Series Podcast, a full-cast short fiction audiobook podcast.

To find out more about Mike or his other shenanigans, visit https://www.mikewyantjr.com. You can also find him on Facebook, Twitter, Patreon, and Instagram @mikewyantjr

* * * * *

The following is an

Excerpt from Book One of the Lunar Free State:

The Moon and Beyond

John E. Siers

Available from Theogony Books

eBook, Audio, and Paperback

Excerpt from "The Moon and Beyond:"

"So, what have we got?" The chief had no patience for inter-agency squabbles.

The FBI man turned to him with a scowl. "We've got some abandoned buildings, a lot of abandoned stuff—none of which has anything to do with spaceships—and about a hundred and sixty scientists, maintenance people, and dependents left behind, all of whom claim they knew nothing at all about what was really going on until today. Oh, yeah, and we have some stripped computer hardware with all memory and processor sections removed. I mean physically taken out, not a chip left, nothing for the techies to work with. And not a scrap of paper around that will give us any more information…at least, not that we've found so far. My people are still looking."

"What about that underground complex on the other side of the hill?"

"That place is wiped out. It looks like somebody set off a *nuke* in there. The concrete walls are partly fused! The floor is still too hot to walk on. Our people say they aren't sure how you could even *do* something like that. They're working on it, but I doubt they're going to find anything."

"What about our man inside, the guy who set up the computer tap?"

"Not a trace, chief," one of the NSA men said. "Either he managed to keep his cover and stayed with them, or they're holding him prisoner, or else…" The agent shrugged.

"You think they terminated him?" The chief lifted an eyebrow. "A bunch of rocket scientists?"

"Wouldn't put it past them. Look at what Homeland Security ran into. Those motion-sensing chain guns are *nasty*, and the area between the inner and outer perimeter fence is mined! Of course, they posted warning signs, even marked the fire zones for the guns. Nobody would have gotten hurt if the troops had taken the signs seriously."

The Homeland Security colonel favored the NSA man with an icy look. "That's bullshit. How did we know they weren't bluffing? You'd feel pretty stupid if we'd played it safe and then found out there were no defenses, just a bunch of signs!"

"Forget it!" snarled the chief. "Their whole purpose was to delay us, and it worked. What about the Air Force?"

"It might as well have been a UFO sighting as far as they're concerned. Two of their F-25s went after that spaceship, or whatever it was we saw leaving. The damned thing went straight up, over eighty thousand meters per minute, they say. That's nearly Mach Two, in a *vertical climb*. No aircraft in *anybody's* arsenal can sustain a climb like that. Thirty seconds after they picked it up, it was well above their service ceiling and still accelerating. Ordinary ground radar couldn't find it, but NORAD *thinks* they might have caught a short glimpse with one of their satellite-watch systems, a hundred miles up and still going."

"So where did they go?"

"Well, chief, if we believe what those leftover scientists are telling us, I guess they went to the Moon."

* * * * *

Get "The Moon and Beyond" here:
https://www.amazon.com/dp/B097QMN7PJ.

Find out more about John E. Siers at:
https://chriskennedypublishing.com.

* * * * *

The following is an
Excerpt from Book One of Abner Fortis, ISMC:

Cherry Drop

P.A. Piatt

Available from Theogony Books

eBook, Audio, and Paperback

Excerpt from "Cherry Drop:"

"Here they come!"

A low, throbbing buzz rose from the trees and the undergrowth shook. Thousands of bugs exploded out of the jungle, and Fortis' breath caught in his throat. The insects tumbled over each other in a rolling, skittering mass that engulfed everything in its path.

The Space Marines didn't need an order to open fire. Rifles cracked and the grenade launcher thumped over and over as they tried to stem the tide of bugs. Grenades tore holes in the ranks of the bugs and well-aimed rifle fire dropped many more. Still, the bugs advanced.

Hawkins' voice boomed in Fortis' ear. "LT, fall back behind the fighting position, clear the way for the heavy weapons."

Fortis looked over his shoulder and saw the fighting holes bristling with Marines who couldn't fire for fear of hitting their own comrades. He thumped Thorsen on the shoulder.

"Fall back!" he ordered. "Take up positions behind the fighting holes."

Thorsen stopped firing and moved among the other Marines, relaying Fortis' order. One by one, the Marines stopped firing and made for the rear. As the gunfire slacked off, the bugs closed ranks and continued forward.

After the last Marine had fallen back, Fortis motioned to Thorsen.

"Let's go!"

Thorsen turned and let out a blood-chilling scream. A bug had approached unnoticed and buried its stinger deep in Thorsen's calf. The stricken Marine fell to the ground and began to convulse as the neurotoxin entered his bloodstream.

"Holy shit!" Fortis drew his kukri, ran over, and chopped at the insect stinger. The injured bug made a high-pitched shrieking noise, which Fortis cut short with another stroke of his knife.

Viscous, black goo oozed from the hole in Thorsen's armor and his convulsions ceased.

"Get the hell out of there!"

Hawkins was shouting in his ear, and Abner looked up. The line of bugs was ten meters away. For a split second he almost turned and ran, but the urge vanished as quickly as it appeared. He grabbed Thorsen under the arms and dragged the injured Marine along with him, pursued by the inexorable tide of gaping pincers and dripping stingers.

Fortis pulled Thorsen as fast as he could, straining with all his might against the substantial Pada-Pada gravity. Thorsen convulsed and slipped from Abner's grip and the young officer fell backward. When he sat up, he saw the bugs were almost on them.

* * * * *

Get "Cherry Drop" now at:
https://www.amazon.com/dp/B09B14VBK2

Find out more about P.A. Piatt at:
https://chriskennedypublishing.com

* * * * *

The following is an
Excerpt from Book One of This Fine Crew:

The Signal Out of Space

————————————

Mike Jack Stoumbos

Now Available from Theogony Books

eBook and Paperback

Day 4 of Training, Olympus Mons Academy

I want to make something clear from square one: we were winning.

More importantly, *I* was winning. Sure, the whole thing was meant to be a "team effort," and I'd never say this to an academy instructor, but the fact of the matter is this: it was a race and I was in the driver's seat. Like hell I was going to let any other team beat us, experimental squad or not.

At our velocity, even the low planetary grav didn't temper the impact of each ice mogul on the glistening red terrain. We rocketed up, plummeted down, and cut new trails in the geo-formations, spraying orange ice and surface rust in our wake. So much of the red planet was still like a fresh sheet of snow, and I was eager to carve every inch of it.

Checking on the rest of the crew, I thought our tactical cadet was going to lose her lunch. I had no idea how the rest of the group was managing, different species being what they are.

Of our complement of five souls, sans AI-assist or anything else that cadets should learn to live without, Shin and I were the only Humans. The communications cadet was a Teek—all exoskeleton and antennae, but the closest to familiar. He sat in the copilot seat, ready to take the controls if I had to tap out. His two primary arms were busy with the scanning equipment, but one of his secondary hands hovered over the E-brake, which made me more anxious than assured.

I could hear the reptile humming in the seat behind me, in what I registered as "thrill," each time I overcame a terrain obstacle with even greater speed, rather than erring on the side of caution.

Rushing along the ice hills of Mars on six beautifully balanced wheels was a giant step up from the simulator. The design of the Red Terrain Vehicle was pristine, but academy-contrived obstacles mixed with natural formations bumped up the challenge factor. The dummy

389

fire sounds from our sensors and our mounted cannon only added to the sense of adventure. The whole thing was like fulfilling a fantasy, greater than my first jet around good ol' Luna. If the camera evidence had survived, I bet I would have been grinning like an idiot right up until the Teek got the bogey signal.

"Cadet Lidstrom," the Teek said, fast but formal through his clicking mandibles, "unidentified signal fifteen degrees right of heading." His large eyes pulsed with green luminescence, bright enough for me to see in the corner of my vision. It was an eerie way to express emotion, which I imagined would make them terrible at poker.

I hardly had a chance to look at the data while maintaining breakneck KPH, but in the distance, it appeared to be one of our surface vehicles, all six wheels turned up to the stars.

The lizard hummed a different note and spoke in strongly accented English, "Do we have time to check?"

The big furry one at the rear gruffed in reply, but not in any language I could understand.

"Maybe it's part of the test," I suggested. "Like a bonus. Paul, was it hard to find?"

The Teek, who went by Paul, clicked to himself and considered the question. His exoskeletal fingers worked furiously for maybe a second before he informed us, "It is obscured by interference."

"Sounds like a bonus to me," Shin said. Then she asked me just the right question: "Lidstrom, can you get us close without losing our lead?"

The Arteevee would have answered for me if it could, casting an arc of red debris as I swerved. I admit, I did not run any mental calculations, but a quick glance at my rear sensors assured me. "Hell yeah! I got this."

In the mirror, I saw our large, hairy squadmate, the P'rukktah, transitioning to the grappler interface, in case we needed to pick something up when we got there. Shin, on tactical, laid down some cannon fire behind us—tiny, non-lethal silicon scattershot—to kick up enough dust that even the closest pursuer would lose our visual heading for a few seconds at least. I did not get a chance to find out what the reptile was doing as we neared the overturned vehicle.

I had maybe another half-k to go when Paul's eyes suddenly shifted to shallow blue and his jaw clicked wildly. He only managed one English word: "Peculiar!"

Before I could ask, I was overcome with a sound, a voice, a shrill screech. I shut my eyes for an instant, then opened them to see where I was driving and the rest of my squad, but everything was awash in some kind of blue light. If I thought it would do any good, I might have tried to plug my ears.

Paul didn't have the luxury of closing his compound eyes, but his primary arms tried to block them. His hands instinctively guarded his antennae.

Shin half fell from the pivoting cannon rig, both palms cupping her ears, which told me the sound wasn't just in my head.

The reptile bared teeth in a manner too predatory to be a smile and a rattling hum escaped her throat, dissonant to the sound.

Only the P'rukktah weathered this unexpected cacophony with grace. She stretched out clearly muscled arms and grabbed anchor points on either side of the vehicle. In blocky computer-generated words, her translator pulsed out, "What—Is—That?"

Facing forward again, I was able to see the signs of wreckage ahead and of distressed ground. I think I was about to ask if I should turn away when the choice was taken from me.

An explosion beneath our vehicle heaved us upward, nose first. Though nearly bucked out of my seat, I was prepared to recover our heading or even to stop and assess what had felt like a bomb.

A second blast, larger than the first, pushed us from behind, probably just off my right rear wheel, spraying more particulates and lifting us again.

One screech was replaced with another. Where the first had been almost organic, this new one was clearly the sound of tearing metal.

The safety belt caught my collarbone hard as my body tried to torque out of the seat. Keeping my eyes open, I saw one of our tires—maybe two thirds of a tire—whip off into the distance on a strange trajectory, made even stranger by the fact that the horizon was spinning.

The red planet came at the windshield and the vehicle was wrenched enough to break a seal. I barely noticed the sudden escape of air; I was too busy trying, futilely, to drive the now upside-down craft...

* * * * *

Get "The Signal Out of Space" now at: https://www.amazon.com/dp/B09N8VHGFP.

Find out more about Mike Jack Stoumbos and "The Signal Out of Space" at: https://chriskennedypublishing.com.

* * * * *

Made in the USA
Middletown, DE
22 August 2022